Praise for *More Than Any River* . . .

"The war for water has come to California's Central Valley. When family farmers find themselves in a desperate battle against agribusiness moguls whose greed knows no bounds, the fight becomes about more than survival. In this gripping novel of loyalty, betrayal, and resilience, Victoria Tatum brings the land itself to vivid life as the most powerful character of all."—**Laura Davis, author of *The Courage to Heal*** and ***The Burning Light of Two Stars***

"As with any consequential novel that demands our attention, as this one does, this book highlights the cost of caring, and for that matter not caring, about the resources, natural and otherwise, that give value to our lives. If water makes our very life possible, so too, in a similar way, does reading Victoria Tatum's *More Than Any River*."—**Joseph Di Prisco, author of *My Last Resume*** and ***Subway to California***

"If you like reading about people who live in interesting but unfamiliar places, you should enjoy this novel, one of lives flowing onwards, ever-changing like flowing rivers, but linked together, with people who see the Delta as home. It is a good read and can serve as a way to learn about the challenges of farming in the Delta and the importance of fishes in the management of the water that flows through it."— **Peter Moyle, Distinguished Professor Emeritus, Center for Watershed Sciences, University of California Davis**

"Victoria Tatum's rich novel, *More Than Any River* starts off as a low, even, and humming narrative of personal stories and grows into a rich fabric of land, river, and delta, wedded to the folks who work it and give it meaning. Like the tributaries that feed the immense Central California Sacramento River Delta, from Mendota Canal to the Friant-Kern Canal and Millerton Lake, we're all connected."—**Joe Ortiz, author of *The Village Baker*** and ***Pastina***

"An important read for these times, when the world faces worsening flooding and drought at the very moment that reaching consensus has become harder than ever."—**Ellen Barker, author of the East of Troost series**

"In the true center of the Golden State you'll find not silicon nor movie stars but North America's largest freshwater swamp, the California Delta. In *More Than Any River*, Victoria Tatum conjures a story as beautiful as the Delta's islands, and as dark as the water at the bottom of its sloughs. This is a novel about the profound love for place and community that compels people to fight against the plans of the powerful."—**Joe Matthews, author of *The California Crackup* and journalist for the *Zocalo Public Square*** and ***Democracy Local***

"This is a story of people and place, revealing how water, history, and human lives are intertwined in ways that are rarely acknowledged but lived every day and carried across generations.

Reminiscent of the geographic immersion of Master Filmmaker Gianfranco Rosi, *More Than Any River* allows us to slow down and consider what is often overlooked, the systems that shape our lives, and the moral choices that determine who benefits and who bears the costs."—**Mark Manning, CEO of ConceptionMedia Films, Co-Founder ENGAGESTREAM**

"*More Than Any River* is set in a California literary tradition that links history to place, and to watersheds, where human beings work, sweat, dream and die. Victoria Tatum has woven a mosaic that matches the land. It is a must read for anyone who loves California, where gold and greed played a critical role in its founding. But surrounding that history was water, and *More Than Any River* reminds us of that throughout."—**Geoffrey Dunn, author of *The Lies of Sarah Palin***

MORE THAN ANY RIVER

MORE THAN ANY RIVER

A NOVEL

VICTORIA TATUM

SHE WRITES PRESS

Published in 2026 by
She Writes Press, an imprint of The Stable Book Group

32 Court Street, Suite 2109
Brooklyn, NY 11201
https://shewritespress.com
Library of Congress Control Number: 2025919167
ISBN: 979-8-89636-030-8
eISBN: 979-8-89636-031-5

Interior Designer: Andrea Reider
Maps: Erin Greb Cartography

Printed in the United States

For Bumps and Bea, Uncle Brud and Aunt Minnie,
whose legacies live on in the Delta.

We came from the border
we go to the border
like our grandparents and our children
eating bread that the Devil kneaded
suffering this end of the world.

We are the border
more than any river and more
way more
than any bridge.

—from *Sixty*, by Fabian Severo

"In the West, it is said, water flows uphill toward money."

—Marc Reisner, *Cadillac Desert*

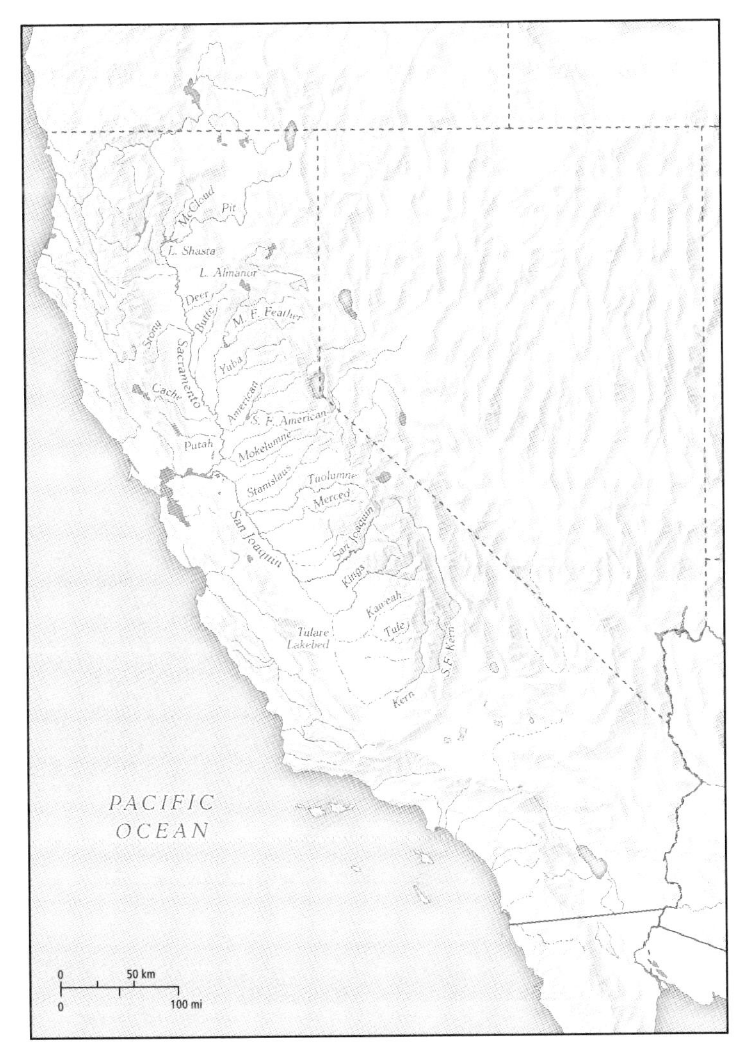

McCloud
Pit
L. Shasta
L. Almanor
Deer
Butte
M. F. Feather
Stony
Sacramento
Yuba
Cache
American
S. F. American
Putah
Mokelumne
Stanislaus
Tuolumne
Merced
San Joaquin
San Joaquin
Kings
Kaweah
Tule
Tulare
Lakebed
S.F. Kern
Kern
PACIFIC
OCEAN
0
50 km
0
100 mi

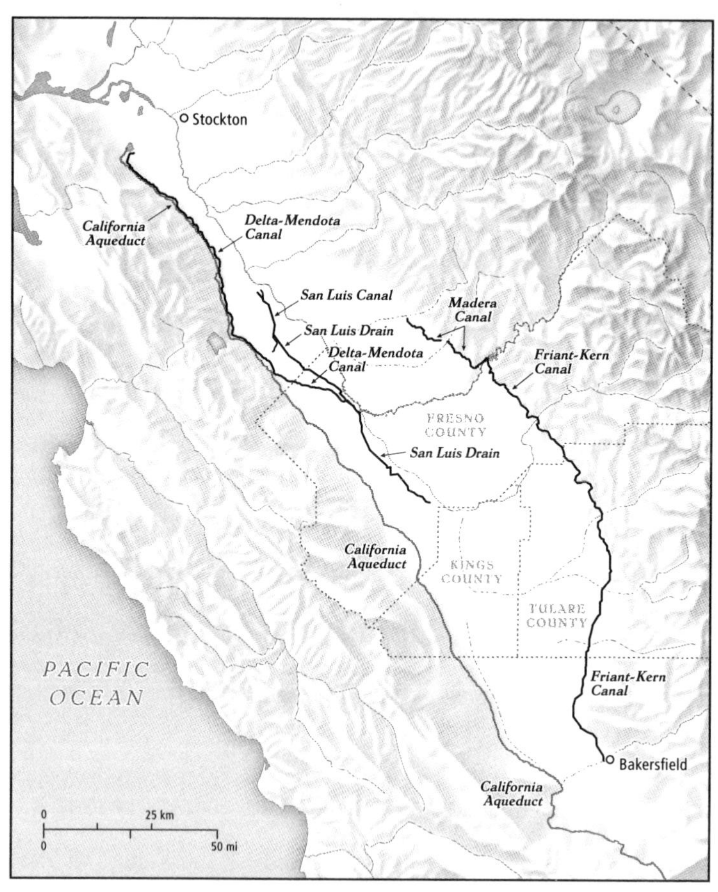
Stockton
California Aqueduct
Delta-Mendota Canal
San Luis Canal
San Luis Drain
Delta-Mendota Canal
Madera Canal
Friant-Kern Canal
FRESNO COUNTY
San Luis Drain
California Aqueduct
KINGS COUNTY
TULARE COUNTY
PACIFIC OCEAN
Friant-Kern Canal
Bakersfield
California Aqueduct
0
25 km
0
50 mi

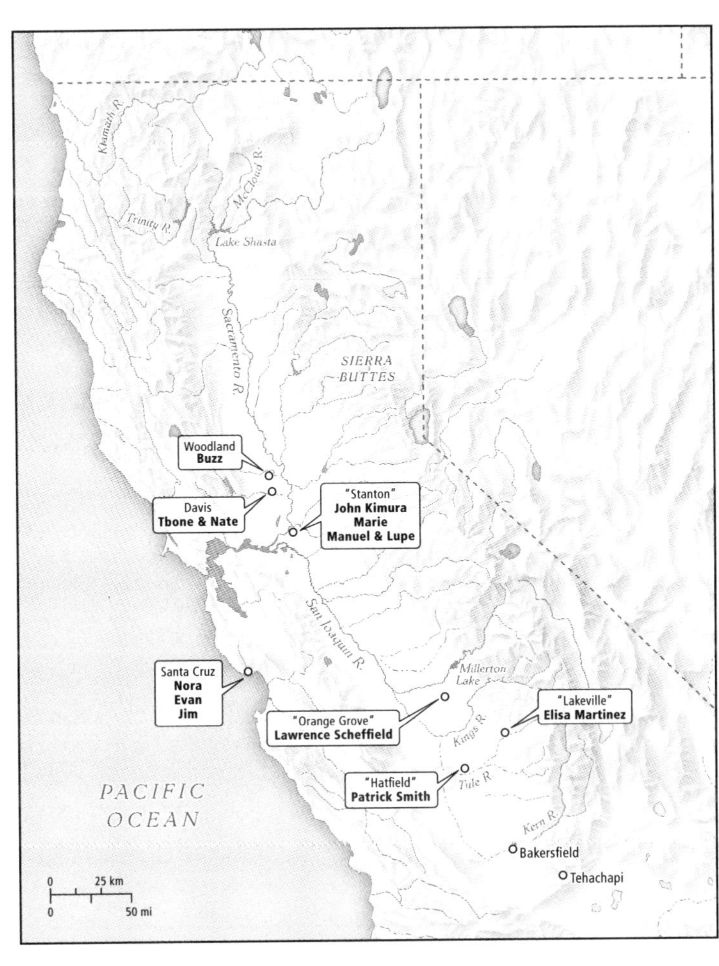

Klamath R.
McCloud R.
Trinity R.
Lake Shasta
Sacramento R.
SIERRA
BUTTES
Woodland
Buzz
Davis
Tbone & Nate
"Stanton"
John Kimura
Marie
Manuel & Lupe
San Joaquin R.
Santa Cruz
Nora
Evan
Jim
Millerton
Lake
"Orange Grove"
Lawrence Scheffield
"Lakeville"
Elisa Martinez
Kings R.
"Hatfield"
Patrick Smith
Tule R.
Kern R.
PACIFIC
OCEAN
Bakersfield
Tehachapi
0
25 km
0
50 mi

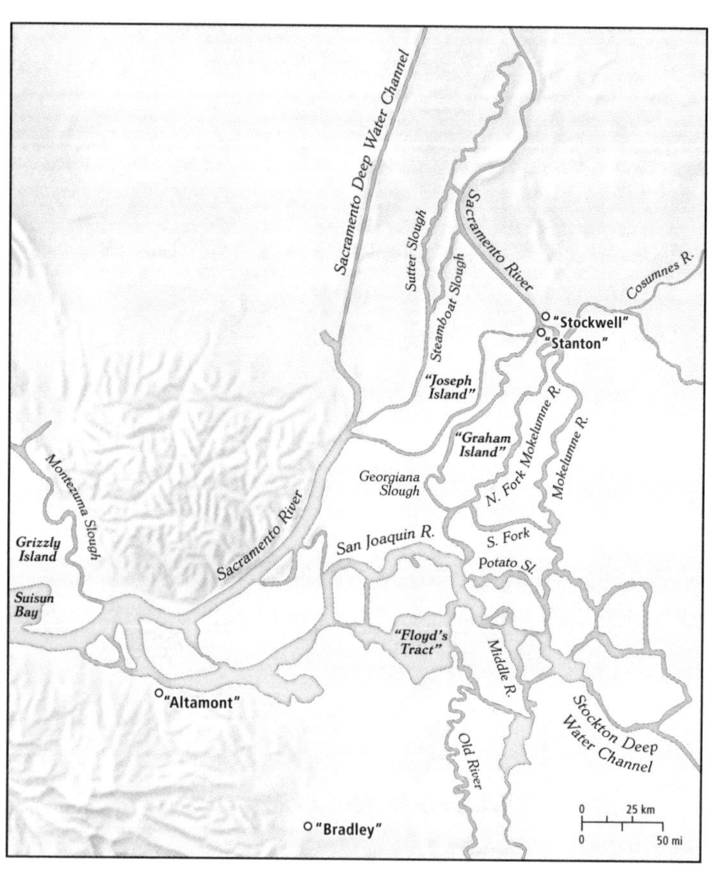

Sacramento Deep Water Channel
Sutter Slough
Steamboat Slough
Sacramento River
Cosumnes R.
"Stockwell"
"Stanton"
"Joseph Island"
"Graham Island"
N. Fork Mokelumne R.
Mokelumne R.
Georgiana Slough
Montezuma Slough
Grizzly Island
Suisun Bay
Sacramento River
San Joaquin R.
S. Fork
Potato Sl.
"Floyd's Tract"
Middle R.
"Altamont"
Old River
Stockton Deep Water Channel
0
25 km
0
50 mi
"Bradley"

SACRAMENTO RIVER

1

The day Eiji fell from the tractor and was crushed by his own machine, Kimiko blamed herself for not having been in the orchard to point out the rut.

"I was there," Takashi told her, "and I didn't see the rut."

"Can't be two places," Kimiko said, more to herself than Takashi. When the accident happened, she'd left the orchard and had been inside making their lunch.

For weeks afterward, Japanese neighbors and friends came to the house and set dishes on the counter. Asparagus that the Issei, first-generation Japanese, had planted themselves, simmered in fish broth, and a pot of short ribs cooked until tender, with potatoes pulled from the dirt. Mixed into those dishes was the unspoken understanding that farming was dreams realized, hard work, and peril all in one, like nori rolled around sticky rice and sweetened with sesame.

Eiji's neighbor Wes showed up with a dish of noodles. "Your father," he said to Takashi, "was happy on Joseph Island."

Takashi nodded. Eiji had escaped war in his own country and then the hard labor of Hawaiian pineapple plantations for an existence coaxing life from the delta soil. That soil had been nourished by water that flowed from the northeastern corner of California, where the Pit River formed the headwaters of the Sacramento. By the time it passed through the far reaches of the Cascade Range, the McCloud River, along with snowmelt and volcanic springs, swelled the Sacramento. It moved through the northern valley in a series of pools and riffles deep enough for a drift boat and wide enough for the cast of three or four fishermen if their skiffs were lined from bank to bank. Cottonwood and willow hung over the banks, the native pink-striped rainbow trout hiding in their shadows.

As the Sacramento wound through the valley, other rivers fed by snowmelt from the Sierra Nevada dropped in to join it. This made fertile ground for rice and alfalfa growing tall in the spring, for olives and stone fruit ripening in the heat of summer.

Out of the Southern Sierra the San Joaquin flowed north. It was joined by the rivers flowing from the gold country that provided rich ground for heat-seeking crops like almonds and peaches, raisins and grapes. The two rivers running the length of the great Central Valley met in a meandering delta at the mouth of the San Francisco Bay.

At one time the Maidu, Wintun, and other native tribes populated the Sacramento Valley, living near the streams where fish were plentiful and antelope, tule elk, and deer came to drink. In the winter when the river flooded, creating a rich marshland of tules, the Native people retreated inland. Their lives ebbed and flowed with the river.

From the beginning the white settlers were different. They tried without succeeding to tame the Sacramento. Large-scale mining dumped vast amounts of gravel and sand into the rivers feeding into the lower Sacramento. When the Sacramento River flooded, fertile delta farmlands were buried under sand. The sand raised the riverbeds so drastically that they were soon higher than the islands, and every time the settlers built up the levees, a raging river tore through them.

That was how Eiji Kimura found his land, a hundred flooded acres in what the Japanese called Kawashimo, or "down river," leased from a white banker in the north delta town of Stanton. Eiji's friends told him rice would be good on an island that might flood again, but Eiji began with fifty acres of potatoes and onions that fattened underground, beans that grew tall on bamboo poles, and fruit trees that blossomed in spring. He saw the bounty and the work that took him from his knees in the soil to a ladder among the trees as being the finest expression of his own name, which meant prosperity and peace.

Eiji's friend leased another hundred acres next door from the same banker and planted asparagus, which with the high water table didn't need to be irrigated. The tules and cattails that grew on those boggy islands turned to peat when they died, and asparagus thrived in the airy soil. When Eiji drove high up on the levee road, he looked down at his friend's fields and saw the crew, mostly Filipinos, with straw hats pulled down over their heads, bandanas covering their faces, and pants tucked into their boots to keep peat dust from lodging in their socks, their hair, their eyes and throats. On land used to grow food, there was always a downside.

Wes was the banker who'd leased Eiji and his friend their land, and as he set the dish of noodles on the counter he said quietly to Takashi, "You're in charge of the farm now."

Takashi swallowed his tears and tried to summon the pride he felt at carrying on his father's legacy. After the funeral at the temple, he and his sisters, along with their mother, buried Eiji on the farm. Eiji had planted a garden of morning glories, asters, and marigolds at the edge of his cherry orchard, and they made his grave there, using stones from the river levee and a headstone with his name—peace and prosperity—carved in Japanese letters.

Sadness lingered like the musky smell of marigolds and flowed with the river washing against the levee. But they got up every morning, pulled up potatoes and onions, and hacked at the weeds the same way they had when Eiji was alive. And they went to family picnics, where Eiji's friends remembered him with comforting stories.

It was when Takashi saw Keiko at a picnic that he was carried back to the stories their fathers had shared of their labor on a pineapple plantation. Grabbing a little bucket of Brooks cherries he'd picked himself, he walked over and offered her the bucket. And although they'd played together in a gaggle of children and flung themselves down with plates of food at many a picnic, that day when Keiko accepted the cherries he could taste their dark sweetness as if he were biting into one himself.

"My father wants me to get an education so I can do more than labor. But your cherries are delicious, so how can picking be bad?" She tilted her head as if she were teasing, the same way she had when they were nine years old.

"Neither picking nor an education is bad," Takashi said.

"Next year," Keiko said, spitting a cherry seed into her palm, "I transfer from junior college to Chico." But instead, that December their parents' native country would bomb the Honolulu harbor and President Roosevelt would order all Japanese Americans into internment camps.

The weekend after the picnic, though, Takashi picked up Keiko in the truck and drove her along the levee road where wood ducks perched in the willows, and down into the orchard he hoped would dazzle her.

As he turned off the engine he was thinking about how his father's trees were watered with the snowmelt from a volcano in the lower reaches of the Cascade Range, and once in the upper limits of that range, farmers had crossed two varieties of cherry to produce the Rainier, named after the volcano they could see from their valley. But that seemed too much to explain, and instead he got lost in a description of the genetic phenomenon that had produced the golden cherry from two dark ones.

Keiko wore a straw hat with a wide brim she pulled down to shade her eyes, and when he looked up she was laughing.

"Sorry," he said. "Too technical."

"Not at all. Life is a mystery," she said, holding his gaze, and it was Takashi who ended up being dazzled.

He started the truck engine, and in that moment the world spread before them like a road running alongside the trees thick with leaves.

The following winter, she and Takashi were stuffing their family's prized belongings into the Buddhist temple, stacking furniture to the ceiling, when they said their goodbyes. But Takashi didn't have time to wallow in his sorrow, because when he returned to the house he found his mother wrapped in a blanket, her breathing labored. One of his sisters held her while the other wiped the sweat from her forehead.

Kimiko spoke and her son moved close. "Your father built up this farm from fifty . . ." She stopped, took a breath. ". . . to a hundred acres. Not leaving home."

Later, when Takashi told his own children Kimiko's story, he would say she died of a broken heart, after war on one continent took away her first home and war on a new continent took away her second. Takashi and his sisters buried her next to Eiji, near the asters and the morning glories with their bright green leaves and purple flutes she had tended alongside her husband.

With the Buddhist temple filled to the ceiling and most of their friends already departed to internment camps, there was no funeral. But as evening shadows fell on the grave where Takashi and his sisters were tossing the last shovelful of dirt, Wes walked up still wearing his suit from work.

"I'll watch over Kimura Farm while you're gone," he said, and Takashi could taste the dish he had set on the counter after Eiji died, noodles and green beans made slippery and salty with butter. Not better than the noodles Takashi was used to, just different, the kindness offered by a neighbor.

War that had stolen their friends and the dignity of a proper funeral for Kimiko would now separate their family, as Takashi's bus was bound for the Tulare Basin at the southern end of the valley, while Keiko and his sisters were headed north toward the state line. The only recourse any of them had was what the son of Eiji's asparagus-growing neighbor had come up with as they were packing their furniture into the temple.

He'd leaned in close and whispered, "Bring seeds."

As able-bodied men during a labor shortage, he and Takashi were being sent to the cotton fields of Tulare, and their sisters sewed beans and marigold seeds into the hems of their coats.

Packed in with the other sweaty young men, Takashi looked out the window of the bus that rolled into a dusty camp. There were creases between his eyes but determination in the set of his jaw. He felt a heaviness come over him unlike even the grief of losing his father and mother, and he stepped from the bus into air as thick as the hyacinth that would one day choke the shores of the delta he called home.

2

Using a piece of broken pipe to pound the hard-packed earth between the barracks and then break up the chunks into soft ground, Takashi pushed in his beans. Next to the beans he spread the marigold seeds and covered them with a thin layer of dirt. He was sprinkling water on his seeds with a coffee can when his neighbor from home picked up the broken pipe and started breaking up the ground next to Takashi's. Once he'd prepared the soil, he dropped in the seeds from the hem of his own coat. Then a man they had never seen before picked up the broken pipe. By summer there were vegetable and flower gardens growing on what was otherwise desolate space.

Like those who came before them, Takashi and his Nisei, or second generation, were gifted at coaxing flowers and plants from the ground, even ground less forgiving than the delta soil, and their captors took notice. An army general called Takashi into his office, a boxy wooden structure that was hotter even than the barracks. But unlike the barracks stuffed with bunk beds, the general's office was nearly empty. In the middle of the space sat a desk, and on a table against the wall rested a coffeemaker holding a drained pot of coffee.

"What messages are you sending with your plants?" the general asked from behind the desk, sweat dripping from his neck onto the collar of his tight, starched uniform.

Takashi blinked.

"You people," he said, which Takashi surmised meant his Japanese friends since the general was white, "arrange your crops to send secret messages to Japanese airmen."

Takashi shook his head. "We're just growing vegetables."

"Where'd you get the seeds?"

That question cornered him, since what few vegetables were served in camp were canned.

"Tear them out," the general said.

Every time Takashi passed the ground where their plants and flowers lay uprooted, wilted and browning in the sun, he was reminded of the fear that motivated the general's suspicions. From Eiji's youth in Japan to the scope of the war that captured his son, there was no time or place Takashi knew of exempt from such fear. Fear that followed a line of immigrants through the Central Valley and said if they looked or talked differently from you and they had something you needed, they might take it from you. If on the other hand you kept them ignorant and wanting, the ignorance of your own white skin prevailed.

Takashi and his fellow prisoners had been uprooted, like the plants the general forced them to tear out, from the homes Eiji and his Issei generation had made for them. The land beyond the guard towers stretched flat to the horizon, and Takashi longed for the Sacramento Valley nestled between the Coast Range and the Sierra Nevada. Every morning they were taken by bus to Tulare landholder Lon Smith's vast empire of cotton on the other side of camp. Picking cotton was harder than any of the work they had done growing up, the endless, dusty rows with nowhere to hide from the sun, the sharp prongs that pricked fingers reaching inside the boll, the canvas sack some managed to fill with five hundred pounds but Takashi never was able to fill with half that.

Before the internment camps brought fresh labor, young people had left the fields for cities in order to avoid the work of picking cotton. Yet Takashi appreciated getting outside the confines of camp with its tasteless food, crowded barracks, and overflowing toilets. Hacking at Johnson grass transported him back to his delta farm. And in the end it was the cotton that released him from the internment camp, when a machine replaced the workers, its pipe like the trunk of an elephant sucking cotton into the belly of the beast. Then prisoners like Takashi and his neighbor, who had Wes to sponsor them, were allowed to return to their fields in the north.

Takashi's and his neighbor's acres were the only Japanese farms protected during the war. Most of their friends would return from internment camps to crops that had been destroyed by night riders carrying torches and guns, the temple holding their families' possessions burned to the ground.

There were cries of surprise and anger from Takashi and his fellow prisoners when the bus rolled up to the burned-down temple in Stanton. A hand-painted sign planted in the ashes read No Japs You Rats. In camp each of the captives had been given a number, and when Takashi read the crudely painted sign, it felt as if a night rider's torch had burned the number on his chest.

By reducing to ashes what to Eiji and his generation was sacred, the night riders had trampled the Buddhist bow of humility and respect. Takashi and his friend averted their eyes and walked straight to the bank where, through the window, they saw Wes rise from his desk. In a moment their fathers' landlord was at the door, holding the lease to his land, which had been locked in the safe. Unable to find the words to properly thank him, Takashi bowed, aware that Wes had never once trampled on that gesture of respect.

In the fields, Takashi's potato plants had flowered, wilted, and died. The vines wrapped around bean poles had turned to sticks, and pears had dropped and shriveled on the ground. But there were potatoes popping out of the dirt, the trees were standing, and three years' worth of weeds were green from Wes's watering.

Takashi was cutting the last of what he'd taken to calling *the war weeds* the day the United States dropped the bomb on Hiroshima. When he saw the pictures in the newspaper, the pain ran so deep he abandoned his work, went out into the cherry orchard, and sat under a tree near his parents' graves. Knots in the trunk of the tree dug into his spine, the ground beneath him was hard, and ants crawled up his arms. He was thirsty and hot and longed for a bowl of rice, but still he sat.

It seemed to Takashi that war was about the soil under our feet and the promises we made to those we loved. The delta might someday reclaim its sinking lands, but until then Takashi promised to tend with every muscle in his body the orchards and fields his parents had planted. It was August and the sun didn't go down until late, but only when it grew dark did he get up and return to the house.

The pain he felt for a Japan no longer his father's stayed with him, like the knots from the tree his back had absorbed. Knots he kneaded with the heel of his hand at night, each day of work bleeding into the next. The letters his sisters wrote from Tule Lake lay open on the kitchen table, like the hands he would clasp when they emerged from the bus. Because the devastating bomb is what ended the war and brought his sisters and Keiko back to him.

Tears streaming down his face, Takashi let go of his sisters and grabbed Keiko. Keiko with the searching eyes, the press of the lips that said, *I will not tell you what I have seen.* During the next year, while she fulfilled her dream of finishing college at Chico, Keiko and Takashi spent weekends helping the community rebuild the temple.

After she and Takashi were married there, and they streamed out of the temple with family and friends, Keiko stopped and put her hands on a set of columns. "We are strong," she whispered to her husband, and Takashi leaned a hand on one of the columns to steady himself. Which was why they gave their children, who were born American citizens, American names.

"That means," Takashi told Betty and John, "you are held to the same laws and privileges as anybody in this country. You belong."

3

Kimura Farm, Joseph Island

Eventually Takashi's neighbor gave up growing the asparagus his father had planted. Asparagus pickers had to dig their knives down into the soil, cut each spear, and run to catch up with the tractor. It was hard work, and when the grandchildren of Eiji's friend didn't want to do it anymore and moved on, Wes leased the land to the Sutton family who planted olive trees.

By the time Takashi's son John was born, the grizzly bears and tule elk had been hunted to extinction, but he lay in bed at night listening to the hooting of owls and the high-pitched bark of coyotes. And when he was a grown man deep into the work of helping his father on the farm, Fish and Wildlife reintroduced the elk to the island named Grizzly, and they nosed across the Montezuma Slough, antlers branching out behind them.

Since their grizzly predators were gone, the elk population was kept in check by hunters, and the farmers John knew couldn't wait to take their rifles to the nuisance deer growing fat on Delta corn and Takashi's pears. While imprisoned in the camp, Takashi had never had to use a gun. The new neighbors who'd planted olive trees had a son, Eric, who was John's age, and when they were grown Eric taught him to use a rifle.

But for John, the early morning walk to the orchard was one he dreaded. Each time a bullet entered the warm flesh of the deer, it felt like taking the bullet himself, and John was sure he didn't have the authority to kill the deer. Except that

Eiji had planted those trees and it was up to John to protect them, just as Eric protected his. One day the two sons would fight together for Joseph Island. In the meantime Eric stuffed his own freezer with venison because his neighbor didn't care for it.

When John saw the bees drawn to Takashi's flower garden, he stacked white boxes housing the honeybees in his orchards to pollinate the blossoms. While commercial hives collecting from vast acres of a single crop lost their queen within a handful of months, on Kimura Farm, with its variety of crops and hedgerows of flowers, the honeybees thrived.

John's father worked alongside him, and stopped for good only when his body wouldn't allow him to pull weeds or dig with a shovel anymore. Then in the cooler evening hours, John took him out in the truck, and Takashi kept a conversation going from the passenger seat while his son repaired a sprinkler or pruned a tree. He was eighty-seven when it became difficult to get into the truck even with John's help.

One evening, watching his son attach a pipe to an irrigation hose, Takashi remarked, "Always running to catch up, aren't we?"

"And we never do," John said.

"How many summers did we leave fruit we didn't have the hands to pick?" his father asked.

"More than I can count."

"And more fruit doesn't always mean more profit," Takashi said.

He seemed to be going back through the years like the stack of bills they sifted through to identify the ones that couldn't wait.

John searched for anger in his father's face but saw none, only contentment. When Takashi died peacefully in his sleep that night, John wondered if he had orchestrated the conversation knowing it would be their last.

By then Keiko was having trouble remembering things. One April night not long after Takashi died, John fell exhausted into bed, only to be awakened by the sound of the front door opening, and his mother's shuffling feet.

"Mom?"

The door slammed.

He jumped out of bed, threw on a pair of pants and ran outside. In the faint light of a quarter moon, he saw the outline of his mother walking toward the orchard. Even without his glasses, he could see the slight puff of her nightgown each time she took a step.

"Mom!" he called, stubbing his toe on a rock.

"Betty's climbing trees for pears again," she said. "We have to get her down."

Having learned in the previous turbulent months not to startle her, John caught up to her and took her shoulders gently between his hands.

"Mom," he said, just above a whisper, "Betty's grown up now. She's married and living in Japan." He hadn't yet learned what to let go when it came to his mother's memory.

Keiko looked alarmed by what he said but let him steer her back to the house where he tucked her into bed. He left the door to both their rooms open, getting up several times in the night to check on her.

A few nights after that she wandered into the orchard again, and John steered her back home. Lying wide awake, he did a quick inventory of their savings, which were not nearly enough for round-the-clock in-home care. A couple of mornings later, he abandoned the plowing and the fence repair and drove with his mother first to Stockton, then to the town two ferry rides over. He told her they were looking at homes where she could live safely without wandering out at night and getting hurt.

The pale walls and creamed-corn smell of the nursing homes depressed him. In one, neglect throbbed from the scuffed-up floors that needed mopping, and Keiko became agitated. John rushed her outside, but she wept in the car, and he told himself he'd find a way to pay for in-home care.

He'd saved the nursing home in Stanton for last. Eric, who had an aunt living there, spoke highly of it, and John was holding out hope. And by some miracle, the nursing home closest to Kimura Farm turned out to be the most welcoming, with decent-looking food and two or three gardens where residents walked or parked their wheelchairs in the sun. For the first time that day, Keiko relaxed.

"What do you think?" he asked her.

"I like the garden," she said.

"Me too."

Three sleep-deprived months later, John moved Keiko into the nursing home in Stanton, where he went to see her every night after dinner. Often when she saw him she looked scared, but his visits seemed to calm her and he always stayed until she fell asleep.

Returning to an empty house, John admitted to himself that he'd like to share his life, as his grandfather had with Kimiko and his father with Keiko. He told Eric, who had the same compact build he did, thick brown hair, and mischievous eyes. Eric had gotten married and was raising a family while tending the olive orchards.

"Come to dinner," Eric said. What was unusual wasn't the dinner invitation but the fact that he invited his daughter's science teacher Benji.

"You a matchmaker now?" John asked, when the night of the dinner he and Eric ducked into the kitchen to grab a beer. But he realized he couldn't wait to talk with the teacher, who smiled at him when they returned to the living room.

"Is Eric's daughter the worst behaved in class?" he asked.

"Not at all," Benji said. "She's delightful."

John looked around for Eric's children.

"They're upstairs doing their homework," Eric said.

"Because they're delightful?" John asked, and Benji's laugh was like a drone catching the queen mid-flight.

"Eric says you grew up on the farm next door," she said, and John found himself telling her about Takashi and the life he built for himself after the war. At dinner when she described her students, her eyes glittered like sun on the water, and her hair would not be contained by the tie she wore loosely at her back.

"I love teaching science to students who live near one of the most threatened estuaries," she said. "Even my boyfriend, who's in Seattle, couldn't keep me from taking this job."

Hearing the word "boyfriend," John told himself it wouldn't have worked anyway. Benji was fifteen years younger than he was.

Then Eric phoned him. "Her boyfriend's not following her from Seattle," he said.

"So?"

"So she's available."

"She's too young."

"She likes you," Eric said, and invited them to dinner again.

John always repaid Eric and his wife by doing the dishes, and this time their hosts retreated to the living room while Benji appeared next to him with a dishtowel. As he handed her a wet pan, he silently chided himself for the thrill he felt at a moment of domestic bliss. After the dishes were done, she walked him to the door and stood outside with him.

"I know Eric told you my boyfriend's not leaving Seattle," she said.

He waited for her to tell him Eric was wrong, but she said nothing more. Before he could second-guess himself he leaned in and kissed her. He'd seen what happened when the honeybee queen died and the drones abandoned the hive in search of a new queen, swarming in a buzzing mass. That night at Eric's, the hive had swarmed in search of a new queen and found her.

John was on the eve of his fiftieth birthday when the midwife handed him his daughter, and he turned to the window looking out on the orchard whose cherries his father had once used as way into a woman's heart. By the time Alexis was born, Kimura Farm was threatened by more than deer and dwindling levees. Landowners to the south wanted the water that flowed past Joseph Island, and John and Eric would need to join forces against them, the same way a kind neighbor had once allied himself with Takashi.

"Kawashimo, downriver," John whispered to the baby in his arms. "You will love living here."

Takashi had always told him, "Only make a promise you can keep." It was as much a promise as John could make to his daughter. Because if water tunnels were built under Joseph Island, no banker in Stanton would be able to save Kimura Farm.

KINGS RIVER

4

Hatfield, California

Around the time Takashi Kimura was born in 1914, Lon Smith bought fifty thousand acres in the Tulare Basin for a dollar an acre. The largest freshwater lake west of the Mississippi, the Tulare ebbed and flowed with the seasons, and was part of a network of wetlands spanning five hundred million acres. The Kings, Kern, Tule, and Kaweah Rivers flowed into the basin, but the ensuing lake was usually dry by September.

In the fields he drilled for oil, Lon planted cotton. Cotton took a lot of water and could be grown cheaper in his native Georgia where it rained all year, but southern farmers were paid not to grow it so western landowners like Lon could sell more.

Before his son Patrick convinced the Army Corps of Engineers to dam all four rivers and divert most of the water to Smith Farm, Lon corralled and hoarded as much as he could and in wet winters collected subsidies from the government for the crops he couldn't grow in his flooded fields. He built a channel to divert water from its riparian owners on the Kings River and, after the stock market crash, increased his claim by buying that land from the same desperate farmers who'd gone belly up. By then Lon had enough money to buy two hundred fifty thousand acres in the Tehachapi Range, with a dream of growing houses on the land where he loosed twelve thousand head of cattle.

For Lon, Beth, and their young son Patrick, the Depression had few adverse effects beyond the fading life of their hometown, which had always shown signs of poverty even in the years it thrived. If anything Lon benefited during the war, with free labor from Takashi and his fellow prisoners.

Patrick was four and the sight of a jackrabbit wasn't yet cause for him to reach for his shotgun when, walking down the road by the barn hand in hand with his mother, he spotted one loping out of the saltbush. The rabbit froze, its nose twitching. Patrick's mother crouched down, and it turned and loped back into the saltbush.

The boy pointed as it disappeared.

"That's a jackrabbit," his mother said, and some days later presented him with a stuffed toy that had long grey ears. "Mr. Jack Rabbit," she said. Beth's eyes, like his own, were the very color of saltbush.

"Hello, Jack," he said, turning over the stuffed toy to examine the stubby tail on its backside. "Do they really stand up like people do?"

She laughed. "No, that just makes it easier to hug." And sure enough, by the time Patrick was nine, Jack was flattened from being hugged and slept on. And his friend Robert, already bullish with the body to match, spotted the stuffed animal on Patrick's bed.

"What's this?" his friend asked, holding it up by the ear.

Patrick grabbed the toy and threw it against the wall, eliciting roars of laughter from Robert, who picked it up and threw it harder. The boys collapsed on the floor, scrambling for the stuffed animal, and each time Patrick threw it he felt his own guts slam against the wall.

After his friend left he hid Jack in a box of outgrown clothes under his bed. Night after night he felt the stare of the black button eyes through the frayed trousers, the lid of the box, and the mattress. Then he forgot about the toy until his mother slid the box out from under the bed.

"May as well give away these clothes," she said. "You're not going to grow back into them."

She pulled out Jack, holding him by the waist, not the ear as Robert had, and asked, "What shall we do with him?"

Patrick's stomach flopped like Jack's, folding under his mother's soft grip. "I'm done with him." He looked down at his sneakers where the rubber curled and peeled away from the canvas. Time for a new pair, Beth would say when she noticed.

She turned Jack over and examined the squashed tail. "He's too worn to give away."

"In the bin he goes," Patrick said, grabbing the stuffed animal and heading outside. But when he lifted the lid off the trash can, he stood holding Jack, blubbering like a baby. Finally, wiping his nose on the sleeve of his sweatshirt, he dropped the stuffed animal in the can and clapped down the lid.

Returning to the house, he found his mother with the box on the living room floor, ducking her head into the clothes as he passed to preserve his dignity.

From then on his vision did not extend beyond the cans he knocked off the fence behind the house with his father's .22. The buckling fence was already the relic of another era, Lon's crop an endless line of white-speckled green stretching beyond it all the way to the horizon.

Patrick was eleven when his father invited him to tag along deer hunting on the Tehachapi ranch, waking him at three in the morning for the long drive south. The sun was just rising when they parked the car and tromped across a rugged hillside. Seventy thousand acres of cotton left little on which to rest the eyes, and Patrick was captivated by the tall black oaks, the red-tailed hawks circling in a pale blue sky. The October air was sweet with the smell of grass, sunbaked and brittle, of mud crusted over and flaking, and Patrick heard the whistle of a hawk in a distant black oak whose leaves had turned yellow.

Carrying a knapsack with their lunch, gun pointed at the ground, Lon wandered the paths deer had cut across the hillside, and his son followed. When they didn't spot a single deer before lunch they settled on a patch of rocks jutting out of the grass and ate hunks of salami Lon cut off with a buck knife, hoping to procure his own trophy antlers like the ones that adorned the handle of the knife.

Hours later they stalked a deer only to have it run away, and the frustration that had been smoldering in Lon erupted in a single growl. He slapped the barrel in Patrick's hand and marched back to the car. Patrick didn't care—he was so happy to be walking the ranch clutching his father's gun. But after his mother got sick he understood the need for retribution.

Every can he riddled with bullets was a tangible antidote to the emotions he couldn't come close to naming when she had one of her endless coughing bouts. The .22 gave him the illusion of being able to do something about it, while his mother shrank further and further into her room with the curtains drawn against the sun.

After the coroner carried her body away, Patrick ran out to the trash can, picked up the lid and slammed it again and again. As if that could bring back the stuffed animal that had long since been hauled away in the garbage truck. When he turned back to the house, Lon was standing on the porch, and although Patrick tried to slip past him, his father seized him by the arms. It was the only time he remembered Lon hugging him, and it seemed to go on forever. After a while Patrick dropped his arms to his sides. His father held on for a few more beats, then let go. Not wanting to blubber as he had the day he threw Jack in the trash, Patrick staggered into the kitchen. Lon followed, closing the door of the room off the kitchen where his wife had slept for the last few months.

In the mornings Patrick examined the hair under his armpits, under the penis that stood stiff when he climbed out of bed to pee. A remoteness settled between father and son, the only sounds at breakfast their chewing on the toast Lon inevitably burnt. Then Patrick turned thirteen, and when he came downstairs Lon laid his present on the kitchen table—a maple Winchester with brass trim.

"Thank you," Patrick said, the toast getting caught in his throat. He swallowed hard and carried the gun outside.

That night he took the Winchester out to the barn, pointing it at bats as they flitted across the beams. But it was dark and they were too fast, and after he'd lodged a slew of bullets in the beams and shot several through the corrugated roof, he slumped back to the house, remembering the deer that had eluded Lon.

In the morning, he pulled on a pair of dirty socks and his boots and slipped outside. He planned to walk out to the road and thumb a ride into town, but parked in front of the house, Lon's brand-new Ford with the whitewall tires looked like a carriage ready to transport him. He eased open the screen door and reached for the ring of keys on the hook. Next thing he knew he was behind the wheel. He told himself that if he'd asked, his father would have given him permission. And as he pulled out of the driveway, Patrick looked in the rearview mirror and saw him standing on the porch. But since Lon didn't wave or otherwise move, Patrick took off with what he wanted to believe was his father's blessing.

It was Saturday, and the glory of two days without school bounced off the hood of the Ford. Patrick passed one old farmer too blinded by the sun to see him behind the wheel. He hadn't even reached the edge of town before he saw Steve and Robert, the friend who'd helped launch Jack Rabbit into the afterlife, moping around in front of the gas station. When they spotted

Patrick driving his father's car, their eyes bugged out of their heads.

"What are you two fools doing," he said after he parked and stepped out of the Ford.

"What are *you* doing in your dad's car?" Steve asked. He was always bouncing and stayed skinny no matter how many burgers he consumed at the Hatfield Frosty.

"Let's go buy some cigarettes," Patrick said in reply, and his friends followed, even though none of them had ever smoked.

The gas station attendant was about their fathers' age, and he looked at Steve as if he knew him, which in a town that size he likely did. But when Patrick fished some coins out of his pocket and asked for a pack of Chesterfields, the man handed them over.

They climbed in the car and drove back to Smith Farm, looking out for police but seeing none. Patrick took the long way home in order to avoid the house, where he knew Lon was waiting. He parked behind the barn and lit the first cigarette, scowling up into the dark where the bats hung from the beams. Robert, stalky with close-cropped hair so thick it stood straight up, leaned a hand up against the barn, took his first puff, and coughed. Steve started coughing and couldn't stop, but the smoke felt oddly comforting to Patrick's empty belly.

"Forget cans. Let's shoot some rabbits," Patrick said, going into the barn.

Steve's eyes widened, but he and Robert followed when Patrick ground out his cigarette with a boot heel and came out of the barn with his Winchester. They walked down the road, scared two jackrabbits out of the saltbush, and Patrick shot them both in the neck. He handed the rifle to Robert, they walked a little farther, and when two more popped out of the brush Robert gunned them down with equal precision.

"Your turn," Robert said, handing the rifle to Steve, who shook his head ever so slightly while accepting the gun.

They kept walking until they stirred three more out of the brush. Steve missed the first one and shot the second one in the leg. It loped away wounded, and Patrick scowled.

"We're here to put them out of their misery," he said.

But Patrick really didn't want to see their rabbit guts. Leaving the carcasses for the buzzards, he drove his friends back to the house, where Lon was standing on the front porch as if he'd been there all morning.

"Take the car again and I'll have your hide," he said.

Steve sucked in his breath, but picturing the dead rabbits, Patrick fought the urge to laugh. He avoided looking at his father as he said, "Sorry about the car."

Gazing at the horizon that shimmered in the noonday heat, Lon motioned to the boys. "Come inside for a sandwich."

In the kitchen he drained two cans of tuna, stirred in a dollop of mayonnaise, and spread the tuna between slices of bread. It was the same lunch he packed his son every day of the week. When Patrick threw the sack in the trash can at school, he felt a pang. Then slamming the lid with the same determination he had when he threw away Jack, he left campus without permission and bought a hamburger at the Frosty.

Patrick didn't have much use for school. Unlike his two friends who couldn't seem to grasp math, he saw the answers right away but got a failing grade because he couldn't show his work. The three of them started smoking behind the building, not bothering to return to class after lunch. By the time they were sixteen, they were skipping school altogether. They dragged an old mattress behind the barn and started skulking around the Friday night dances in Hatfield looking for conquests.

When Patrick saw Genevieve across the room at the Hatfield Town Hall, his first thought was that the flush of her cheeks and the blue in her eyes lit up her face like a goddamn American flag.

"If you get the Waterfield girl pregnant," his dad had been telling him since the first day of high school, "you'll combine two of the biggest empires in California." And now looking at Genevieve he couldn't get his dad's voice out of his head.

He stared her down until she made eye contact, then he turned and walked outside. Patrick seemed taller than he was and, hanging in the shadows behind the building, a brush of sandy hair flopping across his forehead, he thought his chances were pretty good. Sure enough, Genevieve came swinging around the corner like she owned the place, which as the sole heir to her parents' land she pretty much did. Ten minutes later they were all piled in Lon's car headed back to Smith Farm, next over from the Waterfield property that rivaled his family's in size.

By then Patrick had gotten his license and permission to drive his father's car and had moved on to the liquor cabinet, from which he'd stolen a bottle of gin. Sitting on the mattress passing it between the four of them, he felt a surge of passion—whether for the gin, at once both cool on his tongue and burning in his throat, or the live girl next to him, he couldn't say.

Steve and Robert wandered off with the bottle and ended up throwing up in the saltbush, while Patrick and Genevieve looked for something to do. The only thing passing between Patrick's ears was the persistent image of Genevieve naked, her chest as flat as the redwood two-by-fours Lon had used to build the barn. He lurched at her and when she didn't resist, fell back with her on the mattress. She slipped her tongue in his mouth and released the erection from his pants. He moaned, tugged at her underwear, and lost his virginity in what was, after years of lying about it, no time at all. Afterward he wasn't sure whether it was he or Genevieve who'd made the conquest.

Over the ensuing weeks Genevieve started hanging around, and when Robert made a pass at her, she grabbed Patrick's hand as if she were claiming him. That was fine by Patrick, who took her behind the barn and managed to hold out inside her for a couple of minutes, a record in his new ledger.

She avoided him for weeks after that. Patrick was thinking about chasing her down when, driving past the Frosty, he saw her sitting at the picnic table outside sucking on a milkshake. He turned into the lot, rolled up practically to her feet, and stopped. Jangling the keys as he stepped out of the car, he sauntered over and sat across from her.

"You've made yourself scarce," he said.

She didn't look angry, as he'd expected her to. There was a twinkle in her eye like a star on the flag. "I'm pregnant," she said, setting down her milkshake.

Hoping to reverse the urge to throw up, Patrick pulled a cigarette from the carton in his pocket and lit it. When he got his first taste of sex, his father's voice saying "pregnant" had receded. Now here it was again.

"So what are you going to do about it?" she asked, blue eyes penetrating the smoke he blew between them.

He snuffed out his cigarette and when she stood said, "Need a ride home?"

Holding her shake, she climbed in the passenger seat of the Ford and was silent on the drive back to Waterfield Farm.

He parked a distance from the house. "I need some time to think about it," he said.

She got out of the car, leaned in the window, and said, "Don't think too long."

Patrick was smoking a cigarette and pacing in the graveled driveway when Lon emerged from the house.

"Son," he said, squinting through the haze of cigarettes Patrick no longer bothered to hide. "Why don't you marry the

Waterfield girl, quit the school building you haven't seen in months, and help me run this operation." Lon had always called it an operation, and certainly seventy thousand acres was more than a farm.

That was how Lon would get his wish of combining two empires. But he couldn't very well flaunt it when only the year before he'd built a levee that had flooded the Waterfield land while leaving his dry.

Patrick ground his cigarette into the gravel and stormed into the house, furious that ever since his mother got sick his life was moving in a direction he wouldn't have chosen. But if he was being honest with himself, he *had* chosen.

Three days later a black Cadillac pulled up to the house, and Stewart and Ileen Waterfield knocked on the door.

"Come in," Lon said, but Ileen shook her head.

Standing next to her on the porch, her husband said, "We're not planning to have a lavish wedding."

Lon knew exactly what they were talking about, even though his son had told him nothing. "Fair enough, when those two kids are the ones who got themselves into trouble," he said, as if it hadn't been his idea.

That night after dinner Lon placed a small velvet bag on the table. "Open it," he said.

Inserting a finger into the bag, Patrick felt the sharpness of his mother's double diamond ring, and pulling it out, held the silver band between his fingers.

"Your mother would have wanted you to have it," Lon said. His eyes were dry but his mouth was drawn down to his stubbled chin.

A month later Patrick slipped the ring on Genevieve's finger at the Hatfield city hall. She wore a sleek brown skirt and matching jacket. Huddled next to her, her mother looked miserable. On the other side of his wife, Stewart Waterfield was livid, knowing that with this wedding Lon had pulled another flood job.

Patrick seized Genevieve's hand and swaggered out of city hall into the glaring sunlight. It may have been Lon's idea, but with his mother's diamond ring on Genevieve's finger, Patrick saw himself as the vaquero who'd pulled it off. And just like that, at sixteen he was heir to a second cotton operation, an oil company, and the 250,000-acre El Toro Ranch in the Tehachapi Range, whose future was inextricably bound to tunnels under an island two hundred and forty miles away.

5

It was after their third daughter, Maxine, was born, grey eyes with a fleck of her mother's blue, that Patrick realized he loved his wife. They were sipping their evening gin and tonic on the verandah of the big house they'd built next to Lon's, when he said, "I love you."

He heard the surprise in his own voice, but Genevieve didn't blink. She set down her drink and said, "I certainly met my match when you came along."

He hadn't expected her to say I love you. Even as a blind-sided sixteen-year-old, he'd understood the quantifiable terms of their marriage. Genevieve seemed content. Happy even. As the girls grew she poured her energy into the Hatfield Library. In a town that had become mostly weedy parking lots and houses with broken windows, she was the driving force behind the bold, newly built library, with its fresh carpet, air-conditioning that offered relief from the heat of summer, and rows of white shelves waiting to be filled with books, which she purchased by the armload and, after her daughters had devoured them, donated to the library.

As a married man Patrick didn't take orders from Lon any better than he had growing up. It was the day after Maxine's fifth birthday that Lon's heart gave out as he was walking the grounds with a farm manager. For the next week Genevieve took charge of the funeral arrangements, while Patrick was left feeling strangely numb. Standing before the coffin in a mostly empty church, Steve wept and Robert was sniveling because of allergies not Lon. Patrick wasn't sure what he felt, beyond rage at the finality of life and the distant memory of wings in a pale blue sky. And days later, relief that he was free to run the operation as he saw fit.

Lon's genius had been the mechanical picker he adapted from the original elephantine engine his predecessors invented in Georgia. Lon's new picker produced four hundred bales a day of the world's finest cotton, and he had convinced the best tire, T-shirt, and underwear companies to buy exclusively from him. Patrick carried on, persuading big buyers all over the world that not even cotton in the South could compare to Smith's.

Not wanting any part of the plant to go to waste, Lon had sold the seed for everything from vegetable oil to cotton balls. After he died, his son followed suit by doubling the number of calves he raised on El Toro Ranch and building a feedlot just outside Hatfield where he fattened them on cottonseed cake. They were lined up hoof to hoof, munching at a trough as long as the string of cars on the freight train that at night sent its baleful call across the valley. They stood on hills of their own manure, and on hot days the stench in town was enough to burn nostrils and bring tears to eyes. Patrick turned the Tehachapi grazing operation into El Toro Land Company, something Lon had always wanted to do. It was his final tribute to his father, and he knew it would have repercussions from one end of the Central Valley to the other, far beyond the stench of his Hatfield feedlot.

MONTEREY BAY

6

Marie Palvis was fifteen when she told her parents she liked girls, not boys, which was not something people said in 1975.

At five years old on Christmas Eve, lying in front of the fireplace with a warm belly full of lamb stew, she'd asked her mother to read the story of the king and his servant Daniel. Even as she'd gobbled up her mother's cooking, she loved that Daniel, who ate only vegetables, was stronger than the servants who ate meat, and that nobody but he could interpret the king's strange dreams. Curled up to the fire, Marie drifted from her mother's voice toward the rocky plains across which the king, driven out into the wild, crawled to drink from the river like an animal.

Later her mother woke her, and they threw on their coats and climbed in the car, her father driving slowly through the icy streets of Madison, Wisconsin, until the dome appeared in the night sky, rising from the pointed roof of the church. They made their way through the darkened church to the pews and waited.

Then the organ started and the procession came from the back—the first priest with the incense, the second holding the cross high. And last the altar boys, including her brother, holding candles that threw shadows across the half-empty pews.

Sometimes at night Marie crept into Mark's room. "Can't sleep," she'd whisper in the darkness, and Mark would recite the Twenty-Third Psalm, slowing over the words, "Though I may walk in the valley of the shadow of death," so that when she returned to her bed, the sound of feet treading over a mountain path lulled her to sleep. The same way he walked slowly down the aisle with the candles, destined even then for the clergy.

Years after she'd moved away from Wisconsin, she could still smell it—the melting wax and the wet-marble scent of holy water. Her mother's wool coat as Marie leaned sleepily against it and gazed up at the domed ceiling. The bitter pine smoke as the priest passed them waving the censer on a chain. The excitement when they awoke the next morning to snow on the ground outside the window. Their parents in bathrobes, coffee cups clicking against saucers as she and Mark pulled treasures from hand-knit stockings: for Mark a signed baseball, for Marie colored pencils and a Slinky that spiraled from one stair to the next before collapsing under its own weight.

The comfort of it only made it harder to face the stirrings that began inside her as she approached adolescence.

When she said she liked girls, not boys, her dad said, "What do you mean?"

Her mother was stunned into silence.

Then her dad said, "I don't understand," in a tone that meant the conversation was over.

By the time she graduated from the Jesuit college in her home state, Marie felt she was drowning in the thick of her upbringing, like the tapioca her mother used to make cherry pie. If she could get out to the edges she could breathe. So when Mark was assigned the church in California, Marie followed. But the edge of the continent turned out to be a jumping-off point for other destinations—that is, until she found Lydia. Lydia was water glimmering on a rice field that caused the wings to turn, descend, and land, a predetermined stop on a long migration.

She'd met Nora first, and they'd dated for about a year, an unhappy interlude for both of them. They'd found stronger footing on a platonic basis and managed to remain good friends. But

Lydia, she had a way of making a face or saying something funny when Marie got too serious. Like being intercepted with a hug, she stopped you, softened you, dissolved dark thoughts. Much of what made Marie laugh was Lydia's body bending in on itself, her long blonde hair falling over her face. Her whole physical being ran counter to Marie's, Marie's dark hair and the belly she had due to a weakness for avocados and lattes.

"I need somebody like you," Marie said, way too soon after they met. But there was recognition in Lydia's eyes, and that's when Marie knew the person making the jokes needed something too.

Lydia was stable as the concrete slab foundation of her childhood home on the central California coast, earthquake country, where she took Marie to meet her parents, Vera and Walt.

Vera Hayes looked disappointed, as if she'd hoped it would be a man. But she made twice-baked potatoes because her daughter and her friend were vegetarians and drew Marie into the conversation.

Walt's eyes glimmered when Marie talked about chasing volcanoes in Hawaii.

"Dad was stationed in the South Pacific during World War II," Lydia said.

"He was part of the rescue that pulled survivors from the water after Japanese torpedoes hit a ship," Vera said.

Walt peered at his potato skin over the rim of his glasses. "The ship sank in less than fifteen minutes, and the guys floated in their life jackets for five days before they were rescued by a Navy seaplane."

"Weren't there sharks?" Marie asked.

He nodded. "When the pilot saw the men warding off sharks, he touched down on twelve-foot swells. He and his crew kept throwing out the life ring, and once the fuselage was full they tied the survivors to the wings with parachute cord."

Vera took a bite of potato and shifted her slim, sixty-year-old body. "Walt's was the first ship to arrive on the scene," she said.

Lydia's father winced. Seeing he was ready to change the subject, his daughter asked, "You and Dad met at a clambake, didn't you?"

"We did, just weeks before the war started."

"We had time for two dates," Walt said. "Then we corresponded by letter."

"In the last one," Vera said, "he wrote, 'If I make it home alive, will you marry me?'"

After she and Marie did the dishes, Lydia made up the bed on the pull-out sofa in the living room. The sofa where Vera had left her daughter's duffel bag, saying pointedly, "Marie can sleep in your room."

"Maybe I'll sneak in later," Lydia said, slipping a pillow into its case.

But Marie shook her head. "Your parents waited through an entire war. We can wait one night."

"I'm pretty sure they waited until they were married." Lydia closed her eyes on the word "married" because it was a word they'd gotten stuck on.

The idea of marriage gave Lydia pause, but it was the *house* that scared Marie. On her travels west she'd landed on the island of Kauai, where she'd lived in a campground while taking pictures of the active volcano. Luxury was a motel where she occasionally sought refuge from the rain beating against her tent. Returning to the mainland, she'd looked for rentals with short-term leases so she could move with little notice, go somewhere else to shoot pictures.

In the car the next day on the way back north, Marie gazed out the window at rolling hills that recent rains had turned brilliant green. "I think I need to go see my dad," she said.

"I agree," Lydia said.

Before she and Lydia met, Marie had flown back to Wisconsin to be with her mother the last few weeks of her life. Mark could only stay a couple of days, but Marie was able to stay on, able to sink in, knowing it was the last time she would. Her mom slept most of the time, and the three of them fell into a peaceful silence. In that way a treaty was signed and things were left undone.

After the memorial their Lithuanian friends absorbed her dad Dominic, inviting him over, making sure he was never alone too long, and Marie returned to California knowing he had friends looking after him. This would be her first time back in Wisconsin since the memorial.

At the airport when Lydia dropped her off, Marie was surprised at her own tears, and Lydia looked on the verge of asking a question but didn't.

When the taxi dropped her off at her dad's and he answered the door, they hugged. Setting down her suitcase and following him through the living room, Marie spotted a pile of photo albums, and picked up a thick one on top.

In the kitchen, she put the water on to boil and opened the photo album. It wasn't, as she'd expected, childhood pictures of her and Mark, but rather glossy black-and-white photos of her young parents in Lithuania.

"Have you been looking at these?" she asked.

Her father nodded.

When the kettle whistled, she made two cups of his favorite amber tea, as if swallowing the resin-y liquid meant, if not accepting, then making peace with his personal creed. For each photo to which she pointed Dominic had a story, and since none of the faces had followed him to Wisconsin, she knew her parents had left their loved ones behind, much as she had. They'd been older when they had children, and now, studying her dad—thin graying hair, handsome face with the long nose she'd inherited—she saw that she and her father were not so different. And after they'd drained their tea, after they'd come to the last page in the album, Marie pulled a photo out of her daypack and set it on the kitchen table.

"Who's that?" he asked.

"Lydia."

He nodded politely.

Not knowing how else to put it, she said, "We bought a house." Although they hadn't yet.

He frowned and tilted his head as if to say he understood.

The plane had barely lifted off the ground in Madison when Marie thought of beetroot soup, her father hunched over it with his spoon, cheeks reflecting the bright color of the beets, flushed with the happiness of a meal with friends. There had been many meals with friends, the sound of Lithuanian being passed around the table with the crisp fried bread. And staring at the tray table tucked into the seat in front of her, Marie knew the Lithuanian community in Madison, while not family by blood, had brought her parents into the fold. Like the family Lydia was asking her to make with a house.

When she stepped off the plane in San Francisco, the distance up the accordion gangway and through the airport to the waiting area was short, yet it felt like miles. And there was Lydia, gripping a bunch of anemones, flowers as straightforward and wild as the holder herself.

"Yes to the house," Marie said, as they stood holding each other while all around them people called out, hugged, juggled bags and children.

"Yes to getting married," Lydia said.

And in that moment, before they even set foot inside the adobe home, Marie let go of her nomadic existence, setting down roots as tangled and thick as the tomatoes they planted in backyard beds. In the small front yard, bees hovered around the salvia that smelled like pineapple and was a cousin to the variety Marie's mother had planted each summer in pots and added to her potato dumplings. But sage required little water, which was why people in California grew it.

The first decision they had to make was where to put the darkroom. Marie suggested the pantry, but Lydia wanted to convert the old shed in the backyard.

"How much room do you need for a few jars?" Marie asked. But she already knew. Lydia could fill the pantry with her pasta ingredients alone: sesame, coconut, and cashew oil, olive oil local and imported, spaghetti, rigatoni, pappardelle, and fusilli.

Lydia led her outside and yanked open the shed door. "It sticks," she said, "so it's airtight and the light won't get through."

Termite frass covered the shelves and cobwebs obscured the windows. Lydia dragged out a spilling bag of potting soil, grabbed a broom, and swept dirt and frass from the shelves.

Reluctantly, Marie picked up a rag and wiped down the windows. "The chemicals will kill me if the mildew doesn't get me first."

"I can install a vent," Lydia said. Her dad had taught her to use a hammer and screwdriver, and when she was seven, the power drill. By ten she knew how to use the jigsaw and the circular saw and had helped Walt build a table.

"There's no sink or running water," Marie said.

Lydia pointed at the garden hose. "Would the hose and a plastic tub work?"

Marie sighed. Resigned, the following weekend she sealed the windows with cardboard, while Lydia crafted a rudimentary sink with the hose, some jugs, and a plastic tub.

It was when they turned on the battery-operated light and it lit up the darkroom that Lydia brought up church. "I may not believe in God," she said, "but I need to go hear your brother because it's important to you."

For Marie, listening to Mark give the homily on Sunday mornings was like tightening the strings inside her until they hummed. But she knew where Lydia stood.

One clear night early in their courtship they'd gone to the beach with a bottle of wine. They were lying on a blanket looking up when Lydia pointed at the black space between the stars that were the hand and elbow of Orion. "I see the forearm. And when I attach the legs to the seat of a chair, I see a hip socket."

She pointed to Scorpio, where she saw legs in the black space around the stinger. Eventually, Lydia said, the constellations sucked all living matter into their orbits. It was what she and Marie had agreed on, that their bones were the dust of asteroids.

Marie had pointed out what she knew, the Big Dipper, which Lydia said was the Greater She-Bear. She showed Marie how the tip of the handle formed the nose and the dipper rested on the bear's shoulder, and how the star of the dipper pointed to the handle of the Little Dipper, or Little Bear.

"The tip of the little handle," she said, "is Polaris, the North Star, and Little Bear rotates around Polaris." She jumped up and spread her arms wide. "Now we're facing north." She moved her right hand. "This is east." She waved her left hand. "And this is west. Polaris is the navigational star."

That was something Marie would remember after Lydia was gone, and she stood alone in an orchard, looking for a star to navigate by.

The morning Lydia joined Marie in church, she looked around at the statues of Joseph and Mary in every alcove. She spotted the little pilgrim statue a family would host that week and squirmed like a restless animal. Later in the car on the way home she asked, "How is carrying around the Mary statue different from praying to an idol?"

In ancient times, Marie told her, women served in the temple and so did Mary. She might even have vowed herself a virgin before she met Joseph, with the intention of remaining one after they were married.

"The ancient Roman Paula took a vow of chastity after her husband died," Marie said. "She was the one who suggested the Catholic priest Jerome translate the Bible into Latin. Paula taught herself Hebrew and edited the translation that became the Bible for Roman Catholics for fifteen hundred years."

"Celibacy by choice," Lydia said, "is one thing. By order it's another."

Which was true. There were rumors about Paula and Jerome, who were buried next to each other. "After she died Jerome wrote, 'If all the members of my body were to be converted into tongues and if each of my limbs were to be gifted with a human voice, I could still do no justice to the holy and venerable Paula.'"

Lydia looked incredulous. "You memorized that?" When Marie nodded she said, "Sounds to me like Jerome ran his tongue all over her holiness."

And Marie had to agree.

7

In the last year of his life, Marie's dad Dominic came to live with them, and it changed things, with Marie driving him on errands and Lydia making a bigger pot of soup or adding another baked yam to the oven. Late one rainy night when Lydia was working on a grant (in the living room because they'd put Dad's bed in the room that had been Lydia's office), Marie was too tired to get up out of bed to fetch her.

In the morning as they were firing up the espresso machine, she traced her thumbs over the dark circles under Lydia's eyes. It was before Dominic was up, and Lydia said, "I wouldn't change anything."

"Neither would I," Marie said.

Later Marie took him to a doctor's appointment, driving slowly down their street. The rains had passed and the sun was bouncing off fat white clouds. Drops of water glinted at the edges of the fire-red leaves on a liquidambar.

As they rounded the corner her dad said, "Grateful."

Marie assumed he was thanking her for driving him to his appointment, until she saw the tears in his eyes.

"Having you has been a blessing for us, Dad." She wanted to pull over and give the moment its due, but that would have embarrassed him, so she kept driving.

"Lydia," he said. "She's a good egg."

And stopping at a light, Marie pressed the brake twice to mark the moment the fifteen-year-old who'd known with certainty who she was met the eighty-one-year-old who'd needed time to make his peace with it.

When pneumonia landed Dominic in the hospital, Lydia, who'd been her partner for ten years at that point, was not allowed in the ICU because at the time their union was not legal in California. They pleaded with the nurses and doctors to no avail. There was one male nurse who wore lip gloss and tied back his smooth dark hair with a violet ribbon, and he cried when he told them no. Lydia refused to leave the hospital, and in the morning after Dominic died, Marie found her curled up across two chairs in the waiting room.

They had eighteen years. Not long enough, but enough to know someone, to tell her when she had bad breath or when she would repeat herself, to know the first question she would ask every morning was, "How did you sleep?" Long enough to see friends you thought would stay together break up. Long enough to learn how to stop and listen to the other person even when it annoyed you, to know it was a gift for things to be that easy.

Then one Sunday morning they went for a hike, parking on the side of the highway north of town and walking up the packed dirt path of an open field until it meandered into the woods. Lydia was talking about her dad, who at eighty-eight was younger by a decade than Marie's dad and had just retired from the Santa Barbara engineering firm he'd run for sixty-four years. That was what kept surfacing for Marie in the terror of the days following: that while Walt had remained at the helm of his company well into his senior years, Lydia's life had come to a halt just shy of her forty-fifth birthday.

Puma, panther, cougar, the animal was all of these. But in the woods and canyons he roamed on California's central coast, he was known as a mountain lion. His torso reached four feet from head to hind legs, and his tail was almost as long. He hunted at dawn and dusk, and covered miles of his own territory at night. He came from a steep hillside thick with buckeye.

There was no warning, no movement off the trail. Lydia was talking, and then the lion was there. A flash of muscle and fur, it ripped into the conversation between them, pouncing on Lydia's back. The women screamed as the lion sunk its jaws into her head and dragged her face-down into the canyon. Marie lunged for Lydia's legs, hanging on as the lion dragged the two of them deeper into the woods.

She was supposed to stand up, make herself big, but instinct made her hold on. And she continued to hang on as her elbows scraped through redwood needles and a stick jabbed her in the belly. Someone's screams—she wasn't sure whose—pierced her eardrums, which only made her hold tighter.

The screaming stopped. Lydia's body had gone slack. Marie's gaze climbed slowly, not wanting to see redwood needles jammed in the waistline, belt twisted cruelly around Lydia's narrow hips. Her ribcage not rising and falling. And a tangle of hair and blood in the lion's jaws.

The screaming started again, and this time Marie knew it was hers. A rock whizzed past her and hit the lion below the ear. It let go of Lydia and bounded off into the trees.

Marie looked up to see two men, their bikes thrown down on the trail. They dropped the rocks in their hands and ran toward her.

"She's not breathing!" Marie yelled, turning her partner onto her back to search for a pulse.

The men were looking at her, not Lydia. "Are you okay?" the taller one asked.

She wanted to say she was fine, that they should help Lydia, but she saw it on their faces. It wasn't her partner they had saved.

She lunged for Lydia, felt the stick stabbing her and wanted to jab the stick in further. If her partner in life had bled to death, she would too.

One of the men was crouching next to her, his hands on her shoulders, and suddenly she was shivering.

"We're going to get help," he said, his voice so faint she barely heard it. While his friend's voice up the trail, yelling into his cell phone, jarred her hearing.

She tried to break free of the hands and couldn't. It couldn't have happened so fast. But if it had, if that was the case—a strangely rational phrase that popped into her mind amid the rawest cruelty—the man ought to let go, get his friend to stop yelling into the cellphone. Pick up their bikes and ride away. And leave her to die with Lydia.

8

Nora insisted on picking her up and driving her to the yacht harbor. Leaning against the sun-warmed seat of the car, Marie felt the solidity of the friendship that had remained after their romance collapsed two decades before. And when they got out of the car, Nora and Evan's daughter T Bone, Evan, his partner Jim, and Lydia's parents were all waiting on the dock, by the boat Marie had chartered to scatter Lydia's ashes.

With no wind, under a sky that should have been shrouded in summer fog but was instead an absurdly brilliant blue, the crew motored out into the bay. After they emptied the last of the ashes, the wind came up. It dried their eyes, leaving a track of salt Marie could feel on her cheeks, like being left with memories instead of the real person. She was glad of the pressure of bodies in the boat, without whose weight she might have toppled into the water. Might have jumped. Not an impulse as much as an inability to see a way forward, a way around the fact that the lion had taken Lydia and left Marie. Lydia's mom sat next to her gripping her hand.

When the crew hoisted the sails and turned back toward the harbor, Marie gazed at T Bone, whose eyes were fixed on the shore, maybe even inland. She'd left the ocean where she grew up for the Central Valley at the same age Marie had left the inside of the continent. And for an instant, Marie saw movement. Tectonic plates pushing up the earth's surface to form Lake Superior, and farther west, releasing fire that formed mountains that became islands. Tectonic plates moved oceans, and those same forces drove people across the landscape, allowing them a tenuous existence amid its bumps and canyons. For Marie, it was a glimpse of the way forward.

It took weeks for her to brave the farmers' market without Lydia, and when she did she wandered around with an empty bag trying to decide how to fill it. After an hour she settled on some organic peaches. They were expensive, and as the young farmer pulled them from the scale, she asked him where his orchard was.

"Sacramento Delta," he said. She felt something at the base of her skull, electrons colliding. She thanked him and walked away. She wandered the stalls, but when she couldn't decide on anything besides peaches, she went back to the man.

"This is your farm, right?"

"Yes," he said.

"It may seem like a strange question, but if I were looking for work, would you happen to need someone?"

"I don't make enough to properly pay the people I've hired," he said. "You could try John Kimura. He'll probably say the same, but it doesn't hurt to ask."

When she got home she abandoned the bag of peaches on the counter. They had begun to stick together with fur when she tossed them in the compost and looked up the contact for Kimura Farm.

A week after that John emailed her back. "Sorry for the delay," he said. "Summer is busy. If you come out to the farm late Saturday, we can talk."

Saturday Marie made herself a lunch of crackers, which absorbed the stomach acids, and cheese she left mostly uneaten. Then she got in the car and headed over the redwood mountain highway. From there she headed east over the Diablo Range and into the Sacramento Valley.

Driving up the interstate past the Stockton channel, she could see the stacks and masts of ships. Glimmering in the heat, they were just out of focus, the way everything had looked since Lydia died. But as she took her exit at the top of the Delta, things came clear—the river she crossed on a steel-trussed bridge that swung open for larger boats, Joseph Island and the town called Stanton, its neon-signed market and saloon, and the narrow levee road leading to Kimura Farm.

Driving through the orchard, she saw a wide-shouldered man with short dark hair bent over an irrigation pipe. She stopped and lowered the window, heat colliding with the air-conditioned interior of her car.

"Marie? Welcome to my office," he said, setting down his wrench and gesturing toward the tailgate of his truck. He looked to be about her age and rubbed his neck as he stood.

She parked off the road, and when he sat on one end of the tailgate she leaned against the other end. Any earlier in the afternoon and the metal would have been too hot to touch.

"So you want to be a farmer," he said, wiping a muddy glove across his forehead.

He sounded sarcastic, but she nodded.

"Do you have any experience with farm labor?"

"Limited experience, but I'm a quick learner," she said.

He shifted on the tailgate. "Organic farming is hard. Even on large corporate lands someone has to do the back-breaking work. On Kimura Farm that means all of us and long days. My wife is a teacher who calls herself a farm widow."

"I've always looked at the work of farms from behind the lens of a camera," Marie said. "I'd like to be on the other side."

"You're coming from a fertile farming region. So why the Central Valley?"

He sounded skeptical, which did not bode well for getting the job. If the odds were against her she may as well be honest. "Lydia, my partner of eighteen years, was killed by a mountain lion when we were hiking. A farm far from the redwoods seemed like a good idea."

"That was your partner?" John asked.

Mountain lions rarely attacked people and when they did it made the news. She had no idea how he'd react to her honesty, but the corners of his mouth turned down.

"I understand," he said. "My father was one of many Japanese farmers here before they were sent to internment camps. He went from tending his own crops to picking cotton for one of the biggest landowners in the Central Valley.

"He was one of the lucky ones. His neighbor Wes, a banker in Stanton, watched over his farm until he returned. He rarely talked about it, but what he did say was that Wes saved his life. After the war this land gave him something to come back to."

Marie nodded.

"He farmed it until he died," John said. "It has a regenerative history. If you're not afraid of hard work—and you don't look like you are—you're next in line to reap the benefits. In literal terms that means minimum wage for six ten-hour days, but you live on Kimura Farm rent-free. Plus my workers, who are documented, get health benefits. I'm one of the few who includes benefits. They cost me more, but it's the right thing to do."

He slid off the tailgate, eased it back up, and motioned for her to hop in the cab.

Then they drove through the orchards, past workers harvesting cherries, to a row of cabins.

"We cleaned up three," he said, "then our daughter Alexis was born. That was ten years ago, but the dry winter allowed us to finish the fourth. It's vacant and the busiest part of the harvest is now. When can you start?"

The sun had sunk from the sky when Marie arrived back in Santa Cruz and pulled into the driveway of the adobe house she'd put on the market days after Lydia died. When a buyer made an offer, she'd still had no plan. She'd been avoiding the round table, napkins stuffed into their rings after a hasty breakfast. Now she tugged Lydia's from the ring and tossed it in the laundry basket. It sat at the bottom of the empty basket until she brought the hamper from the bedroom and dumped her laundry on top.

Night after night since Lydia's death, the glandular smell of jaws sinking into flesh had flooded her nostrils. Now, after filling the laundry hamper, Marie took a wool scarf of Lydia's and placed it next to her pillow, then pulled their clothes from the closet and stacked them on Lydia's side of the bed. When she crawled into bed the weight of the clothes felt like a second person, and she drifted off to the smell of Lydia's orange blossom face cream.

Lydia had been creeping into her dreams, and when she woke and cut off the dream, she replayed what little reel there was, hoping to return to it. But that never worked, and she found herself wide-awake and worrying, spinning though the past with its jumble of faces, mentally wandering through their backyard, broken eggshell compost, fava bean cover crop, and the smells: orange skins and curried squash. What to do with all those wooden spoons and the cavernous wells of Lydia's cooking pots. She tried reciting the psalm that had always comforted her, but the words wrapped themselves around the deeper track of her worries until the prayer replayed without meaning. Like the mockingbird trilling night and day outside her window, they were stolen songs that had lost their beauty.

Only a year before, a man who lived in a woodsy area of Santa Cruz had heard a loud boom outside his house at dusk. When he looked out the window he saw a mountain lion had driven a deer into the neighbor's fence, the impact killing the deer. He called the police, who chased off the lion and left the deer carcass close to the road. In the morning the carcass was gone. The lion had returned and dragged it into the woods. That was normal, a lion attacking what it could eat, not what had happened to Lydia.

At four-thirty Marie gave up on sleep, went into Lydia's office and sat at her desk. While taking photographs may have fed Marie in the figurative sense, what put food on the table and paid her half of the mortgage for the house was the income from her parents' rental property in Madison, Wisconsin. To pay her share of the bills, Lydia had worked days and the better part of the night writing grants. Often Marie would awaken, go to the room where Lydia sat hunched over her laptop, and beg her to come to bed, and they'd probe the darkness until sleep overcame them.

The morning Marie was to pick up the check from the escrow office, she made and consumed two double lattes while waiting for it to open. Then she drove over to pick up the check and headed to the harbor jetty. Looking over at the windy bay where they'd chartered the boat to spread Lydia's ashes, she thought about ripping up the check from the sale of the house and tossing the pieces skyward like bones to the stars. It was half Lydia's after all, and at that moment money seemed, as Lydia would have said, bronze cast into an idol. But it was also what had allowed them to plant their dreams in the backyard beds.

"If I get hit by a truck tomorrow" was how people who loved each other discussed the unthinkable. She and Lydia had agreed that the sum total of their combined efforts belonged to the person left behind. Marie pushed the check into her bag and drove back to the adobe house that would be her home for just a few more weeks.

SACRAMENTO RIVER

9

2009
Kimura Farm, Joseph Island

Marie left her car packed and followed John into the field, and for the rest of the day they picked tomatoes. The next day would be her first full one, but for now she crawled from the shower to her bed, too tired even to make a salad with the bright red tomatoes she'd brought back to her cabin. Instead of the hollow, gnawing feeling that had followed her everywhere since Lydia's death, she felt only aching muscles. In the morning she stood at the sink and ate one of the tomatoes like an apple, the tang awakening her mouth, seeds dripping down her chin.

"Tired?" a young man one row over asked later in the field as he passed. He lingered over the "r" the way people did whose first language was Spanish.

"Yes," she said. "Are you?"

He didn't answer, and after a week, when she could bend over without feeling as if a knife were wedged between her shin and her tibia, when her rate of picking came closer to the others', she understood why he hadn't answered. With his first days long since behind him, he was not as tired as she and was too kind to say so.

The hour after hour of bending, picking, carrying a box to the truck, and returning to pick again was repetition that calmed her. The pungent smell of tomato stems awakened her senses, and the monotony was broken by the stream of music, upbeat accordion and soulful trumpet coming from the transistor radios a few workers wore strapped to their waists.

After the tomato harvest they turned to apricots. Wanting to prove herself, Marie climbed to the top of the ladder and picked until her apron pouch was heavy, then wobbled to the ground and over to the packing line.

When she returned to the tree, John's foreman Manuel stood next to her and pointed to the top. "Up there," he said quietly. "Fill it halfway. Then come back down and fill it with fruit you can reach from the ground."

Marie followed his instruction, and as she picked the lowest branch, it rose, leaving the last few bunches out of reach. Manuel's wife Lupe walked by with her own pouch and pointed to the fruit just above the lowest branches. "*Esos primero,*" she said. "*La rama subura.*" She raised her arm to show the branch popping up.

"Pick the higher fruit first," said Marie, interpreting the hand motions, and Lupe nodded.

At the packing line John told her, "Lay it so it nestles blushed side up," he said. "And nothing with bruises."

Her first day she packed half as many boxes as Lupe. When she said so to John he reassured her. "Better to do it right. My father always paid by the hour. Then my workers told me they wanted to be paid by the box, so I tried it. But they were rushing, which is dangerous, and the fruit needs to be packed with care. So I went back to paying hourly."

The drought had allowed the bees plenty of time to pollinate the apricots, and they were faced with a crop that was more than they could pick during its window of optimal ripeness. Then Blenheims—the small, bruised apricot that most farmers eschewed in favor of a more perfect, less flavorful orb—rotted on the ground. Yellow jackets were drawn to the rotting fruit. Even with her hair tied up, one got caught under it and stung

Marie on the back of the skull and the neck. After that, when she took to wearing a cap with mosquito netting, the angry approach of a yellowjacket made her jump.

At "lunch" midmorning, Lupe stripped off her own netting and the long sleeves and scarf she wore to keep out the sun. Then she set up a small propane burner on a table at the side of the orchard and heated tortillas. She spooned potatoes and rice from thermoses onto the tortillas and offered some to Marie. Lupe and Manuel had little to spend on food, yet they always shared, and Marie started bringing sandwiches to share as well.

It only took one tortilla wrapped around oily, tomato-reddened rice for Marie to crave the simple comfort of those "lunches." And it only took one lunch for her to understand the wisdom of the midmorning break. Back on the field with a full belly, she was lulled into sleep on her feet by the sun. Staying awake picking after a midday meal would have been impossible.

It was during those first weeks that the nightmare started, the same one every few nights. She and Lydia were in the car careening over the mountain highway, except they were in the back seat and nobody was driving. Marie kept trying to get up front to step on the brake, when the mountain lion appeared out of nowhere and pounced on the windshield. Then somehow they were stopped on the side of the road and the lion was gone. That's when Marie woke up with sweat puddled on her breastbone, aware it would be hours before the night let go of the heat and gave way to the cool of morning.

On Kimura Farm temperatures creeping above the average heat stressed the trees. They flowered but the fruit wouldn't set and mature, or it wouldn't be as sweet. Thirsty coyotes chewed drip lines to suck out the water, and Marie spent the morning helping Manuel repair them.

At the San Luis Reservoir sixty miles to the south, where water from the Delta was stored, layer upon layer of drained basin were exposed like rings in a section of redwood tree. Yet at the Delta all six pumps were running at full capacity, each sucking two million gallons a minute, and salty water from the bay rushed in to fill the void.

When summer turned to fall John said hopefully, "Rain could start as early as November." Instead the leaves turned to a layer of dust in the orchards. Day after day into December the sky was cloudless.

Then in the new year the rain came. It started at midnight like an exhale, and Marie woke to hear it pinging steadily on the overhang of her cabin. Early in the morning the wind rode upriver, tearing dead limbs and scattering them in the orchard, sending the rain sideways. Fat drops collided with the wood sash windows and pattered against hardened ground. Marie dreamt of catching it in barrels and saving it for the dry season.

In the mountains snow buried cabins and covered the landscape in a sparkling layer of white. Where slopes intersected in gullies, it melted deep underneath and gushed into streams. And the dream about the mountain lion washed away, like a river crashing over boulders and flowing under willows as it dropped into the valley.

On the farm the bare-boned trees drank thirstily, and seedlings grew until the fields were gushing with winter squash, onions, and beets. Marie welcomed the mud that stuck to her boots as she trudged back and forth between the field and the truck. In boxes ready for transport to Sacramento and the Bay Area, she packed butternut squash, cauliflower, and beets, leafy greens poking out the sides.

Those were the raw gifts for the punishing labor, the tenderness that accompanied the disking and plowing. Just as they'd packed the fruit gently in summer, they stacked and tied chard so the leaves spooned up against each other, carrying it to the wheelbarrow in a bundle like a baby to keep from breaking leaf or stem. At night they ate the produce they'd planted, harvested, and cooked. Lupe pan-fried the chard with onions and added them to their potatoes for lunchtime tacos.

"It's all about time," John told Marie, handing her a jar of honey. "How to take what there is never enough of and make the most of it in the slower months." Like the honeybees European settlers had brought with them to the valley. Kimura Farm was the perfect environment for them to pollinate and produce honey.

In the morning Marie slathered some of it over almond butter on grainy wheat toast, bringing a bit of summer to her winter breakfast.

10

Lupe heard the heavy sound of boots on the porch before Manuel entered and set them just inside the door so they wouldn't dirty the floor she swept clean every night before bed. He rubbed his hands by the woodstove and breathed in the smell of rice and onions.

"*Tengo hambre*," he said.

Lupe, standing at the stove, turned around and kissed him. He smelled of chopped weeds and sweat.

"*¿Como se fue?*" she asked, turning back to stir the chicken and rice. *How did it go* was the question she asked every night he returned from the field. Manuel got home later than she did because as foreman he had jobs to oversee.

He stood behind her, his body, just a little wider and taller, eclipsing hers.

"*Bien, bien*," he said. "*Que rico, arroz con pollo.*" He was looking forward to dinner, but first he would slip into the tiny bathroom for a shower.

After his shower he took a seat at the table and swallowed deeply from the glass of water she set at his place. Lupe sat down and passed him a container filled with warm tortillas. He took two and helped himself to the chicken and rice.

"We'll go to the church after dinner," he said.

She nodded. For almost two years, they had been trying in the bed tucked into a corner of the room, and lately had taken to visiting Father Larry to pray for a baby.

"What did you pick today?" he asked.

"*Cavó*," she corrected him. Dug, not picked. "Onions and leeks. They were muddy." Mud that embedded itself in the green layers of leek, like bright ribbons the women of Jalisco weaved through their braids. "*¿Y tu?*"

"Helped John replace the belt on a tractor," he said, "And soaped the broccoli for aphids."

"You should have brought me some soap," she said, wiping her hands as if they were still muddy.

He laughed. "*Gracias por la cena.*" Thank you for dinner. He took their plates to the sink, where he washed them and set them in the drying rack, while Lupe wiped the stove and table. Then he put on his boots and they closed the door behind them. It was already growing dark, and it would be dark in the morning when they got up to return to the field.

The headlights flashed on bare branches as Manuel drove through the orchard. Out on the levee road the right side dropped off to the slough, and the left to the olive orchard of the neighboring farm. During the day the rows of dun blue olive leaves cheered her, whereas now the trees were hunched in the darkness like an unknown future.

Manuel drove slowly along the levee to town, where he turned into the parking lot of the Immaculate Heart of Mary Catholic church.

They were about to knock on the parish door when Lupe heard a noise behind the building.

"*Escucha*," she said. Listen.

"*Gato*," he said. Cat. But Lupe heard the more persistent sound of a crying baby.

Suddenly she was a little girl, hearing the baby cry less and less as her mother hurried them toward the border. By the time they reached Arizona the crying had ceased altogether. Lupe moved instinctively toward the sound, sure that this time she could save the baby. She stumbled along the side of the building, Manuel close behind.

"*¿Adonde vas?*" he asked, alarmed that she was moving away from, not toward, the safety of Father Larry's door.

She wondered if it was her imagination that made her see a small lump on the concrete steps. There was silence, and Lupe approached the shape with her hands held out. They closed on the sides of a duffel bag. She saw the outline of a face peering out and jumped back, colliding with Manuel.

"*¡Dios mio!*" she said, even as she reached down and felt a thick blanket wrapped around the baby inside the bag. She lifted the duffel from the step, the baby let out a wail, and Lupe cried out too.

It was a girl. Lupe was not sure how she knew this in the dark.

Gracias a Dios, it had stopped raining the day before. Lupe touched her cheek to the baby's, expecting her face to feel cold, but it was warm and wet with tears. The bundle hadn't been there long.

Manuel stood behind her, squeezing her shoulders and whispering, "*¿Como? Como?*" Then he let go and walked the perimeter of the yard, reaching out in front of him. Lupe might have been scared, watching her husband search for a hiding person, except that she knew there was no one there.

Manuel led Lupe and the baby around to the front of the church and knocked on the parish door, and after a moment it opened. Larry stood in the doorway in the white-collared shirt and black pants a priest wore under his robes. His white hair was swept back on either side of his balding head, and his glasses were slipping down his nose.

Father Larry stared at the duffel. "We pray for a baby and a month later you show up with one," he said to Manuel, opening the door wide so they could step inside.

"It's no joke," Manuel said, turning to Lupe. "*¿Con permiso?*" he asked his wife.

She held out her arms, and he pulled out the baby, letting the duffel drop to the floor. The colors of her blanket reminded Lupe of the one Mamá had wrapped around her baby brother in Jalisco. "Someone left her behind the church."

"That can't be," Larry said. "It's dark back there."

"I know," Manuel said.

Larry headed for the phone. "I'll call the police."

Manuel stood cradling the baby, who hadn't peeped since Lupe had picked her up.

Larry hung up the phone and walked over to peer at her. "I've baptized a lot of them," he said, "but I can't believe what I'm seeing."

Manuel turned to his wife. "Neither can we," he said.

The baby was still looking up into Manuel's face with dark, curious eyes when a female police officer arrived. He told the officer about how they'd found the bundle, then asked, "What will you do with her?"

"I'll call Social Services, and they'll come get her."

"Where will they take her?" Manuel asked.

"She'll be cared for while we wait for a parent or legal guardian to claim her."

"And if no one claims her?" His eyes searched Lupe's.

"Then Social Services arranges for the adoption."

"What if the parent is *ilegal?*"

"The parent wouldn't face criminal charges. We just want to speak with her, or him, and get as much information about the infant as possible."

"Has this happened before? You seem to know a lot about it," Larry said.

"First time for me," the officer said, "But yes, it happens." She looked down at the baby. "I'm going to return to my car and make the call to Social Services. It could take them a while to get here."

"A while?" asked Larry, glancing at the television that had been blaring ever since he answered the door.

"An hour maybe," the officer said. "Are you okay with her?" she asked Manuel and Lupe, who both nodded.

"I've got some milk," Larry said after the officer closed the door. "But I don't have a bottle."

"Of course you don't have a bottle," Manuel said, more to the baby than to Larry, then seeing his wife's face, handed Lupe the bundle, which Lupe offered her finger, and the baby began to suck.

They were on their second round of the news and the baby had tired of Lupe's finger when they heard the knock at the door.

When Larry got up and opened it, a woman with long brown hair and a pale face stood in the doorway, a diaper bag slung over her shoulder. "Hi," she said, extending her hand. "I'm Sherry."

As she entered she looked at the baby, who had resumed her crying. Pulling the bright blanket away to reveal a yellow onesie, she said, "No more than a couple of days old. A girl?"

"*Creo que si*," Lupe said. I think so.

"We'll feed her first, then check to be sure." Sherry dropped the diaper bag onto a chair and pulled out a bottle in a Ziploc bag, along with a can of formula. Washing her hands in the kitchen, she asked Larry, "Do you have a jar or a glass bowl?"

Larry pulled out a bowl, which she filled with water and popped in the microwave. She poured the heated water into the bottle and scooped in some formula, twisted the lid tightly, and shook it.

Squeezing a drop of formula onto her wrist, she handed the bottle to Lupe.

Lupe took the bottle and held the nipple to the baby's wailing mouth. She clamped down, sucking noisily, and Lupe sank onto the couch where they had been watching the news with Larry. For a moment the only sound in the room was the faint bubbly squeal of milk being sucked from the bottle. Lupe tilted up the bottle as the baby drained the milk.

Manuel told Sherry the story. "The officer said the parent will not be arrested if she comes forward."

"That's correct," Sherry said. "The parent has fourteen days. We encourage them to come forward because the more we know about the baby the better. She—assuming it's a girl—was surrendered, for the most part, according to the law."

They looked down at the baby, who had fallen asleep with the nipple of the near-empty bottle in her mouth. Lupe, Manuel, and Sherry watched her sleep, while Larry's eyes wandered back to the television.

Manuel chuckled. Lupe had always thought of priests as being above their parishioners somehow, but Father Larry wasn't that way, and he and Manuel were always bantering.

"What?" Larry asked.

"Your job is not finished," Manuel said.

"I know." Larry grew serious and pressed his hands together. "My job is not done." Because after Sherry took the baby, Lupe, Manuel, and Father Larry would have to pray. Pray that the mother did not change her mind and return, pray that this baby would survive.

On the return to the farm, Lupe fell back in the truck seat and closed her eyes.

She was a girl running across the desert to keep up with Mama. Cristina was fast, burdened as she was with a backpack, the baby in a sling, and Lupe's little brother. She pulled him by the hand while he cried for her to stop.

"I'm tired, Mamá," he wailed.

"Don't stop," she said. "If we do we'll be left to die."

That made Lupe's brother cry harder. Their older sister Juana, who had been lagging, sprinted ahead and grabbed the boy's free hand, so that together she and her mother swung him along. Juana carried the gallon jug they'd emptied of water, and Lupe carried the one whose last cup Mamá would divide between them after dark, when they finally stopped to rest.

The moment the coyote who'd taken Mamá's meager savings showed them the hole in the fence, that was the beginning, not the end, of their hardship. When he delivered them to Mamá's cousin Cristina in Arizona he threatened to take them back to the desert and leave them if they didn't pay him more money. Cristina pulled all the crumpled bills from a pitcher and handed them to him, and although it wasn't the amount he'd demanded, the coyote left.

Mamá had given the last of the water to her children, and her milk dried up. That night the baby, who'd been listless for days, stopped breathing. Mamá held her ear to the baby's face, shook her gently, breathed into her mouth.

Finally Mamá stopped, tears and snot streaming down her face as she held the baby tight to her chest. The children huddled around her on the pillows Cristina had laid on the floor. Lupe was the last to fall asleep, drifting off to the sound of Mamá weeping.

Later, she woke to Juana announcing, "Papá!"

And there he was. Papá, who'd survived his own border-crossing months before, had arrived at Cristina's after taking three buses to get from Northern California to Arizona. While their little brother snored, Lupe and Juana held on to their parents, who clung to each other and wept with the baby between them. After a while they started whispering, and when Lupe and Juana tried to listen, Papá waved them away.

"Time to sleep," he said.

Slowly he and Mamá stood up. Papá took some silverware from the kitchen drawer and the altar candle Cristina had lit for the baby. When Lupe and Juana tried to follow them to the sliding door, Papá shook his head, but they watched through the glass.

Mamá laid down the baby wrapped in his blanket, and she and Papá started hacking at the hard dirt in the yard with forks. The girls were still watching when an hour later they had a hole just deep enough. Not wanting to draw attention to themselves and their family on this side of the border, they buried the baby in Cristina's backyard.

Lupe started to cry. "She can't breathe under the dirt!" she whispered to her sister.

Juana shook her head and held Lupe in an awkward embrace.

Finally the girls crept back to the pillows, lay down on either side of their little brother, and fell asleep. They woke what seemed moments later to pink light and their parents still outside, sleeping spooned up to each other beside their baby's grave.

The sun was creeping like a spider over the horizon when Papá counted out the money in his tattered wallet, setting aside what he needed to buy bus tickets for his family. What was left he dropped in the pitcher Cristina's cousin had emptied for the coyote. Then Mamá, Papá, and their children rode for three days with empty bellies: first a bus across the border into the desert of California. Then another bus on the wide-laned highway crammed with cars, up over mountains that looked as dry as Mexico, across a basin devoid of green, except for the rows and rows of crops where eventually Lupe knew they would stop. They did, in the San Joaquin Valley where they followed the crops from town to town and one migrant camp to the next.

Lupe could still call it up, Mamá and Papá hacking at the dirt with forks. And the camps, the sickening heat, a bandana that hadn't kept the spray from entering her nostrils, the bitterness in the back of her throat. The sharp edges of metal, hands like the scavenging yellow beaks of gulls.

When there were no crops to be picked, Papá tried to hide his worry by whistling with his tongue behind his teeth. On those days he would take Lupe to the dump, which was like a ruined kingdom. A tractor smoothing the mountain of garbage scattered gulls. A glint of color from a broken toy, buried in the pile of soggy mattresses and worn-out brooms, distracted her from the unbearable smell that, made worse by the heat, was a reminder that cream would turn and animals would shrink from their skins.

Once in the middle of summer it rained. The air cleared and puddles formed like a moat around the mountain of garbage. Papá handed Lupe a single yellow glove from the pair they split and told her to grab hold of the strip of metal sticking out of a pile. Sharp edges penetrated the hole in her rain-soaked glove. Together they pulled, and the strip lengthened, but they couldn't tug it loose, so Papá bent it back and forth until the metal grew hot in the crease and broke.

Papá knew an old man who earned his living hauling people's loads to the dump, and they slid into the cab of his truck for a ride to the metal recycling plant twenty miles down the road. Their scraps were meager compared to the mound of metal in the yard, above it a demolished car dangling from the spider-like claw of a crane. But a muscled man in coveralls handed them a few dollars, and that night there was chicken with their usual dinner of beans and tortillas.

Fall came, and they moved on to vineyards. Their father was usually out working by the time Lupe, Juana, and their little brother woke up, but one morning he was waiting outside when they left for school.

"No grapes to pick today, Papá?" Juana asked as they walked along the side of the road.

"Es una huelga," their father said. A strike.

A few days later on the way home from school, Lupe, Juana, and their brother ran across field workers hiding in the vineyards.

"¿Qué pasó, Papá?" Juana asked when they got home.

"Ilegales," their father said. "Hired to break the boycott, but Border Patrol is coming to arrest them."

The next time Lupe passed workers hiding in the vineyards, she was scared, remembering the desert, the greedy coyote, her baby brother's grave. She had always imagined Border Patrol riding the banks of el Rio Grande on horses, wielding guns and machetes, and it wasn't until she was in high school that she discovered they were just men in uniform.

She and Juana spent those years not in school but making their way ever so slowly down a row of crops. In the spring and summer they pulled potatoes from the ground. Their fellow worker, *un hombre* their father's age, told them about the men in uniform. He said it was a laborer, female like themselves, who years ago had demanded they arrest *ilegales* like the ones Lupe had seen hiding in the vineyards. The woman laborer had hitched a ride up to Orange Grove and found seven officers sitting around headquarters playing cards, and only after she rallied college students to protest outside the building did Border Patrol get up from their card game and drive down to arrest the workers so they couldn't cross the picket lines.

Lupe's own legal status came when she made her way to the Sacramento Valley, where she met Manuel, who'd been born in the States and had been working on Kimura Farm for several years. John hired Lupe, and she and Manuel fell in love as the late summer sun cast a blush of red across the yellow pears. Manuel was twenty-six when he married Lupe and John made him foreman.

Juana, who stayed behind in the San Joaquin Valley, also married a man born in the States. She and her husband worked for Sunrise Farms and lived in cramped conditions in an *indegente* town, while the old one-room cabin Manuel now pulled up to in the truck was freshly painted, water running clean from the taps.

Manuel shut off the truck's ignition and they sat with their heads bowed. All those years ago, Mamá had been unable to save her baby, but Lupe and Manuel had saved this one. Now they needed to pray they could adopt the bundle Lupe was certain God had placed that night in her arms.

11

January 2010

They answered the door together. The mother had waves of brown hair and dark eyes that greeted Nate as if she knew him. The girl had her mother's eyes but darker skin, and deep red hair curled into a ponytail.

"This is Ruby," her mother said, "And I'm T Bone."

Nate thought of the grass-fed steak he'd ordered once a week at the Right End Café. It had been seven months since he'd had one. "Like the steak?" he asked before he could stop himself.

"Yes. My real name is Therese if you like that better."

"No," he said, laughing for what felt like the first time since he'd had that steak. "I like T Bone."

"You did know I have an eleven-year-old daughter?" she asked, after Ruby left the room.

"Yes, you said in your ad."

"Where are you moving from?" T Bone asked.

Unsure how much to tell her, he said. "I had a roommate. She left."

"Oh. Would you like to see the house? It's old, but Ruby helped me scrape the windows. A painter finished the outside, and I painted the inside." A fresh coat of white covered the interior.

She showed him the kitchen and the tiny dining room where a door led to the backyard. In her room, he looked out the window at the driveway and yellow oxalis growing at the foot of two bare fruit trees.

"I'm not much of a gardener," she said, "But I did pull out a mass of blackberries." She yanked up one of her sleeves and ran her fingers over faint lines that had once been scratches. "And Ruby helps pick the fruit."

"Persimmon and . . . ?"

"Apple," she said, and led him to the empty bedroom at the front of the house. Looking out the window at the dead lawn, she said, "I taught Ruby how to use the mower, but we don't waste water keeping it green." She looked around the bedroom. "It's sunny in here, though."

"So you own the house?"

"My parents, really," she said.

They climbed a set of steep narrow stairs to Ruby's room, a converted attic with sloping walls. "It gets hot up here in the summer," she said, "but Ruby loves it. It's her little hideaway." She swept her arm across the room. "This was covered in insulation. I spent a sweaty day in safety goggles pulling it out. Then Evan, Jim, and my mom turned it into Ruby's room." She gave Nate a shy smile. "Jim is my dad's partner."

"How did you end up in Davis?"

"I dreamed of becoming a veterinarian. But even with Ruby in kindergarten, there were parent-teacher conferences and field trips to chaperone, and when I finished classes and picked her up from aftercare, I still had grocery shopping, cooking, and dishes to do."

Nate wanted to ask why she'd ended up raising Ruby by herself, but that seemed too personal a question and judging from her forthrightness, if he became her roommate she'd tell him.

T Bone was still talking. "So I went to my biology professor and asked if I could volunteer at the smelt lab. You know about the delta smelt?"

"Do I. I'm a biologist with Fish and Wildlife."

Her eyes lit up. "Then you know their plight. I work for the lab full time now. That's what changed my mind about becoming a vet. Fighting for the smelt's survival makes for a much less emotional equation when caring for one mammal, Ruby."

Nate laughed. "I wish I could say fighting for the fish didn't make me feel emotional."

T Bone threw up her hands. "Then this is the house for *you*."

She handed him an application, which he took with him. Nate and Ana had signed a month-to-month lease, and he knew their landlord would give him a good referral. It was T Bone's question on the application he had trouble with: "Why do you believe you would be a responsible housemate to someone with an eleven-year-old daughter?"

The question seemed intentionally intimidating. T Bone had mentioned she was twenty-seven, which made her four years older than Nate, but he wasn't intimidated. She was direct and he liked direct. The problem was that writing "I'm not a child molester" didn't seem like a good idea, but neither did the truth, that he had hoped he and Ana would have had children of their own.

"I like kids," he wrote, "and Ruby seems like a good kid." Then he folded the application and, on the way to drop it off, stopped and collected a few boxes from behind the liquor store.

An hour later the phone rang.

"Your landlord said she wished you weren't leaving," T Bone said, "And Ruby likes you, so that settles it. Would you like to move in?"

12

Nate grew up an hour north of Davis in a town shadowed by the Sutter Buttes, whose spiky crags rose out of the valley flats. For his tenth birthday his mom and dad took Nate and his sister camping in the Sierra just east of the Buttes. While their parents rested in the campsite, Nate and Deni walked to the river and watched a man in fishing waders cast into the water. He'd let the fly drift then strip in the line. After a while he waded upstream and cast again. That's when he caught a good-sized rainbow and, after deftly removing the tiny hook from its mouth, plunged his hand in the water and waved it back and forth before releasing the fish.

Nate ran with Deni back to camp, where his father was reading and his mother was making sandwiches, and breathlessly retold the story of the man they'd watched catch a sixteen-inch rainbow on a tiny fly.

"Gloria," his father said to his mom, "I believe he's hooked." That was his father's corny sense of humor, and the following summer on Nate's eleventh birthday, his mom and dad gave him a fly rod and took him and Deni camping at the same spot.

He spent a lot of hours untangling his line from the willows, but by the time he left for college, Nate was catching rainbows and browns the size of the one he'd seen that fisherman land. There was no question about what he would study or what field he would go into. As his dad said, he was hooked.

Nate's first job with Fish and Wildlife was a three-month stint hiking California's mountains and rivers, observing, catching, and counting trout. It was the best summer of his life. His dad was not yet sick, he was contemplating asking his girlfriend Ana to marry him, and he was getting paid to backpack and fly-fish.

Dark-haired, athletic, and one class ahead of Nate, Elisa Martinez was the only woman studying to be a game warden, and all the guys in the program were in love with her. Deep in the backcountry, the crew spent long days catching and counting fish and cooking over a camp stove, sleeping on the hard ground and getting dirtier by the day. But on the nights the rain didn't soak their tents, they fell asleep under a sky full of stars, sometimes to the ratchet-y chorus of tree frogs.

In an act of chivalry, the boys wanted to surround Elisa's tent with theirs. But she flipped the idea on its head by pitching hers outside their circle. "I'm the father coyote," she told them. "The mother doesn't allow him all the way in the den with the pups."

Where they were hiking, bears were a problem, and each of them carried a bear-proof canister and hung their excess food in a tree. This required finding a pine branch that was too high for the bear to reach on its hind legs but low enough to pitch the rope over with a rock, a branch heavy enough to hold the bag but too light to hold the bear. One night they awoke to a loud crack, followed by a thump and rustling. When Nate poked his head out, a black bear bigger than his tent was standing three feet away, tearing open the nylon bag.

Knowing the branch wouldn't hold him, the bear had simply broken it and let the food fall. His breath traveling through a long snout was eerily loud, and the smell, given the fact that bears paid for their sweet tooth with cavities, made Nate wish they'd left some toothpaste in the nylon bag.

The bag had also held their lunch, and for the remaining days between breakfast and dinner, their stomachs growled on the trail. On their next trip they camped above the tree line, had to rely on their bear-proof canisters, and were more famished than ever when they came off the mountain. They stopped at a restaurant, and each of them consumed one and a half burritos. Still, the bears out-consumed them. They ate trout from the streams and the frogs that lulled Nate and the crew to sleep, as well as berries and pine nuts. They raided beehives and, while being swarmed and stung, ate the larvae and the bees along with the honey.

Bears are lured by the smell of human food. They raid dumpsters fitted with latches, break into mountain cabins, and tear apart kitchens. They recognize ice chests in cars. After they taste human food, they return again and again to dumpsters and campgrounds. The wardens who Nate knew captured, tranquilized, and relocated them, but homing within seventy miles, the bears came back. Then the wardens had to shoot them.

Elisa Martinez talked about "bagging" her first bear, and Nate was as infatuated with her as any of his classmates. But submerged in a wetsuit and mask in an icy stream, spotting and counting trout, he told himself love and infatuation were two different things. Cold water like a vice grip around his head, he resolved as soon as he got home to give Ana the ring he'd bought.

They'd met in a church group for college students, and it seemed right to marry before either of them graduated from Davis. Corinthians said your body is a temple, given from God. His own father said, "I shall lift up mine eyes to the mountains," and Ana was the creek that dropped from the highest peaks and quenched the summer dust. When Nate got home, he asked her to go with him to the north Delta wildlife refuge. He made a pretense of wanting to show her the loggerhead shrike, one his favorite birds. She went along with little enthusiasm, rolling her eyes about the bird, but he attributed it to her not knowing the real reason for the outing. His hands were shaking on the viewing platform as he took out the ring and went down on one knee, which elicited a real smile out of her. She said yes.

They exchanged vows in Yosemite Valley with just their pastor, their parents, and Deni beside them. In their wedding photo they stood under a giant ponderosa pine, she almost his height, the sun hitting the tops of their heads and lighting up her angel-fine hair, his blond curls and green eyes.

That night on the north rim above valley, Nate was dizzy as he and Ana crawled under his sleeping bag. Whether it was from the 9,000-foot elevation or from having waited two years, as she moved on top of him, the stars above her head spun like a meteor shower.

Afterward he pulled her sleeping bag over his and felt happy, like the down bags puffed up from the warmth of their bodies. He spooned against her on his sleeping pad, her empty pad next to them.

It was on that sleeping pad, shoved to a far corner of the room, where she chose to spend the night they graduated from Davis. Zipped up with the down bag covering her head like she was in an Egyptian tomb, wrapped for burial and ready to depart for the afterlife of their marriage.

At first he mistook it for grief. Because while they were still flirting untethered in youth group, his dad had been diagnosed with cancer, and although he made it to the wedding, by the time they finished school, hospice had taken over. Graduation morning Nate put on his boxers printed with rainbow trout as a tribute to his dad and, after the ceremony, went straight to his parents' house, placing the tasseled cap on his father's head.

"I may have been here," his dad said, patting the reclining chair, "But I walked every step with you to the podium."

"I know you did," Nate said, and his mom snapped a picture of them, Nate still in his gown and his dad wearing the mortarboard.

That night, sitting on the edge of the bed in his boxers, Nate tried to make light of Ana in the mummy bag. "What are you doing over there?" he asked.

She shook her head, making a swishing sound against the nylon bag.

"Is it my dad?"

No answer.

He sat, still as she was, and stared across the empty space of their bedroom, until her breathing turned soft. She was asleep.

Suddenly angry, he switched off the light, but it took him a long time to fall asleep. In the middle of the night a slamming door woke him. He sat up thinking she was gone, but he could hear the soft breathing, could see the hump of her sleeping bag in the dark. He listened for more sounds but the house was quiet. When he finally fell back asleep he dreamt that she left, slamming the door behind her, and when he tried to get up and go after her, he was trapped in a tangle of sheets.

In the morning he decided to force the issue. "There are full-time openings with Fish and Wildlife here in the valley, and I'd like to apply."

"I want to join the Peace Corps," she said, shoving her sleeping bag into the stuff sack. "In Namibia." Halfway around the world on the southern tip of Africa.

"Are you packing for Africa today?"

She said nothing. Making light of it didn't work anymore than it had the night before.

"Why did we get married so young?" she asked.

"For love?" He was remembering their dating days, fully clothed limbs wrapped around each other until he was unsure which were his. He'd stopped to catch his breath, remembered their promise to wait, and slowly they'd unwrapped themselves.

Heart pounding, he'd grabbed for her hand, but already she was up off the couch and at the door, like a loggerhead shrike spooked out of a delta cottonwood.

"I've lived in the Central Valley all my life," she said. "I'm ready to leave."

"But this is my dream job," he said. What was lost, the delta a polluted maze of sloughs whose tiny smelt inhabitants were fighting for their lives, only made him want it more.

It was said in the delta that if you passed the same bridge twice, you'd better cross it because you were stuck on an island. Each time Nate drove through an unfamiliar part, he fitted another piece into the map of wiggly sloughs and amoeba islands he was shaping in his head. It was a puzzle he loved to dive into, while Ana couldn't wait to cross the bridge that would release her.

"I'm sorry," she said. "I can't do this. I'm moving back in with my parents until I leave for the Peace Corps."

And when Ana hauled a backpack full of clothes to her childhood home, Nate wondered if there was a promise he'd still failed to make to her. Before he could do anything about it, though, his mom called and said to come quickly. Deni took the red-eye from Rhode Island, and Nate picked her up at the airport.

It was when he and his sister went back to Nate's house to take showers and change clothes and their mom left the room to use the bathroom that their dad died. On their childhood camping trips as the car began to climb into the Sierra, he had never failed to say, "I will lift up my eyes to the mountains." He died with his head turned toward the window where the Sutter Buttes rose from a haze in the distance.

"We have to go to the river he loved so much," their mother told Nate and Deni.

But once they got to the campground on the Yuba River, Nate pointed to the Sierra Buttes forty-four hundred feet above them and said, "I want to go up there."

His mom took an empty sandwich bag, scooped some of the ashes from the box, tucked the bag in his shirt pocket, and handed the box to Deni. Then the three of them walked to the river and tossed handfuls into the rapids of an early summer snowmelt.

Their mom kept some in the box for the locust tree in the backyard, where in summer their dad liked to "cool in the shade."

Standing at the edge of the Yuba River, Nate looked up at the rocky outcropping above the tree line.

"Go," his mom said.

He drove as far up the narrow road as the car would take him, then hiked the steep trail to the lookout at the top. It was June, right before he started his first paying job with Fish and Wildlife. There was still snow on the ground, and by the time he reached the lookout he was sinking up to his knees.

A grated walkway surrounded the tower, and Nate held onto the railing to keep from being blown off, wondering how he was going to empty the bag in a howling wind. But the far side was protected, and looking down at two glacial lakes, he opened the sandwich bag and poured out the ashes.

"This is your heaven, Dad," he said, gazing over the peaks to the hollowed tops of Lassen and Shasta in the distance.

He made his way back to the car and returned to the campground, where his mother was reading and Deni was napping in a patch of sun. Nate had always been mystified by Deni's ability to drop off anywhere, when it took him a long time to fall asleep. He sat next to her, resting against a boulder, and when he closed his eyes, he saw the two glacial lakes, pockets of deep blue in a rocky landscape. He saw their dad's ashes landing unceremoniously on patches of snow. But as June melted into July, the ashes would seep into the ground, maybe traveling through the aquifer to those little lakes. Maybe sinking deeper to the mantle of the earth and making their way through the magma channels to the chambers of the Cascades' two southernmost volcanoes.

Deni stirred and opened her eyes. "How was your hike to the great beyond?"

Their mother closed her book and turned toward them.

"Still a lot of snow," he said.

"I see that." Deni grabbed the wet muddy calves of his pants.

Like Ana, Deni had always been less attached to the landscape and restless to move away. She'd left for college in Rhode Island, met her boyfriend, and moved in with him in Providence.

"We're going to get married," she'd assured their mother. "And have babies."

"You're going to need help with those babies," their mom said. And having already retired, after their trip to the Yuba with the ashes, she sold the house and moved to Rhode Island.

In their wedding photo Ana's pale eyes gazing at the camera had always reminded Nate of the feathers on those loggerheads hiding in the cottonwoods. But when he got home from spreading his dad's ashes and picked up the frame, those same eyes looked faint and indecipherable. Setting the frame down, he drove to the barber and had his head shaved clean. Blond curls lay around the barber's chair like the fading yellow leaves of his dad's favorite backyard locust in fall.

He started packing as soon as he got home from the interview with T Bone. He would need the twenty days left in the month to sort through their things. The smell of Ana, like ripe lemons, puffed up at him as he dropped her clothes into the first box, but for once he didn't linger, didn't bury his face in them as he had for weeks after she left.

It didn't take long to get through her things. Ana lived a Spartan existence, which was probably why she hadn't hesitated to join the Peace Corps in a poor and remote part of the world. She may have needed to move to another continent, but for Nate, the ad for a room in a house, in the town where he'd lived for five years, made him feel as if he'd won a Lotto scratcher.

There were other differences as well. He could see that now, seven months after their graduation. That she was never with him when he visited his dad. That she listened to music with her earbuds in, even when they were together in the car. That she lived on white rice and raw almonds, and claimed the only fish she liked was filet of sole. Even the name Ana, which had always sounded beautiful to him, was elusive—a single consonant with the vowel floating off either end, just out of reach.

He dropped the boxes by the front door, picked up the phone, and called the therapist he had seen every week since Ana left. When Loretta didn't pick up he left a message.

"I'm taking her stuff to her parents' house," he said when she returned his call, "and I'm ready to call the attorney."

"What was the cataclysmic event?" Loretta asked.

She was referring to the phrase he had used the third time he walked into her office. The first session he'd cried more than he'd talked, and the second session he'd been unable to respond to most of her questions. The next time, before he even sat down, he said he felt paralyzed. She'd asked what it would take to unfreeze him, and it was another week before he had an answer: "A cataclysmic event."

"I found a room for rent in a house with a mom and her eleven-year-old daughter. I think it would be good for me."

"It probably would be."

"I want to send Ana the divorce papers."

"Do you think she'll sign them?"

"Why wouldn't she?" He'd had no word from Ana. Even in

a village on the southern tip of the continent there was internet, and her phone was working. He knew because the cell phone bills came to their house, and he scoured them as if he were a stalker and not her husband. It was time to sever that account, and the paper bills too.

When he hung up from Loretta he called Ana's parents in the suburb of Sacramento where she'd grown up.

"Hello!" Her father greeted him cheerfully over the phone as if nothing had changed.

"I'd like to drop off a few of Ana's things," Nate said. "I'm moving into a room in a house and won't have space for them." Unsure after he said it why he needed to offer an explanation for not keeping her clothes.

Even so, Mr. Streets said, "Oh?" as if he were surprised.

Saturday morning when Nate rang the doorbell, Ana's mother opened the door. "Nate! How are you?" she said, as cheerful as her husband, who was nowhere to be seen.

"Okay." He wanted to ask if they'd heard from Ana but didn't want to hear it if the answer was yes. "Did Mr. Streets tell you I was coming by?"

"He did."

Nate waited for her to say more, and when she didn't he held out the first box. Mrs. Streets, as small and slight as Ana, reached for it without a word. Nor did she say anything when he went to the car for the second or third. She stood in the doorway, the boxes stacked behind her like a family member whose existence she hadn't acknowledged.

"Thank you," she said, and closed the door.

Nate got in the car, drove half a block, pulled over, and sobbed. Big heaving sighs, wiping his nose on his sleeve. But after he started the engine again, his arms floated as if he'd been carrying heavier boxes. He remembered how Mrs. Streets had worn the wrong shoes for an outdoor wedding, had picked her way across the pine needles, how she and Mr. Streets left in the car before he remains of the wedding picnic had even been put away.

"Why?" he'd asked Ana. It was a pastor from their church who'd married them in Yosemite, so that wasn't it.

"She's only comfortable with God inside a church building," Ana had said with a touch of scorn.

"Ridiculous," he said now to nobody, then drove back to Davis and headed straight for the Right End Café at the edge of town.

"Where've you been hiding?" the waitress Bonnie asked when she brought him his steak. "You look like you haven't had one of these in a while." She eyed the shoulders that had gotten bonier since he'd stopped lifting weights.

"Ana left," he said. "Months ago. I wasn't okay for a while, but I am now."

"I'm sorry," she said genuinely, even though Bonnie was the opposite of Ana, a boisterous woman who'd been serving men steak and draft beer for twenty-five years.

Nate's first grass-fed steak after months without left a metallic taste in his mouth, but he ate all of it and gave Bonnie a generous tip. He drove home, fell into bed, and slept through the night. In the morning he went to the gym and lifted weights until his arms couldn't lift anymore.

13

May 2010
Woodland, California

Chester Eberstark awoke in darkness as he had every morning for sixty-six years—except Sundays, when he stayed in bed until the sun came up. People asked him what accounted for the health that kept him on a tractor into his early nineties. They seemed to want him to say it was eating the organic product his family farmed on two-thirds of their nine thousand acres of rice, so he told them it was his Sundays. He didn't like leading questions.

He laced up his boots in the dark, opened the bedroom door, and stomped down the hallway to the kitchen. He couldn't say even in the spryness of youth that he'd been light on his feet.

"Buzz," Margaret called from the pantry, "there's a clean mug in the dishwasher."

He found the mug, took the pot from the coffeemaker, and filled it, slopping coffee on the counter.

Margaret emerged from the pantry with a jar of apricot jam. "Good thing you didn't spill it on your hand," she said. "Coffee's hot."

"The way I like it," Buzz said, as she flipped the eggs bubbling in a pan and slid them onto a plate.

For as long as they'd been married Margaret had gotten up early to make him two eggs over easy, bacon, and toast from her homemade pumpernickel bread. Since at ages ninety-one and eighty-five he and Margaret were still alive and running Eberstark Farm, Buzz didn't see any reason to switch to oatmeal—even after their daughter Alice started making vegetarian dishes from their own brown rice, gently chiding them about their diet.

Alice was all right, though. She managed the farm full time now, a fact for which he was grateful, since her brother Henry hadn't taken to farming. Still, the environmental law Henry practiced in San Francisco kept him involved in the farm. Having seen the Dust Bowl that resulted from poor stewardship of the soil, Buzz had pledged to take good care of his land when he moved his young family to California.

Spreading marmalade on his toast, he eyed the blotter-sized calendar on the wall. There it was in bold red, in a month's time: June 12, "Storm the Meeting." Would Lawrence Scheffield ever be surprised when Buzz, Alice, and her lawyer-brother Henry descended on members of the Saltsink District's secret meeting with the Department of Water Resources, one to which the North Canal District had not been invited.

Not so long ago, Buzz had run for and won a seat on the North Canal Water District. For although Eberstark Farms was north of the delta, it took its water from the Sacramento before it flowed through the estuary. Certainly his engineering degree from Stanford had helped, as well as the fact that he had opinions when it came to water issues in the valley and wasn't shy about expressing them.

It had started with the dam that went in on the Feather River, then the aqueduct Pat Brown built to carry water to Southern California. Southern California paid the bill, but continued to get most of its supply from the Owens River in the eastern Sierra. In the west, water running uphill toward money was being pumped over the Tehachapi Range.

Later, when Jerry filled his father Pat's shoes as governor, he wanted to build a canal to divert more delta water to the aqueduct. When Jerry was elected to two more terms thirty years later, the canal morphed into a tunnel. Two tunnels in fact, behind which the Saltsink District and its business partners were the driving force.

Canal or tunnel, it would divert enough to shut down Delta farmers and kill an estuary that had already gone to shit. Literally. Just below the North Canal, the Uplands Sanitation District was flushing wastewater into the delta, and the Saltsink District was pumping it out.

"Did you say something?" Margaret asked.

Buzz stared at the calendar, and she followed his eyes.

"Why do you let him get to you?" she said.

For Buzz, it came down to the fact that both cotton and rice farmers were compensated by the government and both were major consumers of water. Saltsink's water was subsidized, while Eberstark's wasn't, but that was it in a nutshell. So to speak.

"For Lawrence," he told his wife, "it's about draining us all dry."

Margaret shook her head, not because she disagreed but because she'd been listening to him rant about Lawrence Scheffield for years. The way Buzz saw it, a man was essentially competitive, and the difference between his practices and Scheffield's was bound to piss him off.

The back door opened and Alice entered, graying blond hair tucked under a Chico Wildcats ballcap. Alice was tall and blue-eyed like her dad, beautiful like her mother. The photo from his wedding day had long since been tucked away in a drawer, but Buzz knew it by heart. Margaret had looked like Barbara Stanwyck then, and still did.

On their first date in Red Cloud, he'd convinced Margaret to go with him to see her latest movie.

"What makes you think I look like Barbara Stanwyck?" she'd said, and to this day teased him about his pick-up line.

Alice's marriage had not fared as well as her parents', and both boys had chosen Chico because while it was away from home, it was close enough for them to keep an eye on their mother. Danny, the younger one, wanted to become a professional ballplayer, and Chris, about to graduate with a degree in agriculture, was coming back to help run the farm.

Alice's dog Stix, the terrier mix, slipped in under her feet, licked the toast crumbs off the floor, and lay down.

Margaret was finishing the dishes, and Buzz could see their daughter wanted to take over. Up until a few years ago Margaret had done the housecleaning herself. Now she hired a woman to come in once a week but still made lunch and breakfast, shopped, and did the bookwork for the farm. Alice cooked dinner, but despite being two heads taller, she hadn't been able to wrestle the dishwashing away from her mother. She picked up a towel and dried the frying pan Margaret handed her.

"What's on for today?" Margaret asked.

"We're starting the weed crew on the water grass," Buzz said.

"Why don't you take west field 102," Alice said, "and I'll supervise 105."

Supervising wasn't the half of what Alice would do. She'd pull out the weed grass alongside the rest of them. Even before he got too old to weed, Buzz had always walked out from his truck and watched. His crew knew what they were doing, and it was a chance for him to converse with them.

After more and more of their crew came from Jalisco, Michoacán, or El Salvador, Buzz had started listening to cassette tapes in Spanish. "*¿Donde está la pala?*" he repeated back to the tape as he drove across the farm in his truck. When his hearing got worse, he turned up the volume. He didn't realize how loud it was until he noticed his crew looking up and spotting the truck when he was still two fields away. That was embarrassing, but by then he could carry on a basic conversation, and he gave up the tapes. The only time he lost the thread was when talk with his foreman Diego veered away from farming practices. Then Diego would switch to English, and the two of them engaged in a tug-of-war between Spanish and English.

Buzz put his breakfast plate and cup in the dishwasher and walked down the hallway to the bathroom. He had to pee more often since he turned ninety. He'd bragged about how long he could hold his coffee all the way into his eighties. Not anymore. It took longer with stiff fingers to fasten his pants too, and by the time he'd washed his hands and returned to the kitchen, Alice and Stix were waiting in the truck.

Each field was a rectangular basin enclosed by a lip too narrow for driving, which was why Alice dropped Buzz at the edge of the field she'd assigned him. He walked with his chair out to where the crew was weeding. He might still be able to drive a tractor, but he couldn't stand for long periods anymore.

Spring, when they flooded the fields for planting, was nearly gone. It was his favorite time of year, the little yellow planes buzzing the fields like bees, dropping in low to release their cache of rice seed. Soon after, bright green blades of grass started popping out of the water, and sheets of emerald gleamed to the horizon.

It had been two weeks since they'd drained the fields, and Buzz's boots sank into the ground but came up dry. He unfolded his chair and placed it on the narrow levee of dirt nearest Angel and Jorge.

"*Dime que tenemos*." he said to Angel, tilting his hat to shade his face from the sun. *Tell me what we've got.*

"Water grass . . . red berry," said Angel.

The aquatic weeds would dry up when the field was drained for harvest. That, along with pulling the water grass, was the extent of weed control on most of the farm.

"*¿Como está Yolanda?*"

"Bien. Trabajando," he said, jerking his head toward Inland Fields where his wife was working.

Buzz watched a great blue heron stalking the edge of the next field, the S of its neck straightening toward something in the grass, probably a mouse. The herons hunted the flooded fields too, and fished in the ponds and rivers.

"La niña esta enferma." Angel's daughter was five. *"Tiene un resfriado,"* he said, and shrugged. It was just a cold.

Buzz inhaled the tart smell of new rice and the slightly rancid smell of mud. For forty years, ever since Eberstark Farms had stopped burning the fields, he'd been able to breathe deeper. Some of their methods for working the rice straw into the soil had been a disaster, but the new plows worked. They mixed the cover crop in with the straw. It was more expensive than burning, but it beat air pollution and fertilizers. The last third of Eberstark's fields were not pesticide-free, but they came close.

Not like that bastard Scheffield, CEO of the 118,000-acre Sunrise Farms in the Saltsink District two hundred and thirty-six miles to the south. His biggest crops were cotton and almonds, but his real business was water. The previous year he had sold enough to fill 1,800 acres with a foot of water to his own business partner Patrick Smith for his housing project in the dry Tehachapi mountains. This was after complaining that allocations from the state had deprived Sunrise Farms of the supply it needed. But the selling price per acre-foot that year far exceeded its value for cotton and almonds, so he fallowed some fields, took the water the state had given him, and sold it. Patrick Smith passed the cost of the water on to consumers in the housing project. Scheffield also sold bottled water from halfway around the world, where he extracted more of it than any other company in the South Pacific.

With almonds, grapes, cotton, and tomatoes grown and distributed by the company, Sunrise's motto was "From Our Valley to Your Health," making it sound like a cozy little valley rather than a vast empire of acres. The health part of their motto was full of holes too.

Scheffield's presence was everywhere worldwide: in the almonds people ate by the handful, in their cereal or protein bars, and in the cans of tomatoes they opened for spaghetti sauce, in the cotton T-shirts they wore, the grapefruits they sliced open on Christmas morning, and the plastic-bottled water they were gouged five bucks for in their hotel rooms.

Mad all over again, Buzz snapped his chair shut as Angel and Jorge moved away toward a fresh crop of weeds. He tromped back along the edge of the field to the road, where he unfolded the chair and sat waiting for Alice to appear in the truck.

14

The gold had disappeared from their pans before it stopped gleaming in their eyes, but the river you could see coming. What for months had been immense snowdrifts in the mountains the heat turned to shrinking white lines, and the jowls of rocks grew longer while the shadows across the Sierra recoiled. You could hear it too, boulders rumbling and the white force of water.

The little river raged, sending a wall of water twenty-one feet high through the town in its wake. It raced across the valley below the Buttes and poured into the big river, the Sacramento, tearing out levees and burying barns. People wouldn't be able to contain it, even with a dam higher than two of the world's tallest redwood trees stacked one on top of the other.

Buzz had seen it before, when he was sixteen in Red Cloud, Nebraska. First the winds had come, blasting hot air across the plains, whipping up soil depleted and overgrazed. Storms of brown and yellow dust turned the middle of the day dark, tearing out farmers' corn and wheat. With their crops ruined, nobody was buying the farm equipment Buzz's father sold, and he stopped going to work. He sought refuge inside the house, where electric fans blew hot air and dust around the rooms.

Just as people were bracing themselves for another summer of record-breaking heat, the torrential rains came. Buzz stood with his father on a bluff overlooking the Republican River as it swelled to a thousand times its normal flow. Things floated by that shouldn't have: pig and cow carcasses, a tractor bobbing and tipping in the current like some wild carnival ride, and a man clinging to the roof of a house. As it tilted toward the swirling water, the house swung around and caught in a stand of trees, and the man was able to slide down the roof, grab onto the trunk of a cottonwood, and pull himself up the bank. Just as he scrambled to safety, the current loosed the house from the trees and sent it spinning downriver.

They stood so long Buzz felt the rain soaking through the oilskin of his coat. Eye to eye with his father since he'd grown so much in high school, Buzz saw weary lines around his father's blue eyes and two-day growth on his face, his hat drooping in the rain. They were retreating to the truck when a neighbor pulled up in his car and told them the river was threatening to take out the power plant.

Buzz and his father arrived at the power plant as workers, stranded by a rising river, abandoned their sandbags and climbed onto the roof of the building. Spectators had turned to rescuers and were dragging rowboats to higher ground. They could see the men on the roof shouting, but they couldn't hear them above the roar of the river.

With the current too strong for the boats, Buzz and his father helped fasten ropes and a roller on the power poles. They were pulling the workers across one at a time in a basket when one of the poles toppled and plunged a man into the water. The rescuers locked arms and waded into the river.

Farthest out in the water, Buzz stretched out his arm, and the man grabbed it as he swept past. The force nearly pulled Buzz into the current, but behind him his father thrust backward, falling onto the chain of people and landing Buzz and the swimmer on the muddy bank.

Buzz was on his hands and knees catching his breath when the 25,000-gallon water tank outside the power plant crashed into the river, waves from the impact washing over his shoes. He jumped up and grabbed the swimmer, who stumbled to his feet, and the two of them ran higher up the bank behind Buzz's dad.

"Your mother's worried by now," his dad yelled into his ear. "We have to go."

Sure enough, she opened the door to the kitchen when they pulled up in the truck. Straightforward with a broad body, she was formidable, but with her height just under five feet and the love she dispensed through her stew and cornbread, she was everything a boy needed in a mother.

"I thought you'd drowned in the river!" she barked at them through the rain, pressing her hands into the sides of the apron she wore whether or not she was cooking. But later, when they'd changed into dry clothes and their coats hung dripping onto the kitchen floor, she set plates of fried pork chops and apples before them.

"That's the last of the chops from the freezer," she said. With the drought and her husband not selling farm equipment, it had been a long time since she had bought pork or even eggs, and with the farms swept away by the river, it would be a long time before she did again. They savored every bite of their dinner, while Buzz told the story of the river overtaking Red Cloud Power and Light.

When Buzz's mother heard the workers would have to spend the night on the roof of the plant, she said, "We'll bring them sandwiches tomorrow."

In the morning there was a break in the rain, and they put on their coats. Buzz's and his father's were still heavy from the soaking they'd received the day before. Outside, the air was mercifully clear of dust, although it would return when the storm passed.

Upon reaching the power plant, they saw that the river had subsided enough to launch a rowboat. Buzz's mom set the cheese sandwiches in the boat, alongside gallon cans of water, thermoses of coffee, and biscuits others had brought, and two men rowed the supplies across to the workers.

By the time Buzz and his parents left, half the stranded men had been rowed across. A hundred people would die in the Republican River that day, but all the power plant workers would be rowed to safety. The next morning Buzz read aloud from the newspaper that the men had slept close together on the roof and had traded off sleeping on the outside so those in the middle could be warm.

After that the federal government set to work damming the Republican and many other rivers, in an effort to stop the floods. But the dams would be out of proportion and rushed, hardly a good idea when moving that much earth material.

If the atomic bomb was not what Albert Einstein had ever intended, grandiosity and negligence were not what Buzz strived for when he chose to study civil engineering at Stanford. The flooding of the Republican River would leave an indelible impression on him, and he would carry the sorrow of those years with him to California, where the Feather River breach would inundate more acres and where people were bound to make the same mistakes. He would watch in alarm, just as he and his dad had from the banks of the Republican River, but he would never give in. Not as long as there were living beings, fish or farmer, being overlooked by others' greed. Until he took his dying breath, he would stand waist deep in the current and reach for the hand of the man being swept away.

15

The night before Buzz left for Stanford, he crawled under a wet sheet to stave off the heat, only to find it stiff and brown with dust in the morning. He couldn't wait to board a bus for California.

His mother's attempt at showing happiness could not hide the downturn of her mouth as she loaded him onto the bus with enough food to keep his belly full across three state lines. When school ended for the summer, Buzz did not return home. Instead, he headed to the Sacramento Valley to help his uncle Earl on his Woodland rice farm. He saw it as a way to earn his room and board, rather than give his mother another plate to fill.

Buzz was excited to go home for Christmas. He and his father searched the woods, where the snow was sparse, for the biggest pine tree the two of them could carry, one grand enough to display his mother's handcrafted decorations. Still, by the time she unhooked them from the dying branches, wrapped them in newspaper, and stacked them carefully in a box, Buzz was anxious to get back to his engineering books at Stanford, where he stayed at the library every night until it closed. He loved the challenge of arranging numbers on either side of an equal sign to derive a certain result, loved how building a bridge that could withstand great forces depended on those linear equations and the laws of physics.

Summers continued to lure him back to Woodland, where it was easier to be so far from home because he got to spend time with his uncle. Earl, whose wife and baby had died during childbirth, was shorter and more muscled than Buzz's father, but he had the same eyes, like a Nebraska sky when the clouds parted.

The distance from home was also ameliorated by the presence of a girl he met in French class his senior year. Mostly he was awed by her perfect accent, as his own was terrible. When he graduated and the Second World War started, Buzz enlisted in the Navy and was stationed in Washington, where he did mechanical work on military vehicles. He wrote to her half-heartedly, knowing he wasn't in love with her. By the time the war ended, she was engaged to someone else.

He was drawn again to Woodland, where one fall day his uncle proudly showed him his duck pond. Earl had dug a shallow trench with the tractor, and when he drained the adjacent field, he diverted some of the water to the trench. He promised to teach Buzz how to duck-hunt, but harvest got in the way. At dawn Buzz stood following a pair of flying ducks with his finger, remembering the clay pigeons his dad had taught him to shoot with a twelve-gauge shotgun.

After two years of work that added muscle to Buzz's calves and biceps, his uncle started talking about having Buzz oversee the farm. In Red Cloud, though, farmers were recovering from the drought and buying machinery from his father, and in 1947 Buzz returned to Nebraska to help out. One afternoon when he stepped outside the shop for a breath of fresh air, he ran into an old high school classmate and his younger sister Margaret.

Buzz started stepping outside for a breath of fresh air more often and could hardly believe his luck when the next time she walked by she was alone. A head-tilting, brown-eyed beauty with wavy hair, Margaret looked like Barbara Stanwyck, and he wasted no time in asking her to the movies.

It turned out Margaret had been going out of her way to end up in front of the shop. On their first date, after the movie ended they walked around in front of the house where Margaret claimed Willa Cather had grown up. At the time it was being rented to an unrelated family, and as they wandered around trying not to look as if they were spying, Margaret, having read every one of her books, told Buzz more about Willa Cather than he wanted to know.

Buzz had been courting Margaret for six months when, collecting the mail, he saw the letter addressed to him from his uncle Earl. He was tempted to open it out by the mailbox, but took it inside. After dropping the rest of the mail on the kitchen table, he took the cup of coffee his mother handed him and sat down across from his father.

"If you're serious about taking over the reins," the letter said, "you'll need to move permanently to Woodland in another year or two. I'm not getting any younger."

"It's from Uncle Earl," Buzz said, holding up the letter.

"Oh?"

"He says if I want to take over the farm, it's time."

His father reached for the sugar.

"I would like to, if I have your blessing." Standing at the stove with her back to him, his mother sighed and her shoulders sank, the kind of sign Buzz watched for, as both of his parents were frugal with words.

His father stirred his coffee. "When Earl moved to California, he said Woodland reminded him of Nebraska."

Buzz nodded.

"You've spent a lot of time there," his father said carefully. "Earl says you are a good worker, and he's done well enough with the rice." Each time he said his brother's name his eyes turned down, as if the name were a letter mailed overseas to a loved one. "How does your engineering degree fit into your plans?"

"I've wondered that too," Buzz said. "I'm grateful for the support you gave me that allowed me to go to Stanford. But you always said education had value no matter where it led you."

His father's eyes widened, as if he hadn't expected his words to get through, much less be used to challenge him.

"In school," Buzz said, picking up his cup and setting it down again, "the universe is closed, and the laws of physics and the neat equations fit inside. On Uncle Earl's farm, the universe is open." He held his hands wide. "The same laws of physics apply, but there are more unknowns."

"You lost me," his father said, but when his mother turned around, her teary eyes said she understood.

Buzz wanted to jump up and embrace them both, but they were as parsimonious with affection as they were with words. Their presence every night across from him at the dinner table had taught him what he needed to know about love.

"What it comes down to without physics," he said shrugging, "is I like being outside."

His father nodded and drained his coffee.

"But what about the shop?" Buzz asked.

"I suspect William can handle it," his father said, suppressing a smile. His assistant William had been doing fine before Buzz came home to help and almost put him out of a job.

It wouldn't be until his own son talked about becoming an attorney that Buzz would understand the enormity of a father's hopes for his son. That evening over coffee, he took the sum of what his father hadn't said to mean Buzz had his blessing. It would be years before he knew it to be much more than that.

It was difficult to sleep that night, and on the following evening's walk with Margaret, his uncle's letter weighed on him.

"What is it?" she asked. She had a way of reading him that made it easy to confide in her.

"If you married me," he said, "I'm not sure how useful the English classes you took would be in running a farm."

"Yes!" she said, making him jump.

"Yes what?"

"Yes, I'll marry you."

"That wasn't a proposal," he said.

She frowned. And knowing what he wanted, Buzz dropped to one knee under a towering white maple and asked properly, "Margaret Thorman, will you marry me?"

"Yes," she said, impatient. "And if it's an accountant you need, math was never a problem."

Buzz took her in his arms and kissed her. A breeze moved through the maple tree, leaves glittering in the last of the sunlight.

"What about Woodland?" he asked.

"Yes!" she said, as if he'd invited her to Paris.

She took his hand and they walked. "The way you described school as a closed universe? Willa Cather or the laws of physics, it's the same thing. It's all very safe. I'm ready for the open universe."

A few months later, when the summer heat was giving way to fall, Buzz and his new bride emerged from Red Cloud's Lutheran Church to see his dad standing at the curb next to a brand-new Nash. Its roomy beige body, green hardtop, and bubble headlights shone in the midday sun.

"Where'd you find that beauty?" Buzz asked, thinking his father had hired a driver to take them to the reception at the hotel downtown.

"You're going to need a car to get to California," he said.

The gift just about knocked Buzz over. Because it was a surprise, but also because the car he and Margaret beheld, as they stood holding hands, meant many things at once: the success of their father's business after the war, his parents' endorsement of their move, and the fact that a parent's love was so enormous it outweighed his own desire to keep his child close by. Buzz understood all of this even before he had a son of his own.

A year later he and Margaret slipped into the front seat of the Nash, with the newborn Henry in a basket between them, and headed for California.

16

Woodland, California

When he was a boy fishing on the Republican River, Buzz's biggest catch was a catfish, but he had dreams of landing a sturgeon. Prehistoric bottom-feeders, lake sturgeon were as much as twice a boy's height, could live to be a hundred and fifty years old, and had already been overfished before Buzz was even born.

The fate of the delta sturgeon that lived in the San Francisco Bay and came upstream to spawn was the same. Before netting was banned and the dam on the Feather River blocked the sturgeon's migration, fishermen caught them and sold them at markets from the state capitol to San Francisco. By the time Buzz moved to Eberstark Farm with his young family, the green sturgeon was almost gone. And Earl's duck blind, a deep hole he'd dug in a clearing and lined with plywood, was overgrown with blackberries.

Uncle Earl had been gone for four years when Buzz loaded his young daughter and their Labrador, Murray, into the truck, drove out to the pond, and, instructing her to hold the dog, took a pair of hedge clippers to the brambles.

"Horseradish!" he said when he got tangled, and thorns tore at his neck and arms.

Murray, ninety-seven pounds of muscle under a butterscotch coat, strained at the leash.

"Sit!" five-year-old Alice said, and Murray sat. Panting, tongue hanging sideways.

On Thanksgiving Day Buzz planted Earl's wooden decoys in the pond to attract real ducks, and early that Sunday morning headed out to the blind. He whispered to Murray to lie down. Creeping up to his blind in the dark, he could see the outline of ducks floating next to the decoys. Murray, whose DNA told him what to do when he'd never hunted a day in his life, stayed quiet. Buzz was so excited to see ducks on the pond that when a flock of mallards swung by, his shaking hands made a lousy shot. The mallards scattered, and the ducks on the pond, widgeons as it turned out, flew away.

For Christmas Margaret gave him a book on duck hunting, and every night he managed to read a page or two before his eyes grew heavy and the book, propped on his chest, hit him in the forehead.

"Maybe that'll make the information stick," he said to Margaret, before turning out the light on his side of the bed.

On New Year's Day he shot his first duck, a mallard, and Murray, sitting quietly next to the blind, knew what to do. He trotted into the water and retrieved the fallen duck.

Buzz brought the mallard back to the house, upended a bucket, and sat outside plucking the feathers. Murray stayed close sniffing at the duck, while Alice and Henry watched.

"Want to learn how to hunt?" Buzz asked his son.

"No," said Henry, who at seven had picked up the duck hunting book when Buzz finally finished it and read it in one day.

"I do!" his daughter said, which was how, a few years later, Alice learned to hunt with Murray.

Although he didn't take to hunting, Henry loved the dog as much as Alice did and would run with Murray from the house all the way to a distant rice field, just to say hello to his dad. In middle school, when he had already grown a foot taller than most of his classmates, he started a self-training regimen for the high school track team. With Murray at his side, his "training" was a perfect outlet for the excess energy plaguing an adolescent boy, not unlike the adrenaline rush that had come each time the young Buzz had shattered a clay pigeon. When Henry got to high school, the stride of his long legs was too much for a ten-year-old dog, but every time he came home from a track meet he hung his medal around Murray's neck.

Henry's first choice of college was his father's alma mater, and by the time he was accepted and left for Stanford, Murray was thirteen and so arthritic he didn't bother to get up for meals. Alice knelt by his bowl, trying to get him to eat. It remained full of dry dog food, and she sat next to him, rubbing his coat where the ribs showed through.

"It's time to take him to the vet," Margaret said one evening when Buzz came in from the fields.

The next morning Buzz picked up the dog and carried him to the truck, with a teary Alice following. He laid Murray on the seat, and the dog rested his head on Alice's lap.

When the vet said it was time to put Murray down, Buzz felt brave agreeing to do so in front of his daughter. Then he went outside and bawled, leaving Alice to stay with Murray while the vet injected him.

Buzz heard her sobbing when Murray was gone, went back in, and put his arms around her. Alice never questioned his need to go outside, nor did she hold it against him.

"Want to come with me to pick them up?" he asked his daughter, when the vet called to say Murray's ashes were ready.

It sounded more like begging than an invitation, but Alice took command the same way she'd held so tenaciously to Murray's leash when he'd outweighed her by fifty pounds. After Buzz got weepy at the sight of the smooth pine box holding Murray's ashes, Alice stepped in and picked it up.

"It's okay, Dad," she said.

Buzz had boarded a bus for California even as his mother dabbed at her eyes with a handkerchief, had enlisted for his country when a duck was the only living being he ever wanted to shoot, and had turned his eyes toward Woodland when part of him would always remain in Red Cloud. Yet he'd never felt so weak as in the letting go of his dog.

A few mornings later Buzz and Alice were packing the truck for the blind, when Margaret came out, handed her daughter the box with Murray's ashes, and pressed a bottle of Old Overholt against her husband's chest. Buzz tucked the bottle under the seat, climbed into the truck beside his daughter, and drove to the other side of the farm under a sky full of stars.

When they got there Alice slipped out of the truck, leaving the box on the seat, and headed for the blind with her flashlight. Then she shrieked and leapt backward. Buzz shone his flashlight on a two-foot garter snake, curled up under the stool in the blind. Seizing the opportunity to look brave, he picked up the snake and tossed it into the field behind them. Then, retrieving his own flashlight and a whisk broom from the truck, he brushed three black widows out of the blind.

No ducks had flown at their noisy approach, and the pond was empty. The stars faded, and light appeared at the edge of a clear sky that didn't bode well for shooting. The best time to hunt was just after a storm, when the ducks flew against the wind. You could watch the backside of the storm beyond the Sierra, and sometimes a flight of geese would pass in front of the mountains, their feathers shining fluorescent white in the sun against the black backdrop of clouds.

High up out of shooting range they saw a V formation of pintail. Buzz liked to say they were "on oxygen" because in a jet stream they could fly from Canada to Mexico in two days. He and Alice waited, the quiet broken occasionally by their gritty boots scraping against the plywood. It was a rare lull, both in the flight of ducks and in the rice fields. That morning as Buzz sat in the blind, the fields were plowed and the smell of rotting rice straw mixed with the swampy smell of pond wafted toward them.

As they passed the flooded acres on the way home, Buzz pointed to a blue heron skimming low over the water. It landed and lowered its neck, but when it took flight again its beak was empty. Alice had been as unlucky in the hunt as the heron and, when they went into the house for breakfast, she left the box of ashes in the truck, determined to go back in the evening.

Back at the pond after supper, as the sun sank behind the coastal range, Buzz heard the beating of their wings before he saw the flight of teal.

"There!" he said, pointing his gun.

Alice pointed and fired. The ducks scattered, and a green-winged teal fell to the pond.

Elation crossed her face, then vanished when she realized Murray wasn't there to retrieve it. Her eyes welled with tears, and Buzz waded into the pond. When he turned around, expecting his daughter to be cheered by his second act of chivalry in one day, Alice was standing at the edge of the water with the box of ashes in one hand and the bottle of whiskey in the other.

"Aren't you a little young for whiskey?" he asked, trying to put off the inevitable. But those blue eyes looking back at him bolstered him. He handed her the duck in exchange for the box and started to work at the seal.

"Damn thing's taped up so you can't get in it," he said.

Alice ran to the truck and returned with a Swiss Army knife. He wedged open the lid and pulled out a clear plastic bag containing Murray's remains. The first evening stars emerged, blinking like fireflies, and their reflection rippled as Buzz waded into the pond. Whistling once lightly, he emptied the bag, the mirror of stars momentarily drowned by a cloud of ashes.

"Goodbye, Murray," Alice said, but Buzz couldn't speak.

Alice twisted the top off the Old Overholt and handed him the bottle. He took a swallow of the liquor he rarely drank. It burned sweet in his throat and unlocked his tongue. "Goodbye, Murray," he said, in a whisper that sounded like the breeze moving through dry reeds.

Buzz handed Alice the empty box, picked up his gun, and walked with her to the truck. The headlights shone on the road like the Milky Way stretching across the sky before them as they made their way back to the house.

Their boys would be in diapers when Alice's husband Sully brought her home a yellow Labrador pup they named Barclay. That was Sully, always looking for ways to make her weak in the knees. He would build a house that brought her back to her childhood, then abandon her and the house. He would buy a dog that reminded her of Murray, then leave her with the boys just as both the older one and the pup were being potty trained.

But Alice showed her usual tenacity in raising the children herself. She could be found driving a tractor around the farm with them seat-belted in, Danny in his car seat and Chris on his booster. And when Danny took to hunting the same way Alice had, she taught him to hunt with Barclay, no longer a pup, just as her father had taught her with Murray.

The boys were both in finals week at Chico when Alice had to put Barclay down. After which she drove straight to the shelter and picked out the dog that was the least like a Labrador—a two-year-old terrier mix yapping at them from inside the cage. But the woman at the shelter said the dog loved to fetch, which is how he got the name Stix. Stix followed Alice from the truck to the house and everywhere between, and when she shushed him the way Margaret did, it put an end to his yapping. Except when the mail truck came and he yapped and jumped up against the white picket fence Sully had put around the house in an ironic token of his domesticity. Then Alice would come out of the house and shush the dog.

"Sit," she'd say, and he'd sit.

If Sully were the kind to bring home an irresistible purebred pup, Buzz proudly noted that Alice was the kind to go the shelter, pick out the neediest dog, and turn it into a winner.

SAN JOAQUIN RIVER

17

By the time the ground was littered with shiny chestnut buckeyes, the flow of streams from the Tulare Basin to Southern California had slowed to a trickle. If a wet winter left the hills green through spring, a dry winter was never far behind. Yet people vying for water had always hedged their bets on the wetter years, and those in the southern Central Valley with the most land increased their allocations by creating family affiliation where there was none.

Once the San Joaquin River was as mighty as the Sacramento, until the dam went in at Millerton and a hundred and fifty miles of river dried up. At the delta, tidal flow and farm drainage refilled the San Joaquin with salty and polluted water, and when the pumps were running the water sucked backward.

Twenty-five miles southwest of Millerton was the city of Orange Grove where Salvatore Giangrande built his empire. Salvatore hailed from a rocky coastline of Sardinia, where the Mediterranean sun beat down on his back as he helped his father tend Carignan vines growing out of the sandy soil. He was just fourteen when he took a small sample of the lemon crop his father grew alongside his vineyards and boarded a ship bound for America.

Sal sold lemons and bananas from a cart in New Jersey until he had enough money to import the fruit himself. A force to be reckoned with in the business before he was twenty, he once again looked west. With money in his pocket, he made his way to Chicago, embarked on a westbound train, and arrived four days later in the high desert town of Barstow. From the arched balcony of the station hotel, he gazed out at the Tehachapis where a late snowstorm had dusted the peaks like the powdered sugar his mother dispensed over a cake.

Boarding a train that took him over those mountains, over the rocky range that separated the Los Angeles Basin from the Central Valley, he was captivated by the phenomenon of an engine managing the 4,000-foot climb. Built by Chinese laborers, the tracks passed through tunnels and bridges to gain seventy-five feet of elevation in less than a mile, looping over themselves like the mouth of a cannoli.

Coming off the pass, Salvatore looked down on green stripes of irrigated land that, as the train moved north through the valley, he saw were vineyards like the ones he'd tended with his father on the island of Sardinia. He debarked in Orange Grove, where the cold front that had produced a late snowstorm in the Tehachapis quickly gave way to longer days and dry heat that reminded him of his native Italy. He wasted no time in procuring eight thousand acres of what was "dirt cheap" desert land in the region he'd just passed through on the train and used what money was left to buy a couple of plows and a horse.

While Lon Smith wrangled the King's River, Salvatore took advantage of the canals that diverted so much water from the San Joaquin that by the time he planted his grapes the river was no longer navigable for ships.

The year his first grandson was born, the skies dried up and Sal's grapes shriveled on the vine. But the next year was better, for both the sweet grapes his family passed around the table, and the smaller, juicier ones he grew for wine. He kept his business alive when lice attacked his vineyards and doubled his acres by the time Prohibition came around. Even an early frost that ruined his table grapes turned out to be a boon when he discovered he could sell them for fermentation. He struck a deal with a San Joaquin Valley winery, where in exchange for each ton of grapes his company delivered for free, he took a hundred gallons of wine. When Prohibition ended he had six hundred thousand gallons aging in barrels in a warehouse, which the winery was only too happy to buy back.

Sal then turned his attention to the north, where he bought thirty-five acres in the town of Altamont at the mouth of the Sacramento Delta. The sandy soil failed the vegetables that farmers had planted there but was inhospitable to the lice that had threatened Sal's vineyards. It lacked the salt content of his sixteen thousand acres south of Orange Grove, and he never had to irrigate. On top of that, the conditions, heat with cool evening winds coming off the bay, were perfect for the red Carignan grapes he had helped his father grow on Sardinia.

Sal bought the San Joaquin Valley winery from the vintners with whom he'd done business so he had a place to make jug wine from his Carignan grapes. On his eightieth birthday, he handed over the winery and Giangrande Farms to his son. Sal II turned to Texas, where warm, stable temperatures helped grow the best grapefruits in the world, adding nine thousand acres of sweet Texas Rubies to the Giangrande empire.

Salvatore's ventures were renowned in the Central Valley, where the young Lawrence Scheffield had every intention of achieving more. Lawrence's father delivered the morning and evening newspapers in addition to working a full day at the fruit packinghouse. Humiliated every time his father fell asleep at the dinner table, Lawrence swore he would one day be the owner of that packinghouse.

His sophomore year at Orange Grove High, he got bumped up to calculus, where he introduced himself to Nina, the great granddaughter of Salvatore Giangrande.

He nodded at the chalkboard dusty with graphs and polynomials and said, "If you need a study partner, I'm pretty good at this stuff."

"I'm not sure I need a study partner," Nina said.

There was a pause, just long enough for Lawrence to squirm in his loafers. Then she said, "But I could use someone to lug these heavy books."

Buoying up the books she'd unceremoniously dumped in his arms, he walked alongside her. Every day from then on, he ate lunch with her under the ash tree that provided an island of shade on a campus sprawling under the sun. The shade was crowded with students, but Nina and Lawrence garnered enough respect to secure the spot where she could sit against the trunk of the tree. They were a good-looking couple, Nina tanned and lithe, Lawrence with his beach-blond hair.

Straight out of high school Lawrence went to work in a fruit packinghouse, making his way from the floor to vice president in less time than it took Nina to graduate from college. Those were the credentials he took to Nina's father the day he put on a suit, drove over to her house, and parked his red Buick Skylark in front. Sal III, answering the door wearing a maroon silk smoking jacket and holding a fresh Campari and soda, spotted the car over Lawrence's shoulder exactly as the young man had intended.

"Lawrence," he said, grabbing the suitor's hand in a firm shake, "can I get you a drink?"

"That would be great," Lawrence said.

Salvatore handed him his own glass and retreated to the kitchen to make another. The house smelled of garlic, and Lawrence could hear Mrs. Giangrande chopping something in the kitchen. Nina appeared at the top of the stairs, held her finger to her lips, and winked conspiratorially.

Salvatore emerged from the kitchen with his cocktail and, after they toasted, led Lawrence over to the fireplace, which was swept clean, the grate holding a decorative arrangement of pinecones. Standing with Salvatore in front of the fireplace, Lawrence launched into the speech he had been rehearsing on the way over in the Buick: "Sir, I am vice president of Sweeney Fruit Company, and I'm in a position to invest in a parcel of land in the valley."

"Yes?"

"I intend to expand my business to crops, and I believe I am secure enough financially to be a good husband. As you know, I have loved your daughter since our sophomore year in high school. Mr. Giangrande, I am asking for Nina's hand in marriage."

Salvatore's jowly cheeks sank, and Lawrence wondered how he'd misstepped. "You are trying to sell me on your merits as a husband."

"Yes, sir."

"This is where you are wrong," Salvatore said, taking a sip of his Campari with an index finger pointed at Lawrence.

"Wrong, sir?"

Salvatore set his drink on top of a coaster on the mantel. "I will give you my daughter's hand in marriage because she is in love, and nothing is more important than my daughter's happiness."

Lawrence almost dropped his Campari. From upstairs where she had been spying, Nina squealed, ran down the stairs, and threw her arms around her father. The kiss she planted on Lawrence's cheek was almost a letdown after the relief he felt knowing he had Sal III's approval.

Before they were married, Lawrence bought a lot overlooking the San Joaquin River and started meeting with the architect, who expanded the foyer three times before Nina was satisfied.

The house had six three-story bulwarks, like a wedding cake that had multiplied, and balustrades across the roofline, as if one day Lawrence would have to defend his fortress.

Just as the first Salvatore had, Lawrence and his business partners lived in Orange Grove, which since their childhood had grown into a bustling town, rather than in the destitute towns of the Saltsink Water District. From the bedroom window he and Nina could see the San Joaquin River, while the land further south, where he would add his crops to Nina's great-grandfather's, was in a hydrologically closed basin.

Lawrence kept his promise and, in 1973, on the eve of his first wedding anniversary, invested in more farmland with the money he'd made packing, distributing, and shipping fruit out of the Central Valley. To that land he added exponentially by buying out Sal III, using his wife's dividends as well as those of her brothers, whom he named as owners of Sunrise Farms. Then he took his wife to London. And on to Italy to see her relatives, drinking wine with them in the family vineyard on Sardinia. He did it because it made her happy, and that was the difference between them. Nina wanted the sun to crown her regal head from all parts of the world, while Lawrence knew all he needed for the world to come to him was the punishing sun of the South Central Valley.

18

May 2010

In Lawrence and Nina's garage there were four cars. First was Nina's Mercedes, with its stretch hood and premium rims on the tires like the prongs of a diamond ring. Next to that was the red Buick Skylark Lawrence had parked in front of her house the day he asked for Nina's hand in marriage. They still took it out on special occasions. Then came the new Buick he drove most days, and next to that was the Hummer, the bright-yellow, military-style tank he drove down to his fields late on Saturdays. With his business partner Patrick Smith mining his Tulare land for oil, Lawrence felt proud to be driving through Sunrise's seventy thousand acres of almonds riding high on the leather seat of a gas-guzzler.

On the straight, four-lane highway, Lawrence's Hummer bore down on cars in the fast lane, forcing them to move over. He turned west into the vast patch of land that was the Saltsink Water District and drove down the main street that served as the highway, through the railroad towns Salvatore Giangrande had seen from the train.

Passing through Highland, he hit the red light just as the men, his own employees, piled out of a battered four-door sedan, stiff from a day in the fields, and walked with their five-gallon jugs across the weedy parking lot to the water-vending machine just outside the supermarket. A woman he recognized as

Employee of the Month—Luna? Juana?—was massaging the base of her spine while greeting her fellow workers. Followed by another woman and their strollers, she pushed open the broken automatic door of the supermarket.

From outside the market, he saw the gritty concrete floor where multiple squares of vinyl were missing, saw the women walking the aisles pulling dish soap and bags of pinto beans from half-empty shelves. He saw because this was the intersection he passed through every evening on his way to check his fields. He saw because the light turned red, and this was the existence he'd strived so hard to overcome. He saw because he didn't want to see.

Back outside, the women would fill their water jugs. Shifting two toddlers to one stroller and loading their jugs onto the other, they would navigate sidewalk cracks, the result of subsidence caused by Sunrise Farms overdrawing the aquifers. They would cross the main street and walk along the shoulder, where pavement met the dusty fields, parting at the house with bedsheets covering the aluminum windows. He saw the single bedroom where Juana—not Luna—and her husband slept with their three children, while two more adults slept in the living room. He saw the house because it was everything he'd avoided when he built his own on the San Joaquin River.

Lawrence's employees lived just outside the Highland city limits, where they couldn't drink the water piped into their homes. Juana and her husband were legal and lucky to have year-round work, but they needed the two men in the living room to help meet the rent. The men, who were illegals and also worked for Lawrence, returned to their families in Mexico for the half a year they had no work. All of them labored sixty-hour weeks on Sunrise Farms, the world's number one supplier of almonds, which drew clean water from the aqueduct running past town. They liked working for him because he was the first boss this side of the border who'd given them gloves and goggles for spraying the crops.

When Lawrence reached the almond orchards, he left the engine running and, descending from the driver's seat of the Hummer, approached his trees. With the toes of the snakeskin boots Nina had given him for his sixtieth birthday, he dug into the white crust on the surface of the soil. It was selenium, what likely had caused the demise of ancient irrigated civilizations. Normal drainage would have taken care of it, but drainage in Lawrence's district was poor due to an impermeable layer of clay beneath the surface. So workers wearing white-hooded coveralls and masks, along with the goggles and gloves, would spray a sulfuric acid amendment at the base of the trees. After spraying they would irrigate frequently to leach out the salt.

Never knowing how much water he would end up with, Lawrence used the aqueduct for the early stages of his crops, then switched to the wells that had become Salvatore Giangrande's primary source of water. But the wells had long since overdrawn the aquifer, which only increased the salinity.

That was what irked his nemesis Buzz Eberstark. The Sacramento River flowed right past Buzz's Woodland farm and the saturated islands of all those delta farmers whose riparian rights he protected when he got elected to the North Canal Water District. Lawrence and Patrick's rights were by appropriation of all the rivers in the arid part of the Central Valley. But as Buzz's lawyer son himself would tell you, both appropriation and riparian rights were covered by the law. Furthermore, Buzz flooded his fields to grow rice, and the government paid him a certain amount no matter the going price, just as they supplemented Lawrence and Patrick's prices for cotton. So as far as Lawrence was concerned, he and Buzz were even.

Back in the Hummer and rolling past the orchards, Lawrence came to the fields where he'd decided not to replant tomatoes. Cotton required more irrigation than most crops, but it tolerated the salt. In the most recent years of drought, though, Lawrence had been forced to abandon his cotton to water the orchards. Row crops could be fallowed, while permanent crops were too much of an investment to let go. Which was why he was replacing his tomatoes with more almonds and grapes.

Sunrise Farms was still new when Lawrence convinced buyers the Carignan grapes Salvatore had planted at the mouth of the delta were worth more than jug wine prices. Thirty-five years later his hair had receded and he shaved his head clean, but the list of top California wineries buying his grapes was extensive. However, it took nearly three hundred gallons of water to produce one bottle of wine, whether it was a Carignan or a Chianti. And each almond tree took several acre-feet of water a year to yield full production.

That was where the four islands came in, starting with the one just east of Lawrence's delta vineyard near the town of Bradley, where Patrick Smith had converted two hundred prime grazing acres into a housing development. Patrick and Lawrence had just entered into an agreement to purchase the islands from a Swiss company that had been trying for fifteen years to flood them for commodity water. Both northern islands, Graham and the neighboring Joseph, were in the line of sight of the proposed tunnels, and Joseph could be used to stockpile fill dirt.

The other two islands near Bradley could be flooded to expand Floyd's Tract, which, after the Feather River flood had put them under water, had never been restored to farming. A resort had sprung up, but that too had been abandoned. People still stored their boats near the docks where boards were missing and the invasive hyacinth choked the marina.

Lawrence and Patrick maintained that flooding and habitat restoration were one and the same, but the southern delta was twenty to thirty feet below sea level. Expanding Floyd's Tract would produce a lake, not marshland—which was the point, since it translated to water storage. Pulling back onto the highway in the Hummer, Lawrence offered up a prayer of thanks to Salvatore Giangrande for the Altamont vineyard that inadvertently put a few more slices of delta pie on the Sunrise map.

SACRAMENTO RIVER

19

June 2010

Buzz tightened the knot on the tie Margaret had chosen for him and slipped on his tan blazer. If they were going to storm this meeting, they had to look like more than a couple of farmers. But he was proud of his vocation, which is why he completed the outfit with his work boots. Margaret rolled her eyes and said nothing.

Clomping down the hallway, he reflected on how his boots didn't find the brake pedal as easily as they once had, which was why Alice was in the driver's seat for the trip to Sacramento. But he was proud of the fact that up until a year ago he'd been driving the tractor.

"Good luck," Margaret said, kissing him as he went out the door.

"How'd I ever persuade a girl like you to marry me?" he asked, stumbling as the toe of his boot caught the gravel.

His wife's eyes registered panic before Buzz braced his hand on the side of the house to right himself. Alice jumped out of the truck and opened the passenger door, but he waved her away, climbed in, and pulled the door shut, feeling a sting in the wrist of the hand that had pushed off the house.

The truck tires crackled and bounced along the road traversing the fields. Then they turned onto the two-lane highway and headed east toward the interstate. Vast squares of rice field unfurled behind them, and they rolled through acres of almond trees exploding with green. They passed a row of domed silos, the fields combed brown and covered in tomato plants bearing new fruit.

Buzz was made for wide-open spaces. He loved being surrounded by farmland so that from his bedroom windows all he could see was the coastal range to the west, to the north a scattering of low buildings whose lights twinkled at night.

In Germany, every winter by New Year's, his father and uncle had dragged a toboggan up the hill behind their house. Buzz wasn't even a notion in his father's mind at the time, yet he could feel the weight of the wooden sled, hear the blades slicing through snow as the two boys struggled uphill, their boots sinking deep in the powder. Winters were shorter now, and that snow was gone. A million square feet of snowpack, vanished from the Northern Hemisphere.

Buzz pointed to an orchard where the fuzzy green hulls of almonds were sprouting from branches. The tule fog they depended on to form buds was disappearing. "You used to complain," he teased his daughter, "when the fog obscured our view from the duck blind."

As if on cue, when they approached the bypass a flock of waterfowl rose from the flooded fields. It was a sight that brought Buzz as close as he would ever come to religion. He didn't believe in God, just the earth beneath his boots, where if he had his way he'd be buried. In a plain wooden box that would break down, so that he could sprout up one day, maybe as water grass. Nothing more than a weed that would disintegrate in the dry season, particles rising in the wind to meet the geese as they flew toward Canada.

"Remind me," Alice said as she turned off the Garden Highway. "What was their rationale for keeping this meeting a secret?"

"Jamie Cannigan says the ASD work is 'at a very delicate stage.' Advocates of a Sustainable Delta, there's an ironic name if I've ever heard one."

Alice laughed.

When they arrived at the Farm Bureau building, John Kimura was waiting on the sidewalk. John was one of the few in the next generation who'd chosen to carry on his family's heritage of farming—along with Alice and, in his own way, her brother Henry, who now approached with a newspaper reporter in tow.

"It's not just your height that makes you stand out." Buzz nodded affectionately at his son's coat and the colorful mallards flying across his sky-blue tie.

From the Thanksgivings he spent at his son's house in San Francisco, he knew Henry's closet held a whole row of suits, while his own held two.

"Wondering where you went wrong?" Henry asked, hand on his mallard tie.

"Where I went right's more like it," Buzz said.

Henry grinned. It was as near as Buzz could come to saying, "I'm proud of you."

Parents were different now. Buzz saw it in the way Henry held his children when they were little, in how easily he told them he loved them. The distance he moved from the farm was twenty times smaller than the one Buzz had put between himself and his parents, and Henry closed it every time he crossed the valley to fight for the delta. But Buzz didn't have the words any more than his father had to let Henry know how much it mattered to him.

Henry's dress shoes struck the pavement like a judge's gavel as they approached the building, and Buzz felt the adrenaline pumping through him. In the elevator the reporter, a young woman from the *San Francisco Chronicle*, located the recording device on her phone and turned up the volume.

"Room 205," Henry said, his long legs reaching the door first, which he held open.

Buzz relished the look of surprise on Lawrence Scheffield's face when they walked in. Jamie Cannigan—thin tanned face, hazel eyes, and blue denim sleeves pushed up above the elbows—stood up from the table. Behind him on the other side of the vast window flowed the seemingly endless waters of the Sacramento River.

For years the ASD's predecessor, a panel formed to resolve water issues in the delta, had floundered and squandered millions of dollars, and in an effort to move things along, the state's Department of Water Resources had called for a series of closed meetings with a select group of players. The few organic farmers present, who along with one of their attorney sons had formed Save the Delta to face off against the ASD, were not invited.

There were a couple of problems with these secret meetings. For one, in addition to heading the Department of Water, Jamie Cannigan, as Director of the Conservancy of Biological Resources, had signed an agreement aligning his organization with the tunnels. For another, he was wooing back to the table the water lords who had walked out on previous meetings in order to subvert them—subversion that from the looks of things was working.

"This is a closed meeting," Jamie told Buzz. "You may not report to the public the names of the participants or quote them in any way."

"And if we do?" Buzz asked.

Jamie raised his eyebrows.

"We have no intention," Henry said, "of withholding information from the public."

"Let's be reasonable," Lawrence said.

"Reasonable?" Henry moved around to stand in front of Jamie Cannigan. "How are your two planned multi-billion-dollar pipes that would dwarf the Chunnel reasonable?"

“We have a plan to flood the Uplands,” said Jamie. “For smelt habitat.”

“With most of the water gone to the tunnels,” Henry said, “nothing would save the fish.”

Which was true, since the smelt were almost gone. But that was the point: secretly they believed the delta was beyond saving.

“Water minimums for salmon have already taken half the supply,” Lawrence said.

“You can’t just drain the streams for your water supply,” said Buzz.

“We need sound science,” the agribusinessman said.

“How much more sound can science get than your own team of Davis biologists?” Buzz asked. He knew his question was ironic, as water contractors got the results they wanted from the scientists they hired themselves.

“And you must not be that worried about water,” Henry added, “when you just sold a bunch of it to Southern California.”

“It’s not a sale,” Lawrence countered. “It’s a transaction that enables us to bank water in the southern part of the state.” It was the kind of hogwash Lawrence was bound to come up with, and the reason Patrick Smith, absent as usual, tended to let Lawrence stand in for him at these meetings.

“Speaking of banks,” Henry said, “have you paid the fees associated with transferring water you got for free from the state?”

“All of you need to leave,” Jamie Cannigan said.

“And if we don’t?”

Jamie stood up. “This meeting is over.”

“For the record,” Henry said as he moved to the door, “this secret gathering is a violation of the First Amendment and the Open Meeting Act.”

Buzz followed Henry, with Alice, John, and the young reporter—whose story in the *Chronicle* would be picked up by *The Sacramento Bee*—not far behind.

In the hallway, the walls were lined with scenic delta shots: ducks rising off a flooded cornfield, a tractor in a pear orchard, the Paintersville Bridge at sunset. Maybe, Buzz thought, they wanted to chronicle the delta before its demise.

Back on the first floor, they passed a sign in the lobby that read: CALIFORNIA FARMERS, FEEDING THE WORLD. Buzz let out a guffaw. Lawrence always said Saltsink's allotment of water supplied the world with food, and Saltsink had recently doubled its export of almonds to China. Americans could not possibly eat all the almonds Sunrise Farms produced, so the company had developed an aggressive marketing campaign to create a global taste for the nuts, espousing their health benefits. Almonds had never been a traditional part of people's diets in China, but the country's population was the perfect target for America's overproduction.

Chinese farmers with small family operations were encouraged to sell to large mechanized ones and join the mass migration to cities, while America was growing and exporting corn for ethanol and soy for animals. Chinese pigs were growing fat on cheap soybean meal, and more people in China were buying pork and less of the produce they used to grow themselves. That was how America was "feeding the world."

Buzz had a sudden image of his son crossing the Bay Bridge, blue tie waving out the open window like mallards on their spring migration. How many times had Henry made the drive back to his nesting grounds to defend a fading way of life?

Feeling a surge of pride, Buzz fell into stride with his son. "Keep defending us like that," he said to Henry, "and you'll be putting that closet full of suits to good use."

20

Woodland, California

The rain made one last appearance in June, and it was still wet the morning Margaret got ready to drive to town.

"Can't you wait?" Buzz asked.

"We can't wait another day for toilet paper or milk," she said.

There was a brief respite as Buzz and Alice headed out to the fields, but he kept his eye on the darkening sky. Though they seldom reached the enormity of a thunderstorm in the Midwest, big California rains carried Buzz back to the flooding Republican River, and picturing Margaret driving slippery roads didn't help.

Margaret kept the books in order along with the house. She listened to Buzz and Alice's talk over lunch to get a sense of which fields were producing or which methods for incorporating the rice straw worked and which didn't. It made it easier for her to see where the money followed the rice. And they had done all right. Buzz always said it was more profitable to be good stewards of the land, and mostly the books reflected his views.

The rain started as Alice combed one of the south fields for weeds. Retreating to the truck, Buzz watched his daughter bend in high boots, rubber overalls, and slicker to pull the offending plants from between blades of rice. Then fat drops began pelting the truck and plastering the windshield, and he tried not to think about where Margaret was. The east–west road could be flooding. Normally the ditches channeled rain away from the road, but a tomato truck had veered off and toppled, and a car rolled in the same place on the opposite side, so the ditches had been filled in. He leaned his head against the back window of the cab, closed his eyes, and willed the hammering rain to drive the worries from his mind.

Moments later the truck door slammed as Alice climbed in, water pouring off her overalls.

"Guess the slicker didn't hold you for long," he said.

Pushing the hood and a wet strand of hair away from her face, Alice looked surprised. "Almost an hour."

He must have dozed off.

She started the engine. "Let's go see if Mom's back."

So Alice was worried too.

The driveway was empty. Buzz and Alice took off their boots and slickers in the mudroom, and he put on a dry pair of shoes. Standing by the kitchen door in her socks, Alice hesitated. Margaret had mopped before she left, even though they had a cleaning person now.

"Floor's dry," Alice said, crossing to her cell phone, which she tapped and held to her ear.

There was a muffled chiming sound and Alice threw open the gadget drawer, pulling out Margaret's cell phone. Just then the kitchen door opened and in came Margaret, wet and empty-handed.

"Mom, what happened?"

"I had to turn around," Margaret said. "The east–west was flooded. There was a detour and I got lost trying to find the north–south."

How that could be, even in a downpour, when they'd been driving those roads for sixty years, Buzz didn't know.

"Good thing *you* weren't driving," Margaret told him.

She must have read alarm on his face or she wouldn't have said something cruel. But she had a point since Buzz had no sense of direction.

Alice held up the cell phone.

"I don't see how calling from a tomato field in the middle of a squall would have helped," Margaret said.

Having refused a cell phone himself, Buzz turned away so their daughter wouldn't see him smile.

Alice washed her hands at the sink and plunked a jar of peanut butter on the counter. As she spread it on slices of bread, Buzz saw with relief that on a less eventful shopping trip Margaret had bought the natural peanut butter their daughter insisted upon.

When they sat at the table (with glasses of orange juice because there was no milk), Margaret said, "The east–west was closed, so I backtracked to the north–south. But I got confused when I passed the Michaels' place and saw, through sheets of rain, not orchard but the frames of new houses. There must have been thirty of them."

Alice shook her head.

"I'm not losing my mind," Margaret said.

"No you're not," said Alice.

"Still, I've never gotten lost on these roads, so I told myself if that's where the Michaels' orchard was supposed to be, I'd reach the north–south in five minutes." She set down the sandwich she'd been holding, uneaten. "Fifteen minutes later I hadn't reached it, and I pulled over in a tomato field to collect myself. At that point getting home seemed more important than toilet paper. So I turned around and crossed the north–south I missed the first time."

Alice swallowed a thick bite of sandwich and said, "What if we all go into town together?" She held her breath, waiting to see how her mother, who didn't easily accept help, would respond.

"Fine by me," Margaret said.

So after lunch the three of them set out in the truck, Alice driving and Margaret in the middle. The rain had lightened to a heavy mist, and the tule fog had set in. The wipers couldn't erase the fog creeping over the car, and the visibility might have been worse than it had been in a downpour.

"Take the lower east–west," Margaret told her daughter. "I want you to see the houses."

Alice sighed.

"You knew about it," Margaret said.

"I didn't have the heart to tell you," Alice said, when they passed the spot where their friends' orchard had been, seventy-five acres of almonds farmed by a couple Buzz and Margaret had known for the duration of their time in Woodland. Both the man and his wife had died the year before.

"None of the kids wanted to farm," Alice said.

Where there should have been trees Buzz saw a jungle of crosshatched two-by-fours. "Shame," he said, "tearing out small family orchards so Lawrence Scheffield can plant more."

Then he pointed at the north–south road his wife had missed. Alice turned onto it, and Margaret scowled. But on the return trip, with the bag of groceries at his feet as the truck rumbled along and his thigh rested comfortably against her knee, she reached over and took his hand.

Buzz held on tightly. He held on as they turned into the farm, as they drove by rain-soaked fields and the pond Earl had built long ago. When Buzz had finished cleaning it up he'd begged her, after the children fell asleep, to drive out with him to see it. As they'd approached in the truck, a nearly full moon had cast its sheen across the pond. He'd guided her to a clearing between the blind and the blackberry bushes, and they'd made love in the stubbly grass.

He was afraid to look at her now, in case she was overcome by the same memory. Why that fear after sixty-two years of marriage, he didn't know. But in the face of a deluge and concrete pads covering their friends' orchard like gravestones, Margaret's hand was the north–south road that had seemingly appeared out of nowhere, and it pulled them toward the open universe they had chosen so many years before.

21

June 2010

Six months after moving into T Bone's house, Nate was in a convoy of tanker trucks buzzing down the highway toward the mouth of the delta. Sloshing around inside the tanks were tens of thousands of fingerling Chinooks a crew of biologists was transporting from the Mokelumne Fish Hatchery to the ocean. The Chinooks' imprint cues were so strong that they would return from the ocean in three years to spawn in the very same part of the river where they had hatched, even after being trucked around the delta.

Nate hadn't been born when the salmon in California's rivers were so plentiful people caught them with spears, but he would never forget when he saw the Chinook spawning in a creek just north of the Feather River. The riffles were alive with the silver-skinned salmon digging in the gravel to deposit their eggs, and the water was loud with the sound of them flopping and waving their tails. He'd stood for a long time in the peppered shade of the alders, stunned by the noise.

On almost every West Coast river, spawning took place below a major dam that precluded fish from migrating farther. Whenever he drove north, Nate imagined himself a salmon swimming through a host of obstacles. The hatcheries for one. While they gave the salmon a fighting chance, the fish were not nearly as strong as their wild predecessors.

Then there were the lower stream flows two winters before, which the young salmon had been unable to survive. Higher water exports from the delta also mimicked the pull toward the ocean, drawing delta fish to their death at the pumps. Fish and Wildlife's last salvage count of splittail at the facility near the pumps had yielded seven hundred thousand dead in one day.

The convoy of tankers crossed a bridge and headed south on Mare Island, until they reached the tip where it jutted out into San Pablo Bay. The drivers backed up the trucks to the marina and hopped out. Nate's driver attached an accordion hose to the tank and told him to grab the other end.

Nate tugged the hose toward the docks, where volunteers tied it to one of the holding pens. The drivers opened the valves at the tanks, a rush of water snaked through the hoses, and hundreds of thousands of six-inch salmon leapt into the pens. Then Nate and the crew waited. They ate lunch, talked, and took naps in their trucks while the salmon acclimated in the pens.

In limbo with the fish was the ocean tide. As it began to flow back out, Nate and the others climbed in boats and towed the pens into open water. Then, lowering the pens below the surface and away from the birds, they released the salmon.

The bass-fishing boats floated close by, and fishermen would likely find a handful of young salmon in the stomach of each striped bass they caught. Nate hoped most of the salmon would escape to swim through the bay and out to the Pacific, and he'd be there to see the results when the salmon returned to the Sacramento River. He'd helped tag the fish at the hatchery, injecting a one-millimeter coded tag into the snout of each fingerling, and after they spawned and died he and a crew would cut open the carcasses to retrieve the tags.

That was where the science got murky, when samplers used calculations to estimate the fish population. But the science was what Nate loved most about his job. People liked to hold up science as being the standard by which faith in God looked absurd, when in fact scientists made leaps of faith all the time.

Nate's young and failed marriage and Ana's parents' attachment to the inside of a church had soured the wide-eyed believer in him, but he still saw a higher power in the mysteries of the natural world. And the most he could hope for was that humans would understand their place in the scheme of things in a valley where salmon no longer thrived. With the dams, the hatcheries, and the new levees rising like pyramids from the floor of the delta, scientists were grasping at threads of a wilderness long gone, yet grasping was the only choice they had.

22

Squatting at low tide on a rock bench below the Paintersville Bridge, Nate stared at a colony of button-sized clams protruding from the mud. Their appearance had caused a steady decrease in vital native organisms, but the clam wasn't the only threat. Samples from the water treatment plant's discharge had revealed DDT, mercury, and industrial chemicals.

The Uplands Sanitation District, one of the last in the area using an antiquated system, was a primary discharger of wastewater into the delta. The state had urged the USD to upgrade its treatment system, but the USD had protested that the discharge met the Environmental Protection Agency's criteria for bathing beaches.

And the EPA criteria for bathing beaches? Nate had taken enough water samples from those beaches to be leery of swimming. He trudged back up to his truck and drove toward the town of Stockwell, where he was meeting T Bone for lunch.

He pulled into the parking lot at the Rush Inn, a turn-of-the-century wood plank building in Stockwell's one-block town of Western storefronts built, along with the railroads and the levees, by Chinese laborers.

He pushed open the door and walked through the dark front room where the bartender was wiping down the ancient mahogany bar. The low ceiling was a collage of business cards: engineers, electricians and plumbers, yardwork and hauling. T Bone was sitting in the back of the crowded café at a table that overlooked the slough. She stood ceremoniously when she saw him enter the room, and he was acutely aware of his chest and shoulders filling out the T-shirt that had hung baggy when he'd moved in half a year before.

Used to the high turnover at lunch, the waitress was immediately at their table.

"I'll have the burger," Nate said. "Cheddar, no mayo." She scribbled on her pad.

"I'll have the minestrone," T Bone said, "and a salad with ranch, please."

As the waitress headed for the kitchen, T Bone peered out the window. "Any sign of Wallace?"

Wallace was the humpback whale that weeks before had swum seventy miles up the Sacramento River. With their ocean food supply depleted, humpbacks had been swimming into new territory, but this one seemed to be floundering in the slough right below the Rush Inn. Nate's coworkers had tried and failed to lure him back to the ocean. Everyone in the café now spent lunch watching out the window for signs of Wallace.

"He surfaced once yesterday looking pretty listless," Nate said. "But we got a transducer."

"A what?"

"A high-power underwater speaker. We're borrowing it from the Navy, and are going to try luring Wallace out with humpback feeding songs."

"When?"

"Tomorrow morning," he said, grinning like a schoolboy.

The next morning, a Saturday, Nate got up early and drove to Stockwell to meet his coworkers down at the docks below the Rush Inn. Tied to the dock was the yacht with the name *Pirate Booty* painted on the stern. This was the boat they were using to lure Wallace out of the slough.

By the time they'd set up the equipment there was still no sign of Wallace, but the scent of hash browns mingled with the swampy smell of the slough. The Rush Inn was buzzing with customers, which Nate knew included T Bone and Ruby, who were hoping for a table close to the windows. From there they could watch the action while enjoying a breakfast that was as good as the Inn's famous minestrone.

Nate's stomach grumbled as he and a coworker picked up a heavy-duty speaker encased in steel, carried it to the side of the yacht, and lowered it into the slough. The crowd standing on the levee above the docks hushed as the speaker emitted eerie feeding songs just before it sank underwater.

That's when Wallace emerged next to the boat. Nate backed up, surprised by the eye gazing up at him, and the crowd along the levee broke into applause. The captain of the *Pirate Booty* rushed to the helm and started downriver, with Wallace following.

As the *Pirate Booty* made its way downstream, Wallace emerged less and less frequently behind them.

"Turn off the music for a moment," Nate's coworker said, and Nate flipped the switch. Behind them the water was still.

After a couple of minutes his coworker said, "Now switch it back on." Nate did, and a few minutes later the surface broke, Wallace emitted a puff of water from his blowhole, and sank back down.

For the rest of the ride down the slough, Nate switched the speaker off and on to keep Wallace following. When they reached the Deepwater Ship Channel, wind on the surface made it harder to spot the whale. He started diving and staying down for longer.

In Suisun Bay they slowed, gulped down sandwiches, and scanned the water for Wallace, who was wandering farther. They spotted him only two more times before the sun got low and they harbored for the night.

When Nate got home, all the windows were steamed up from the pasta T Bone was boiling, and Ruby opened them to let in the air that was beginning to cool as the sun went down. The table was set, and there were carrots arranged in a cup like a bouquet.

"Pretty flowers," Nate said to Ruby.

She shrugged. "The lettuce was rotten and I threw it in the compost."

Nate laughed and headed to the bathroom to wash his hands. He felt the occasion warranted a shower, but T Bone had already dumped the pasta into a strainer. Sniffing his shirt, he didn't detect body odor, only the faint scent of mud and kelp, which seemed appropriate for celebrating Wallace's journey.

At the table he sat down next to Ruby, and T Bone set a steaming plate in front of him. As they dug in he caught them up on Wallace's journey, finishing with, "We'll look for him in the morning."

"I'm not going to be able to sleep!" Ruby said.

"Me neither," Nate said.

He got up before dawn and drove to the marina at the mouth of Suisun Bay. A thin fog lifted, and a breeze textured the water as the captain started the engine of the *Pirate Booty*. They hoped to spot Wallace as the channel narrowed under the Benicia Bridge, but there was no sign of him. Nate kept the speaker turned on.

Just as they passed under the Carquinez Bridge, they saw the white spray a hundred yards off the port side, and beat a path southwest in the direction of the whale.

They had passed through the San Pablo Bay and under the Richmond Bridge before Wallace emerged again, this time not far behind the boat. Nate, his coworkers, and the captain cheered.

They thought they might have to double back when they passed under the Golden Gate Bridge without spotting him again. But just as the Farallon Islands came into view, Wallace surfaced seventy-five yards behind them. Then he dove, slapping his tail as if in thank-you to the boat that had escorted him back to sea.

23

Kimura Farm, Joseph Island
July 2010

Marie had been on the farm for a year when she woke to the sound of heavy boots running past her cabin. Heart pounding, she rushed to the front window to see someone with a flashlight heading down the road toward a pair of fading taillights. By the time she threw on pants and a sweatshirt, her fellow laborer, Manuel, was walking back down the road with the flashlight. Shirtless, boots unlaced, he was talking on his cell phone.

"What's going on?" she asked.

"They stole the bees," he said, pocketing his phone.

Manuel's wife Lupe and the other workers emerged from their cabins, children huddled around them, and John roared up in his truck. "Did you see the license plate?" he asked.

Manuel shook his head.

"But those boxes are heavy," Marie said.

"They had a flatbed and a forklift," Manuel said.

"Since when do people steal bees?"

John kicked at a tire on his truck. "Since disease has taken out so many and they can get a hundred dollars per hive."

"The boxes were marked. Can you get them back?"

"Doubtful," John said. "They might even burn them. I'll replace the hives. I can't afford not to. Which, by the way, Lawrence Scheffield can, especially now that he's bought the biggest beekeeping business in the country. Nothing like having your hand in every honey jar." He shook his head. "Of course, when he closes escrow on this island it won't matter where my bees come from."

If Marie was frightened at the prospect of Kimura Farm being dug up for the tunnels, she couldn't imagine how John felt.

"I'll lie down on my parents' graves," he said, "and they'll have to bulldoze over me."

The thought of this job, this farm going away made Marie feel as if she were bending over to pick in the heat of the afternoon and couldn't make the spinning stop. This fertile valley was the ground she stood on, in more than the literal sense. Going back to the place where she'd last felt that kind of permanence wasn't an option. Pulled toward Kimura Farm the way the bees, with their ultraviolet vision, were lured to the red at the heart of the flower, Marie knew the bulldozers would have to run her over too.

True to his word, John replaced the bees, and Marie found herself in the company of hundreds of them as they drifted over the squash plants where she was kneeling and picking. The vines turned up their yellow mouths and the bees floated from blossom to blossom, grains of pollen stuck to their tiny legs.

She couldn't get enough of them, the thousands of bees collecting from millions of flowers a day to produce the batch of honey John extracted from the drum. Shaving the cap off the honeycomb left a sheet he dug into with a knife, removing pieces dribbling with honey, which they popped in their mouths, sucking every last drop of the thick, pear- and apricot-infused liquid from its waxy cells.

At first eating the honey had felt like betrayal. But she knew Lydia would have loved the bees. Every Christmas Lydia had helped a friend make baklava, a Mediterranean treat, and the sweet waxy compartments of the hive took Marie back to those paper-thin layers of pastry dripping with honey.

Loss was like the hexagons built one on another, and she thought back to her mother, her reading voice the hum of twenty thousand wings luring Marie to the hive. On Kimura Farm in the middle of the night when the hum was loudest, she reached for her worn-out Bible and turned to the story of the miracle baby who, when he grew up, camped out by the river where he baptized Jesus. Marie envisioned him in his rough, camel-hair tunic, dipping a claw-like hand in the hive, and derived strength from that image the way John the Baptist had from the locusts and wild honey. That story, on pages thin as the dough Lydia had made at Christmas, helped propel her out of bed on Kimura Farm's darkest mornings.

24

Marie was sweating the instant she stepped into the heavy white suit John handed her. At the hive she pulled the screened hood over her head, while John removed wood frames weighted with wax and honey, brushing into the box any bees that hadn't dropped down. They carried the frames over to the honey-making equipment in the garage where it was cooler.

"My queens were two years old when the hives were stolen," John said, shaving the wax caps off a frame of honeycomb. "Most people can't keep their bees alive nearly that long."

He placed the frames, loaded with honey, in a centrifuge and spun it, driving the honey from the combs down into the drum.

Marie leaned over the faucet outside the garage and splashed cold water on her neck. She wiped the hair away from her face and tied it back again. She saw how Kimura Farm was a salve to the bees. By evening they'd strained and jarred almost sixty pounds of honey, and had nearly emptied the drum.

"Come have a bowl of soup," he said. "We'll finish after dinner."

They washed their hands in the kitchen of the house where John lived with Benji and their ten-year-old daughter Alexis.

"Do we get to taste the honey?" Alexis asked.

"Yes!" John said, setting his glasses on the kitchen counter. While Alexis's long flighty hair was light brown like her mother's, John's was as black as the frames of his glasses.

Washing her hands, Marie saw there was still dirt under her nails from the onions and potatoes they'd dug up the day before.

Benji had made potato soup, which she was ladling into bowls as they sat at the table.

"Too hot for soup," Alexis said, fanning her face.

"On the contrary," John said. "Hot fluids cool you down."

As they ate the soup, thick and oily with the flavor of onions, Benji passed around a green salad and a warm loaf of crusty bread from the bakery in Stanton. When all that was left of the loaf were crumbs, John opened a jar of honey and drizzled some onto a spoon, which Alexis popped into her mouth with a loud, "*Mmm!*"

Marie took the spoon Benji handed her and, as the honey slid down her throat, she once again tasted the pear and apricot blossoms the bees had fed off in the spring.

"Do you know about the honeybird in Africa?" John asked Alexis.

Hearing his storytelling voice, she rolled her eyes.

"The honeybird finds the nest and sounds the alert for the badger. You know what a badger is, right?"

Alexis was listening in spite of herself. "It's like a weasel with a very long nose."

"Anyway, the badger climbs the tree and tears up the nest, then they eat the honey together."

Alexis laughed.

"The honeybird is actually a very clever pest. Hunters follow the bird and take the honey without sharing, so the honeybird tricks the hunters and leads them to a hippopotamus."

Alexis and Benji looked dubious, but John said, "It's true."

Marie helped clear the table and load the dishwasher.

"Want to help jar the end of the drum?" John asked Benji.

"I do, but—" She pointed at the pile of papers she needed to grade.

"I will!" Alexis cried.

"You have homework too," Benji reminded her. "And then bed." Her eyes wandered sadly over her husband's face.

"We're almost done," John said. "I won't be late. Except I need to go see Mom . . ."

The sun was sinking below the horizon when John and Marie sealed the lid on the last jar. Marie drove back to her cabin, past the fields where they had dug up the onions and potatoes, and through the pear orchard nearly ready to harvest. She showered and, slipping into bed, saw a sliver of moon rising above the orchard. Having read only a few pages of her book before her eyelids began to droop, she turned off the light and fell almost instantly into a dream about a man who looked like John following a honeybird on grassland. The bird led the man to a wide, flowing river, where Marie was standing at the edge, licking honey from a spoon. All around her were wandering ribbons of stream and banks thick with willow. Then the water retreated, and she was standing in a dry riverbed, peering down through a hole in the ground to a vast tunnel of water rushing by.

On the other side of the tunnel was a field gone to seed, and in the middle of the field was a cluster of houses half-built and abandoned. Crossing to the field, she saw another man sitting against the side of a house with a sign that said: Will Work for Food. She was holding beets bunched with a wire tie, and she handed them to him. He bit into one like an apple.

Returning to the riverbed, she walked upstream. The honeybird follower was standing on the levee, and as she climbed up, the rocks beneath her feet gave way and water started flooding over the levee into the dry riverbed. Struggling to the top, she stood with the man, watching the sides of the levee collapse. "It's not working," he said, and Marie woke up.

She padded to the bathroom to pee, then went back to bed. Out the window, the moon was sinking below the trees.

"For the land you are entering to possess," the ancient scripture read, "is not like the land of Egypt from which you came . . . where you used to sow your seed and water it with your foot . . . but the land you are about to cross, a land of hills and valleys, drinks water from the rain of heaven."

As waves of cool air from the open window washed over her, Marie imagined irrigation channels dug by foot bringing water from the Nile to the gardens of Egypt. And she knew south-of-delta channel-diggers thought of the rivers feeding into the Sacramento as their land of Canaan.

25

September 2010

Every morning Lawrence's wife Nina made a cappuccino from the machine in their kitchen and said, "Tastes like Sardinia." But all Lawrence needed was a plain cup of black coffee. He wasn't picky about the brand either. On the other hand, Jamie Cannigan, head of California's Department of Water, swore by the bag of Ecuadoran beans he'd brought to the Trout Club. And sipping a cup on the shaded clubhouse porch fifty feet above the McCloud River, Lawrence had to admit it tasted pretty good.

The clubhouse porch was the perfect place to spot the dark shapes moving in the water below, where a rainbow had just taken the nymph on Jamie's fly line. Forty million dollars was the asking price for this vantage point, but the Saltsink Water District had offered six million more. Boom, fish on.

The Trout Club sat on four thousand acres of Shasta forest, but the gold mine was the nine miles of river that ran from the north end of the property to Lake Shasta. It just so happened that Jamie Cannigan was director of the conservancy whose preserve was on the other side of the property boundary, and he had been the one to alert Lawrence when the fishing camp went on the market.

The real treasure wasn't the run of deep pools and riffles full of wild rainbow trout or the big browns that migrated up from Shasta Lake. It wasn't the mountain lions the previous landowners had hunted. It wasn't even the huge caddis that in the next few weeks Jamie had told him would draw the biggest trout, from their larvae at the bottom of the river to their hatch in the evenings when trout snatched them out of the air. No, the real gold mine was the design of Shasta Dam that allowed it to be raised from fifty stories to seventy—the height of the dam on the Feather River—should the need arise. And the need had arisen, with the Saltsink Water District now sitting on the shoreline of a reservoir they hoped to extend two-thirds of a mile up the McCloud River from the dam.

Jamie had used the pliers attached to his vest to extract the hook from the fish's mouth and was laying the trout on a bed of grass when his cell phone rang. From fifty feet above, Lawrence heard it ring once and stop. Jamie pulled it from the inside pocket of his vest, held it up to his face, and shook his head.

"One bar of reception," he called up to Lawrence. He opened another pocket and exchanged it for a tin of flies. He'd just selected one when he pulled the phone out again, held it to his face, and motioned for Lawrence to come down.

Lawrence drained his coffee and took the stairs off the porch. Docksiders, the outdoor equivalent of loafers, were not the ideal shoes for a steep hillside, and he slipped and slid down the trail, grabbing onto tree branches, until he was close enough to talk to Jamie, who was attaching the new fly to his line. On the bed of grass next to his creel, the eye of the dead trout stared vacantly skyward.

"I just got a text from the Indian chief," Jamie said. "The Forest Service is hassling them at their ceremony."

The day before, Lawrence had agreed to go with Jamie to the Shasta fish hatchery for what was essentially an appeasement of the Native people whose land—what little of it was still above water—would be washed out by the new reservoir. The chief, a middle-aged woman with long braids, introduced herself as Audrey. Standing with Audrey in front of the cameras, Jamie had said, "The Conservancy of Biological Resources and the Saltsink Water District are happy to partner with our Winnemen Wintu neighbors on the McCloud River. The Winnemen Wintu were the first to spear the giant salmon in what is now Shasta Lake."

Audrey had a tongue that could talk an osprey out of a four-pound trout. She told Jamie and Lawrence the Forest Service had given her tribe permission to close the McCloud at the end of Shasta Lake for four days during a girl's coming-of-age ceremony, on what was sacred ground for a people whose numbers had severely diminished. "But we're not a federally recognized tribe." That meant the closure was voluntary, and people might ignore it and harass the tribe.

"The Forest Service is there now?" Lawrence asked Jamie.

Jamie kept his eyes fixed on his fishing line. "You'll be a hero if you show up."

Lawrence wondered why Jamie didn't just turn off his damn cell phone.

Jamie dropped the fly he'd just tied on and cast across the pool in front of him. "We have a fight ahead of us," he said. "We need to be good neighbors."

It was easy to be a good neighbor, Lawrence thought as he scrambled back up the trail, when you were standing under a dogwood next to your sixteen-inch catch.

He drove to the lake and parked his Hummer behind three white Forest Service trucks, one that said CANINE. Under a stand of oaks on the other side of the trucks was a Forest Service ranger who couldn't have been more than a day out of training. Next to him, surrounded by a ragtag group of tribal members, was Audrey.

The Forest Service could have sent out a ranger familiar with the tribe, but instead they'd sent one who'd barely passed puberty, along with two fledgling agents who leaned against the hood of the truck hiding behind their dark glasses. No one, Lawrence was relieved to see, had a canine.

Out on the water, a powerboat with a rumbling engine and an American flag waving off the stern had ignored the closure and was spinning donuts in the canyon. In the boat two men and a woman holding tall cans of beer heckled white hippies in kayaks who'd come in support of the tribe. Their wakes flipped one of the protestors, along with a hand-painted sign reading Sacred Land.

"What's going on?" Lawrence asked the ranger.

"The tribe is being fined . . ." He held up a pad of citations. "For operating a motorized vessel in a closed area."

The power boaters laughed as the protestor slid back in the water attempting to right her flipped kayak.

"This vessel," the ranger said, pointing to an old boat pushed up against the shore, "isn't registered."

"We were transporting our elders over to the camp on the other side of the river," Audrey said. "Our girl Marisa is coming of age and is going to swim across to them."

"And I'm going to ask again," the ranger said, "who operated the motor vehicle?"

"She already told you," a tribal member said. "She doesn't know."

"If you interfere with us," the ranger told the tribal member, "y'all will be arrested for obstruction. Do I make myself clear?"

What a twit, Lawrence thought.

A young man with his hair tied behind his back said to Audrey, "The only information you have to give is your name, your birth date, and where you live."

"I'm asking for other information," the ranger said. "I'm asking who operated the motor vehicle and who it was registered to."

"I don't know," Audrey said.

"You don't know, or you don't want to provide that information?"

"I don't know."

"The other citation"—he pushed at the bridge of his dark glasses—"is a violation of the special use permit."

"What's that?"

"Like I said, we're not here to discuss anything. You can go to court to discuss it further."

"Why should I sign something if I don't know what it is?"

"Are you refusing to sign it, Ma'am?"

"I'll sign the one I understand, the boat one," she said, taking the pen he held out.

"Not signing the other one won't make it go away," the ranger said, pulling two citations from the pad.

Audrey held them up for Lawrence to see. They were ten thousand dollars apiece.

"I'm going to ask one more time. Does anyone in the tribe know who the boat is registered to or who was operating it?"

"No," the group said in unison.

"Then my business here is concluded." Passing Lawrence without looking at him, although it was hard to tell through the dark glasses, the ranger climbed in his truck. The other two agents, who were there strictly as reinforcement since they hadn't uttered a word, got in their vehicles, and they all drove away.

Lawrence turned to the chief. "Now what."

"Now we have our ceremony."

"And them?" He pointed at the power boaters whose marine stereo was playing country music at high volume.

"We'll ignore them," she said. "Which is not something we'll be able to do with your dam when our land is under water."

True, Lawrence thought.

"Tomorrow we protest at the Redding Library," she said. "I'll let Jamie Cannigan know how it goes."

Lawrence wondered if Jamie regretted giving her his phone number. The tribal members turned away from Lawrence, and he beat a quick retreat to his Hummer.

He got a text from Jamie the next day as he was filling up at a gas station on I-5: "The tribe protested at the library and the US Attorney's Office dropped the charges."

If the dam went in, Lawrence thought as he screwed the gas cap back on, *there'd be fourteen million more acre-feet of water.* But there ought to be a few sacred rocks still sticking up somewhere.

The same went for the fishing tribes north of Lake Shasta, who had a voice in how much water was released from the Klamath River into its principal tributary, the Trinity. More water for spawning salmon meant less piped from the Trinity to the Sacramento River, which was why the Saltsink District had sued the Bureau of Reclamation and won back its water allocation from the Trinity River.

Roshambo: If the Klamath Tribe's ten thousand salmon were the scissors, a hundred thousand acres of crops were the rock that crushed the scissors, and south-of-delta agribusiness bested the protestors every time.

26

Standing on the angular rocks of a levee barrier, Nate pulled out his pocketknife and sliced diagonally across the thick stalk of a Himalayan blackberry jutting out of a planter box. He'd helped Fish and Wildlife build up these levees. They'd planted native cottonwood, elder, and willow scrub in the boxes, and the roots had grown around the rocks to strengthen the levees.

The Corps of Engineers had always promoted levee vegetation, but after a hurricane wreaked havoc on New Orleans they'd reversed their policy. This meant the delta would get no federal funding in the event of a flood, and in an effort to get them to come back around, state Fish and Wildlife had sued the Corps.

He climbed back up the rocks, spooking a kingfisher out of the willows. It soared across the water stuttering in alarm. In the new trees he'd seen herons, egrets, and the shrikes with their icy grey feathers that still reminded him of Ana. The trees had grown ten feet with that winter's heavy rain, and they would grow much taller. He knew Ana had felt stuck in a young marriage in the Central Valley, impaled on a thorn like the prey of the shrike.

Nate pulled a sandwich from an ice chest on the floor of his truck, and since he was due in Sacramento in an hour for a meeting, ate as he drove. At the north end of the levee, oak trees hung so close to the road that crews had hedge-trimmed the undersides, and where they hung over both sides they formed a tunnel. Harmless, he thought, as he drove through it, compared to bigger tunnels the state had in mind.

After late rains had relieved the drought, talk at the state capitol had turned to flooding the Yolo Bypass in order to create more habitat for a declining fish population. But there were farmers who objected, never having imagined they'd have to make good on a flooding easement on their land. One of them was Diana Shumaker, who, along with her husband, grew a hundred acres of sunflowers just east of the bypass. Twenty years after they'd signed the papers on the farm, she had applied for and landed a job with state Fish and Wildlife, and by the time Nate came on board, she had worked her way up to a position in Washington, where she'd decided to throw up a few barriers.

Knowing that if their property were flooded, they and their suppliers would be held accountable for whatever showed up in their water samples, Diana sent out an email to Patrick Smith, who extracted the petroleum that was a major component of the fertilizer used on her farm. She attached a document from the EPA that called for stricter water-quality regulations in the Central Valley.

Then she forwarded to a friend who lobbied for the Farm Bureau a document she'd received from the smelt lab showing the adverse effects on the fish from trace amounts of chemicals in their water. What she did wasn't technically illegal, but it was ethically murky, since her distribution of information showed a clear bias—namely her own crops that would end up underwater.

She also tampered with a document regarding the splittail in the Napa River, which emptied into the bay west of Grizzly Island. Where Fish and Wildlife cited the presence of splittail in the Napa River after heavy rains when the salinity was zero and their absence the previous drought year when salinity was higher, Diana inserted her own conclusion. "There is no evidence," she wrote, "to suggest a decline in water flow has had a significant effect on the population of the species. Therefore listing the Sacramento splittail as endangered or threatened is not warranted."

Eight days after Shumaker made her edits, US Fish and Wildlife took the splittail off the list of threatened species. Since then the federal government had investigated her actions, but that didn't mean they would change the status of the splittail or the red-legged frog that laid its eggs among the cattails and bulrushes of the delta.

After the Corps of Engineers ripped out trees along the levees, water temperatures soared and the number of bullfrogs—non-native predators of the red-legged frog—soared too. That was when Diana Shumaker, spurred by her victory with the splittail, altered Fish and Wildlife documents again. Already having convinced her department to reduce the four million acres of frog habitat they'd originally designated in California, she convinced them a second time to reduce it to a mere 10 percent of its original acres. When the state Fish and Wildlife's lead biologist questioned her delisting of the species, the Washington office relocated him to New Mexico.

Nate took his downtown exit and, after pulling into a spot and feeding the meter, walked the half block to the tall building that housed the Department of Water Resources. He pushed the button and the doors were closing when he heard someone running toward the elevator. The elevator dinged, the doors slid open, and in stepped Jamie Cannigan. He shook Nate's hand and, holding up his watch, said, "We have two minutes."

Nate was first out of the elevator. Clutching his satchel of papers, he held open the door to the glassy conference room for Jamie. Through the opposite wall of windows, the sun was emerging from behind the clouds and the Sacramento basked in the sparkling light.

Patrick Smith and Lawrence Scheffield were already seated. In the middle of the table were Lawrence's bottles of South

Pacific water for thirsty participants. And they were thirsty. Up for discussion were the two massive tunnels, for which the ASD had been commissioned by the state to come up with a plan. This time Buzz and Henry had been invited to the table.

Nate, who had been invited to speak about the amount of water Fish and Wildlife believed was necessary to sustain California fish populations, took a seat next to Henry. Buzz, seated on Henry's other side, offered him one of the bottles of water, a gleam of mischief in his eye. Suppressing a smile, Nate shook his head.

Jamie Cannigan jumped in. "We're here to discuss what we have narrowed down to the most viable options for the tunnels." Nate knew there were still a number of options on the table, even after years of studies, meetings, and millions of dollars spent.

During the PowerPoint presentation Nate went over his notes. He was third on the agenda, and as his turn grew nearer his heart was hammering. But when he began, the urgency of what he had to say overtook him.

"Less than a decade ago, the fall run of Chinook on the Sacramento River numbered eight hundred thousand. At least a quarter of that is needed for optimal spawning, but last year the number fell to under forty thousand."

"There is no evidence," Lawrence said, "that water flow is the only factor. There's been a decrease in ocean nutrients."

Nate couldn't deny that. He thought of Wallace swimming up the delta in search of food. But he said, "Fish didn't start dying until the pumps were turned up."

"Three years ago Northern California users received their full water allocation," said Lawrence, "while users south of the delta including Saltsink, the largest irrigation district in the nation, got half. A year later we received ten percent. This is not equitable, and mid-rank biologists should not determine water levels for the delta."

"If not the 'mid-rank' biologists," Buzz said, "then who?" Buzz, tall as a hawk on a telephone wire, fixed his gaze on Lawrence. "I can answer that question. Water contractors, not biologists, are calling the shots."

Nate took a deep breath. State Fish and Wildlife had signed an agreement supporting the tunnels. And as one of their biologists he was essentially employed by the ASD's biggest benefactor, Lawrence Scheffield, who had so far refrained from getting him fired but had stopped shaking his hand. That was reason enough for him to be nervous, without the recent relocation of the Fish and Wildlife biologist to New Mexico. Although in that case justice had prevailed. There'd been an investigation into Diana Shumaker's conduct. The Inspector General had described Shumaker's edits on the final documents, which resulted in the removal of the splittail from the list of protected species, as "voluminous," and Shumaker had immediately resigned.

"If the tunnels are not built," Jamie said, "habitat conditions are likely to get worse."

"Habitat conditions are already worse." Buzz turned to Jamie. "Pardon the pun, but you seem to be telling us we're dammed if we do, dammed if we don't."

"If we don't get the water we need for crops," Lawrence said, driving the tip of his pen into the table, "California farmers lose tens of billions of dollars and our state economy shuts down."

"A chunk of that economy and four hundred thousand acres of prime farmland lie in the delta," Buzz said.

"I would think," Henry said to Lawrence, "you had enough supply with the Kern Water Bank you and Mr. Smith purchased from the state. That purchase gave you seven thousand acres of recharge ponds fed by state aqueducts. Not to mention your nearly one hundred wells that have sucked enough from the aquifers to turn them concave."

"It's a dog-eat-dog world," Patrick said.

If Henry was surprised by Patrick's comment he didn't show it.

"The Water Bank," Lawrence said, "is owned by a handful of agencies. Not two people."

"The two largest being the Kern and Saltsink water agencies, owned by you and Mr. Smith," Henry pointed out.

"A functioning water bank did not exist until we invested millions in the project," Patrick said.

"Millions, which for you," Henry said, "is a drop in the bucket—so to speak."

"Henry," Buzz said, "tell us about the Democratic senator from California whose campaign Mr. Scheffield helped fund."

"The senator who inserted a single-sentence provision into the Farm Bill? That one sentence," Henry said, "allows Water Bank agencies to sell their federally subsidized contents for a hundred and fifty times what they paid for it."

"Water that if we didn't capture and store," Lawrence said, "would flow to the Pacific Ocean with no measurable benefit."

"There *are* economic benefits for adequate flow to the fishing and farming industries," Henry said. "The ASD plan cites increased urbanization as a rationale for the tunnels, and in fact what you want to 'protect' isn't the delta but the conversion of delta land from agriculture to concrete."

"Your sarcasm," Jamie said, "is counterproductive to this meeting."

"Plain and simple." Lawrence stood and dropped his tablet into his briefcase. "We get our water or we pull out of the commission."

Since the Saltsink and Kern water districts had contributed a hundred and fifty million dollars to the ASD, this was essentially blackmail. Having made their point, Lawrence and Patrick picked up their briefcases and walked out of the meeting.

Like a fish gulping for oxygen, Nate inhaled the rush of air following their exit through the glass door.

27

Kimura Farm, Joseph Island

Marie watched as John swung himself onto the tractor and fastened the seat belt. Pressing one foot on the clutch and other on the brake, he turned the key and the engine rumbled to life. Diesel fumes filled the air as he let the engine warm up. Then he drove over to the star thistle that grew tall at the perimeter of his fields. He'd tackle them one field at a time, he told her, first the leafy greens, then the winter squash, then the onions.

Down the line, purple flowers pointed their thorns at the October sun. He backed over the first row and it fell like dominoes. At the end of the row he turned on the blades and pulled forward, mouth of the mower coughing out pulverized star thistle.

Once he mowed the last of the thistle—last until next season, anyway—he encountered the sorghum growing just out of sight along the edge of the beet field. Sorghum, corn's ugly brother, was just as destructive as thistle. It sent a jolt up Marie's spine every time her shovel hit those roots.

"Sorghum is the weed in Lon Smith's fields that helped stave off my father's homesickness," John once told her, frowning when she asked if it grew all over the state. "It spread across the country after the government introduced it as an easy way to feed cattle." *Spread* was the operative word for what at its roots was a noxious weed. Seeds lay dormant, chopping or burning the stalks only stimulated growth, and both sorghum and thistle had roots like concrete.

"The makers of Roundup have grown rich on sorghum," John said. "The more it develops a tolerance to Roundup, the more farmers buy and spray."

Often as Marie was getting ready for bed, she would see John's tractor lights scroll across the wall of her cabin as he tried to stay ahead of the weeds.

"My dad said you have to decide which weeds are worth the fight and make peace with the rest. You can't get rid of them," he said. "So you may as well learn from them."

As Marie left John mowing star thistle and walked back to her cabin, she supposed what she'd learned was a muscle memory. The trapezius between her neck and shoulders felt sore just thinking about her shovel hitting those weeds. She banged off the dirt caked to the treads of her boots, setting them inside the door, peeled off her socks and sweat-stained shirt, and threw them in a pile of clothes mounting in the corner. In the narrow shower stall, holding her arms in close to keep from bumping her elbows, she scrubbed the dirt from under her nails with a brush, then scrubbed them a second time with shampoo against her scalp. Once she was clean, walking barefoot across the cabin made her feet ache, and she massaged the spot at the base of her spine.

It being Friday, after a quick dinner she picked up the armload of laundry and lugged it over to the shed where John had installed a couple of washers and dryers. She looked for Lupe as she turned gritty socks right side out and tossed them in the washer. She looked for her again as she separated out the shirts to hang on the line outside her cabin, even though she knew Lupe would appear, as she always did, when Marie was emptying the rest of her clothes from the dryer.

"The washers are ready for you," she said when Lupe appeared.

"*¿Ah si?*" Lupe always sounded surprised, even though they staggered their trips intentionally so the washers were free when Lupe showed up.

"How was the chard?" It was what they'd picked that day.

"*Muy sabrosa,*" Lupe said. "*En tacos con potatoes.*"

"Sounds delicious."

Marie spoke in her native tongue and Lupe responded in a mix of Spanish and English, and each understood most of what the other said. With Lupe she was standing on the other side of a slot canyon narrow enough for them to talk but too wide to jump over. She wanted to. She wanted *sabrosa,* oily rice in a tortilla, versus the plain brown rice she had made with her own chard. She folded slowly to draw out their time.

Pushing her clothes down in the washer and pouring in detergent, Lupe said, "You are a photographer."

One evening early in her first year on Kimura Farm, when the summer temperatures were easing and the sun hadn't yet dropped from the sky, Marie had asked Manuel and Lupe if she could take their pictures. After she switched to digital photography, she and Lydia had dismantled the darkroom, letting the spiders reclaim the shed. And while the outcome of chemical photography was always a surprise, with the digital camera she could see the results and adjust in the moment. The sun, like a light bulb behind a thin blanket of clouds, had lit up Manuel's white cowboy hat, the crow's feet around his eyes. When she'd seen this in her camera, it struck her that three decades after her parents emigrated from Lithuania, Manuel's parents had emigrated from Mexico to support a family working the land under their boots. The land where John Kimura's grandfather planted a flower garden at the edge of his cherry orchard, and his children made his grave near the marigolds, the same orange flowers families gathered in Mexico to honor their dead.

"The photos I took of you and Manuel are still in the camera," Marie said. "Who knows when I'll have time to do anything with them."

Lupe smiled. Free time for laborers was rare. "Why did you come to Kimura Farm?" she asked, closing the lid on the washer.

Marie decided to be honest, just as she had been with John. "My partner, Lydia, was killed by a mountain lion."

Lupe gasped and held a hand to her face. "Mountain lion!"

"Yes."

"Partner?"

"The love of my life. I needed a change of scenery."

Suddenly Lupe's eyes were anywhere but on Marie.

"I'm sorry if—" Tears sprung to Marie's eyes and she saw them in Lupe's too.

"What." Lupe looked at her now.

"If I offended you, talking about Lydia."

She shook her head. "*Es triste.*"

"Very sad," Marie said. "We were together for eighteen years."

"Eighteen! *Han pasado tres desde que Manuel y yo nos casamos.*"

"Three years is a long time too," Marie acknowledged.

"I believe love *es entre hombre y mujer.*" Between a man and a woman. "But you make me cry."

"From now on," Marie said, "we talk about laundry."

Lupe laughed.

"Or the baby," Marie said.

"*Tiene nueve meses.*"

"Nine months! And no one's come forward?"

"Nobody." Lupe's face showed relief.

"I'm happy for you."

"*Gracias*." Lupe picked up her bottle of detergent. "See you tomorrow."

"Bright and early," Marie said.

Marie wondered if their conversation had moved them closer or farther apart. She could have just told Lupe she took the job on Kimura Farm because she needed a change of scenery. But laundry night was the extent of her social life, and other than John and Benji, Lupe was the best friend she'd made.

Lupe must have told Manuel because the next evening as he and Marie walked off the field, he said, first in English, "Don't worry. On the farm we are a team. Out here, we are all together." Then he repeated it in Spanish, walking alongside her.

Back at her cabin, the words *juntos,* together, and *equipo,* team, stayed with her as she showered and ate dinner. An acquired family, in a row of cabins facing an orchard, separated by two ranges of mountains from the edge of the continent where she last saw Lydia. Reminding her of the faces of her parents' Lithuanian friends around a table laden with bowls of soup, in Wisconsin and a sea away from their homeland.

28

That night she had a dream about the grizzlies, bears that likely foraged on their namesake island at the mouth of the delta. In the dream Marie and Lydia were having a picnic on the island, while a mama grizzly caught salmon in the slough that emptied into the bay. Male grizzlies were double the size of a black bear, but this grizzly, a female gorging on salmon, was unconcerned with Marie and Lydia. Their blanket was spread under an oak tree, and her cub was up in the tree shaking the branches.

Acorns rained down on the blanket as Lydia said, "They're having a picnic too."

That she spoke was the best part about dreams with Lydia. When she said the bears were having a picnic, they fell back laughing, but even in the dream Marie was careful not to laugh so hard she'd wake up.

Lydia was pulling food out of a basket—apples, aged Gouda, and roasted almonds. Then she pulled out a foil package of barbecued ribs, which was strange because they were vegetarians.

Pointing to the grizzly, she said, "She took one out of you and made me." That's when Marie woke up. The taste of the picnic turned thick and fatty in her mouth, and she was glad to have awakened before the dream took another turn.

A few years before, a man named Timothy Treadwell had planted his tent in the middle of what he knew to be a grizzly trail. Without a healthy supply of salmon, the grizzlies were hungry and had to compete with each other for the fish rich in fatty acids. When the "bear whisperer" approached a malnourished grizzly instead of teaming up with his girlfriend to stave it off, he became food. And his girlfriend became the grizzly's competition for food. By the time rangers found the camp, the pilot flying above could see the bear feeding on a human rib cage. The rangers made a lot of noise to scare off the bear, but instead it approached them, and they fired at it with a 12-gauge shotgun.

The grizzly would rather have nothing to do with people. It was the bear whisperer's behavior that had gotten him, his girlfriend, and the bear killed. Like Lydia, who may not have made the same mistake, but whose path intersected with a lion that had less room to roam.

Grief was like the mountain lion nightmare that had washed away or the grizzly dream that had taken a dark turn. It took hold of Marie and plunged her into the murky depths, then lifted like a shaft elevator to daylight. She seldom knew which direction she was going.

She pulled a blanket off the bed in her cabin, wrapped it around her shoulders, and walked outside. She hadn't eaten meat since she left Wisconsin, but she was still nourished by animals. John Kimura, who raised chickens, modeled his farm on the ones preceding Eiji, when farmers raised sheep and pigs, pulled their plows with horses, and fertilized the soil with the manure and bones of their animals. The bones returned to the ground under their feet and made life.

Marie searched the sky for the Big Dipper that Lydia had said was the Greater She-Bear.

And there above the pear orchard, she found the star of the She-Bear that pointed to the handle of the Little Dipper, or Little Bear. Like the one shaking the branches in her dream.

Marie faced the star and spread the edges of her blanket wide, just as Lydia had the night she taught her about Little Bear and Polaris. Inland from the ocean, the She-Bear was still above Marie in the night sky, and she had only to look up.

They had agreed the dust of asteroids was what would become of their bones, and Lydia was the star she navigated by. Lydia had been skeptical that Mary was a virgin in the Catholic sense, or that the nun Paula had remained chaste with Jerome, but disagreement was what had allowed Marie and Lydia to grow, separately and together. Now Lydia was gone and Marie was free to take her own vow of chastity, like Paula or Mary, or the half-wild, bee-taming John the Baptist.

KINGS RIVER

29

After Elisa Martinez graduated and became a warden, she had spent a year in the Sacramento Valley. That was around the time she'd met Gilbert, they'd become serious, and she'd sent Nate a text that said, "You have to come see this."

"I'm going on a night mission," Nate told T Bone as he grabbed his keys.

"Hurry, and no flashlight," Elisa texted.

He drove toward a slough at the upper end of the delta, and with little traffic at that time of night, made it in twenty-five minutes. Parking next to Elisa's truck, he ducked under a gate and walked up a dirt road. Under the light of a quarter moon, he could see the road in front of him and, after he walked a ways, Elisa's head in the tules below the levee.

"*Shh,*" she said, as he slid down the levee and landed in the muck, water seeping into his socks.

Elisa handed him her night-vision goggles, and he held them up to his eyes and turned them downstream until they settled on a man standing on a gravel bank holding a heavy rod. Suddenly the man dropped the rod and, lunging for the shallows, grabbed the sides of a thrashing, four-foot sturgeon.

Snagging sturgeon like that was illegal. "Let's go," Elisa said, scrambling up the levee.

Nate sloshed up the bank, the goggles swinging across his chest. Ahead of him Elisa ran down the road, gun drawn.

"Stop!" she called, and the man wrestling the white sturgeon froze.

As Nate made his way behind her down a steep, worn levee path, the sturgeon was no longer moving. Elisa shone a flashlight on the female fish, and the four-inch hooks the man had sunk into her sides to drag her up the bank. She was probably carrying thirty pounds of eggs, translating to three grand in caviar. He had grabbed her when she was spawning.

A medium-set man in snug-fitting jeans with a handlebar mustache, he shrank when Elisa shone the flashlight at his chest.

"Have a truck around here?" she asked him.

"Yes."

"You lead the way," she said, "and carry the fish."

The man hoisted the sturgeon, slung it over his shoulder, and slumped up the path ahead of them.

As they approached the road where Nate and Elisa were parked, they heard a rustling in the brush and footsteps running away. The man with the sturgeon led them to a truck parked behind a stand of weeds. Milkweed shone dully in the moonlight, and the outline of star thistle bristled against the sky. In the back of the truck were what appeared to be logs but were two more sturgeon, likely caught with the help of the friend who'd just run away.

Elisa called the sheriff.

"You can go as soon as he gets here," she told Nate. "It will take a while to write this up."

That was when Nate saw her all over again in the outermost tent, guarding the males who may have been physically stronger than she was but were nowhere near as brave.

Now that Fish and Wildlife had relocated her from the Sacramento Valley to the Tulare Basin, Elisa was calling again. Over the phone, Nate told her he needed to do a water check in Mendota and could meet her at what she said was the site of another cheater.

From the shuttered mercury mine in the foothills of the Diablo Range, whose namesake mountain pointed delta drivers southwest, the San Carlos Creek crawled with a rust-colored, mercury-laden sludge toward a stream system that in the winter's heavy rains had connected with the San Joaquin River. It was at their confluence in Mendota that Nate stopped to record flows and temperatures at the dam.

He drove through the park where trees, stubbornly anchored in ground hardened by years of drought and neglect, provided meager shade for a few picnic tables. Nate parked his truck by the dam and waded into the pool as the detritus of picnics—Styrofoam bowls, candy wrappers, and plastic utensils—lapped up against his rubber boots. He stood and looked out over the dam toward the dry creek bed, envisioning cinnabar clawed from the earth that in the rain caused rusty water to gush through the creek. Already he was thinking about what he would tell T Bone, who had as much reason as he did to care about a failing estuary. Standing in the park, he had to admit that moving in with her and Ruby had lifted him out of a deep funk, and that it was more than a room in a house that accounted for his happiness.

His cell phone buzzed a text from Elisa. He texted back. "I'll be there in an hour."

Nate packed up his meter and drove back out to the highway. He looked for the signs of crops Saltsink landowners claimed they had to fallow due to water restrictions, but what he saw were burlap sacks stuffed with onions slumping in a field, and a mechanized picker dumping canning tomatoes into overflowing bins. It would be difficult anyway to spot a thousand acres of fallowed field on a plot ten times as big. He saw mountains of almond shells at a processing plant. And a dairy, black-and-white cows lined up like piano keys, heads poking through the guillotine holes of the feed trough.

On the interstate he passed the signs that read CONGRESS CREATED DROUGHT, and as he dropped down into the Tulare Basin, NEW ADDITION TO THE ENDANGERED SPECIES LIST: TULARE FARMERS. Then there was the sign in response to the nation's first African American president whose campaign slogan had been "Hope": HOW'S THAT HOPE WORKING OUT FOR YOU NOW?

He arrived at the four hundred yards of concrete Patrick Smith had poured alongside a cotton field for his personal runway and turned left into the town of Hatfield. Crossing the railroad tracks, he drove past the towering wheat silos and the high school with its new library and baseball field, both built by the nonprofit Smith's wife had founded.

At the other end of town, the single block of tree-lined, brick-storefront main street gave way to rundown apartments, trash strewn along cyclone fences, and a neon sign that flashed CAMBIO DE CHEQUES AQUI. Then out into a ghostly landscape of grey dust and, stretching to the horizon, tens of thousands of acres of cotton, brown and bursting with puffs of white in anticipation of the harvest. You could drive for hours and still be on Patrick Smith's land.

Following the directions Elisa had texted him, he turned onto one of the grey roads. By then the reek of fish rotting in the heat had permeated his truck. He headed for the Fish and Wildlife vehicle parked next to the canal about a quarter mile down, where Elisa was standing with a bandana over her face. Nate pulled his shirt up over his nose as he approached her. The face above the bandana looked the same: dark hair and skin, maybe a few more wrinkles around her eyes.

She hugged him quickly, then they peered over the edge of the canal, where millions of shad lay dead, bumping against the banks in a pea-soup film of algae. They jumped in her truck and drove down the canal alongside a trail of dead fish that went on and on.

"Still loving the life of a warden?" he asked ironically, as she pulled over next to a plastic tank with a diameter twice Nate's height, suspended over the bank of the canal.

"Not when I see this sh-t," she said, getting out and kicking at the tank. "I caught the guy dumping fertilizer in the canal yesterday."

"Do you know who it was?"

She nodded. "One of Smith's foremen." Not that it mattered. Dumping ammonia nitrogen fertilizer into the water before pumping it onto their fields was a regular practice for farmers in the area.

"You know what Patrick Smith said killed all these shad? Poor families dumping gasoline and motor oil in the water." Elisa shook her head. "My neighbors fished in sloughs and canals like these."

"I know," Nate said. "I remember."

Nate and Ana had been invited a few times for dinner at the Martinez apartment in Stockton, and they'd gorged on chorizo. Or Nate had gorged. Ana had eaten plain tortillas. But one night they'd been invited to eat with Elisa's Cambodian neighbors. Ana had been studying for an exam, which turned out to be a good thing, as it allowed her to avoid the paste made from garlic and fermented fish they'd spread on their vegetables.

Elisa had grown up with the Chin boys Heng and Tom in a cinderblock complex where her brothers slept in one bedroom, her parents slept in the other, and she slept on the couch. After everyone went to bed and the apartment was quiet, Elisa did her homework. She was the only one in the family who went to college.

The night she and Nate stayed for dinner, Sothy Chin, the boys' mother, made vegetable soup and Cambodian stew, served from a straw mat on the floor of a tidy apartment identical to the Martinez family's with twice as many occupants. Wearing a bright orange sarong with her hair pulled back in a scrunchy, Sothy, who was a head shorter than Elisa, used a pair of chopsticks to spread on her greens a paste she'd made from fish.

While they ate, the boys' father, Amara, talked about growing up fishing in Cambodia, which he and Sothy had fled with their families when the Khmer Rouge killed millions. Their children had never seen Cambodia or traveled outside California.

The next day Heng and Tom let Nate and Elisa tag along when they went fishing below the Stockton Ship Channel. The brothers filled their buckets with delta water and set them on a bank of hard-packed dirt and broken concrete. Elisa pointed to a sign on a nearby chain-link fence that said DON'T EAT THE FISH CAUGHT HERE, in English, Khmer, and other languages, but Heng and Tom shrugged. They pushed pieces of sardine onto hooks nearly the size of their pinkies and cast.

The water their father fished in the Mekong Delta may have been muddy but it was basically clean. The water the brothers cast into on the San Joaquin Delta was clear but far from clean. It was one thing for their guests to eat methylmercury-laden fish when they were invited to a home-cooked meal, and it was another to eat it several times a week as the Chins did.

Tom caught a twelve-inch bass that day and Heng pulled in a catfish—two weeks' worth of meals for a family who had little to spend on groceries.

"My neighbors would never intentionally pollute what they were cooking for dinner," Elisa said, holding up her cell phone. "I took pictures."

For years Nate and Elisa's bosses had closed their eyes to farmers' violations of the law. "This will force an investigation," she said.

As they drove back to Nate's truck he asked, "How's Gilbert?" While Gilbert was in medical school, he and Elisa were long-distance.

"He's good. He left yesterday after a four-day visit. Now I'm adjusting to him being gone, and it's back to catching rule-breakers."

Nate took a breath of the rancid air and kept quiet. On a strictly platonic basis, she had let him in more than Ana ever had, and he'd learned that usually a woman just wanted someone to listen. Besides, even if he could have done anything about it, Elisa was more than capable of handling the enforcement end of her job.

"Buy you a soda?" he asked, when she dropped him at his truck.

"Of course."

Nate followed Elisa to Carter's Grocery, a block off the main street just past the Cambio de Cheques. Traces of the store's former self remained: concrete stumps in the driveway where the gas pumps had been, and a Coca-Cola sign that no longer lit up. Inside, Joe had decided not to replace the broken air conditioner, and there was a gap in the linoleum where he had taken out the freezer.

Lemoore, two towns over, had continued to grow, while a once-thriving Hatfield was left behind. As time went on, more and more of Joe's customers worked for Smith Farms. Most of them couldn't afford Joe's meat, which was why he had taken out the freezer. Patrick Smith's wife and anyone with a car went to Lemoore for their groceries.

Joe's customers did most of their shopping at the little supermarket just outside town, walking half a mile along the side of the highway to buy food at prices he couldn't compete with. Chips and candy, aspirin and cold medicine still moved off his shelves, while lettuce wilted, potatoes went soft, and the milk sat past its sell-by date. So he had gotten rid of the dairy and produce too.

But people still came every day to get Joe's help translating and paying their utility bills. He was sitting on the stool he called his "office" when Elisa and Nate walked in.

He jumped up to greet her and shook Nate's hand. "How are you doing?"

"Tired of policing the cheaters," she said.

"Tell me about it." Joe looked around the empty store. "I may have to close this place."

"No!" Elisa walked past the liters of soda to the cooler with glass bottles, where she pulled out two Cokes. Nate paid for them, and Joe upended a couple of milk crates, inviting them to sit.

"At least I still have soda," he said. "I stopped selling beer when it attracted too many bums in need of a bath."

"Which they won't get in the canals around here." She rolled her eyes at Nate. "Not funny, I know."

"Smith's employees come in here and count out coins just to pay off one dollar on a thirty-dollar credit." Joe's eyes grew wet.

"A week ago a man in a red ball cap stabbed a man in a blue jersey right outside the store. Next it'll be guns."

"Where I grew up in Stockton," Elisa said, "we didn't go outside at night."

Joe shook his head. "This store used to provide a nice living for me and my wife. She works at the supermarket in Lemoore now, but she wants to retire." He looked up at the ceiling. "I could spend my days fishing."

"That wouldn't be bad," Elisa said. Living in a farmhouse rental now, nestled between an olive orchard and the foothill town of Lakeville, she spent her days off exploring King's Canyon. "Gilbert and I fly-fished the lower river last week." Her voice trailed off. "We didn't catch anything."

Nate laughed.

"You can fish the stocked runs near the dam year-round," Joe said, suddenly cheered.

The bell on the door rang as a young woman walked in with two little girls. "*¿Está abierta?*" she asked.

"*Si, si,*" Joe said, rising from his stool as she pulled out an electric bill.

Nate drained the last of his Coke, and Elisa gave Joe a goodbye hug.

"I'm sorry about Joe," Nate said as they stood outside the store. "And I'm sorry about the canal. I don't know that I helped much."

"You did. You gave me someone to vent to."

"Owe me a Coke," he said. It was their joke based on the old saying.

Nate and Elisa parted under the rippling blue heat of an endless sky. Heading toward the interstate, he passed the little supermarket and drove through the next town that looked worse off than Hatfield. In the front yard of a rundown house, bags of garbage sat in a pile as if even garbage service was unaffordable. Abutting the house was a field gone dry. Tumbleweed rolled across it and stopped up against a falling-down fence.

Right before hitting the interstate, Nate passed a stucco housing complex with rolling lawns and sprinklers blasting in the middle of the afternoon. It was a sight he saw too often, sprinklers flooding the orchards, carpeting the ground with weeds. Plenty of farmers and landowners still hadn't converted to drip lines, but operators like Patrick Smith had no incentive with the state subsidizing their water.

Nate hoped that, no matter where Elisa and Gilberto landed for his residency, she would keep policing the rule-breakers and the water hogs. He was afraid it was the last time he would see an OPEN sign hanging in the window of Carter's Grocery.

30

Hatfield, California
1978

Patrick's Falcon 50 landed with a thud on his Hatfield runway. His daughter Katherine's older child, now belted in after having spent the duration of the flight running around the cabin, screamed and lunged for his mother, thereby knocking the baby off Katherine's breast so that both children were wailing as the jet taxied to a stop. Patrick could remember Genevieve switching to the bottle as soon as possible and had no memories of nursing at his own mother's breast, which in his mind meant it was of little importance. But it was preferable to the diaper-change Katherine had started right before the Falcon began its descent. That could have waited.

Patrick's older daughters couldn't wait to get away from Smith Farm, which by the time they married encompassed a hundred and forty thousand acres. Yet Katherine and her husband, both physicians, were settled in Atlanta, in the state where Lon Smith had long ago grown cotton. And Samantha had chosen college in Southern California, which was bound with agribusiness in the Tulare Basin. But Samantha had muddied the waters, so to speak. After studying biology at her Jesuit college, she became interested in pesticide-free farming, and applied to do her graduate work under the tutelage of a horticultural guru in Santa Cruz. Admittedly, even though it was on Patrick's dime, he was proud that two of his daughters' schooling had gone so far past his own.

Every time she came home for Christmas, though, Samantha peppered him with questions about Smith Farm. After graduating the second time, she took a job with a company that bottled soap, claiming it was as effective an insecticide as the chemicals that had been killing bugs for eons.

The only one of his three daughters who wanted children was Katherine, and unless Patrick and Genevieve traveled to Atlanta, they saw their grandchildren just once a year at Christmas. That was okay by the fifty-three-year-old Patrick. But it was unacceptable to Genevieve, who convinced their daughter and her husband to fly in to Los Angeles with three children in tow so Patrick could fly with his own pilot to Santa Monica to pick them up. Meanwhile, Samantha and her husband drove down from Northern California in their Toyota Corolla, which they'd bought for its fuel economy and was of course forest green.

Katherine's family had an inordinate amount of luggage, including a portable crib and a gigantic folding stroller, all of which needed to be transferred from the plane to the car, but the spacious trunk of Patrick's Lincoln took care of it. Genevieve had baked cookies so the children could spend the whole visit hopped up on sugar, and she was standing on the verandah in her apron when Patrick pulled up in the Lincoln. She was thrilled to see all the luggage emerge from the trunk like the contents of Mary Poppins's carpetbag.

The only daughter who'd opted to stay on Smith Farm was the grey-eyed Maxine, who was busy making dinner for the arrivals. She had moved into the old house of Patrick's childhood, next door to the one Patrick built for his young bride. Working alongside a contractor, she tore down the wall between the kitchen and the room whose door Lon had left closed after his wife died. Once her state-of-the-art kitchen was complete, Maxine made pan-fried steaks and lasagnas thick with a portabella mushroom that relegated Lon's canned corned beef to a distant memory. Her husband, a well-driller, endeared himself to the family by drilling deeper and deeper into the Hatfield soil for his father-in-law's crop.

While Genevieve was baking cookies for the arrivals, Maxine had been roasting chickens and enough vegetables to feed an army. Dumping the luggage in the front room, Samantha, who couldn't cook worth a damn, started chasing the kids around the house, getting them even more wound up. Patrick was already looking forward to jetting the kids home, even though he knew that after they left, Genevieve wouldn't speak for days. So it was no surprise that after Samantha's Corolla rumbled out of the driveway, after all the baby equipment had been disgorged from the Falcon in Santa Monica and Patrick had returned to a gloriously empty house, he found Genevieve sitting in her armchair holding a pink sock that had been left behind.

"Honey?"

No response. He patted her on the knee and ducked into his office.

For two nights she served dinner in silence and turned away from him at bedtime. On the second morning when he handed her a cup of coffee in bed, she wiped away a tear.

He sat on the edge of the bed. "Honey?"

When there was no response, he went to get Maxine, glad once again for their youngest daughter. By noon Genevieve was up and dressed Hepburn-style in khakis and white button-down shirt, chopping celery for chicken salad and chatting as if nothing had happened.

It was Maxine who buoyed up her mother by talking about the nonprofit they'd started together. Although Maxine stood poised to take over Smith Farm, Patrick had no intention of handing it over as long as he remained standing. All three daughters held title, and each of his grandchildren was beneficiary to a parcel of land that allowed him to irrigate ever more acres. Patrick never asked himself why that lifted his heart more than having a houseful of them at Christmas.

Patrick's childhood friends had remained in Hatfield as well, although they were hanging on by their fingernails. Steve's father was one of the Kings River farmers Lon had bought out after the crash in 1929, and after he paid the bank what he owed on the farm, he'd borrowed again to open the hardware store. The family was in debt, and Steve seemed to take more comfort in knowing everyone who came through the door than he did in balancing the books. Patrick benefited from that too, since everything he needed for Smith Farm Steve sold him at cost.

Patrick's childhood friends were like his prized Lincoln. He could have bought a new car, but they didn't make them like the one he'd bought himself for his thirtieth birthday, with its power steering and wide comfortable seat that Genevieve, sleek as a cat in her mink stole, slid across to lean against him when he took her to dinner in Lemoore. There was no point in trading in old friends for new ones that wouldn't be the same.

As for Robert, Lon had bought out his father's farm too, and Robert worked for Patrick now. After their adolescent rabbit massacre, Robert had taken to shooting at anything that moved, and Patrick had ensconced him on Smith Farm to scare off the trespassers. But he spent most of his time at the bar in Hatfield. Although the kitchen with its terrible food had finally closed, the bar continued serving doubles to Robert as it had to his father.

One morning just as he sat down at his desk, Patrick received a phone call from his foreman. "I was out last night checking the fields, and I saw your Security"—he said the word as if he were placing quotation marks around it—"drive his truck into the canal."

"Oh, for crying out loud." Patrick set down his cup of coffee.

"He climbed out the window onto the roof of the truck, and I grabbed a rope from my cab to pull him out. We got the truck out this morning, but it's ruined."

"Good God, of course it is. Thank you, Hernando. I'll call him and wake him up."

To his surprise Robert answered on the first ring.

"What were you thinking?" Patrick scowled into the phone. "Meet me in my office. Pronto."

"Boss . . ." Robert said when he walked in fifteen minutes later. It was his nickname for Patrick, and the more he had to drink the more he pronounced it with sarcasm. But he was sober now, if a bit bleary, as he dropped into the chair on the other side of Patrick's desk. "I'm swearing off drink."

"I'm not worried about that," said Patrick, who didn't believe him and pictured "the drink" where Robert's submerged truck had been removed that morning with a crane. "But last week I sold thirty-three hundred acres of Buena Vista wetlands to the Conservancy of Biological Resources."

"Congratulations," mumbled Robert, rubbing at his eyes with his palms, hair, although grey now, still close-cropped and standing on end.

"I'm transferring you to the preserve." Banishing was more like it.

Robert sat up, suddenly alert.

"Your truck is ruined, but I'll give you one of the old jeeps so you can do your job, which is to flush out the poachers those wetlands will attract like flies."

After Robert moved into an abandoned hunting cabin on the preserve, he kept his word about hard liquor. But beer was a different story. Patrick walked in one day to find the utility sink, normally used for cleaning ducks, filled with ice and stocked with beer, the kitchen sink bloodied with duck guts, and the counters littered with empty cans. That was fine with Patrick, as long as Robert, whose gun was visible in the rack he mounted on the hood of the Jeep, kept the preserve free of vandals and people who thought they could drive out there for a picnic.

By then it had been more than two decades since the Corps of Engineers had dammed the last of the Tulare rivers, diverting the water from all four to the basin's largest landholders, including Patrick, and sucking dry the lake where one wet year in high school, Patrick, Robert, and Steve had rowed in a canoe from one lake to the next, Tulare to Goose to Vista. They'd packed food and sleeping bags and, when they reached the San Joaquin River, had slept on its banks like Huckleberry Finn, the book they'd been assigned in school that all of them had failed to read.

They ended up paddling for days, all the way to the mouth of the San Francisco Bay, and Steve kept jabbering about panning for gold. In order to shut him up, Patrick repeated what Lon always said: "By the time we're forty," Patrick told his friends, "I'll make more in one year's harvest than all the gold ever mined from these rivers."

Steve and Robert had laughed and splashed him with their paddles, but looking at his friends whose fathers had already lost everything to Lon, he'd known even then that Lon's prediction would prove true.

31

After eighty-five years the hair Patrick kept brushed away from his forehead was a swath of white. His blood was running in three great-grandchildren and counting. He hadn't had a cigarette in half a century and limited his drinking to a tall gin and tonic in the evenings with his wife. To his Tehachapi grazing operation, where an eight-lane highway had long since replaced passenger service on the train, Patrick had added a subdivision of three-acre ranch estates, so that thousands more commuting souls could live the ranch dream while fighting LA gridlock to get there.

Just west of the interstate, miles of canyon cut through the brown, stream-terraced mountains, and tributaries of the seasonal Santa Clara River ran through the canyon until they were dammed by the state during Patrick's fourth decade. The ensuing reservoirs were used for water storage, as well as relief from the heat for Southern California boaters and swimmers. In the most recent drought, the state had borrowed water from one lake to fill the other for the boaters.

Running parallel to the state's water channels, the eight-lane highway bisected the Tehachapi town of Dubois. Along with Patrick's cattle, Dubois had always relied on a spring for its water, until El Toro Land Company built its subdivision. Then the spring dried up, and the town of Dubois looked down thirstily on the lake nestled in the canyon.

Knowing he had to do something, Patrick tapped into the reservoir. But it was not just the disgruntled people of Dubois he had to contend with. Ever since Fish and Wildlife had reintroduced elk, condor, and bighorn sheep to the Tehachapis, the environmentalists were up in arms about his subdivision. So Patrick took another chunk of his Tehachapi ranch and sold it as a conservation easement. Conveniently, he sold it to the Conservancy of Biological Resources, partners in the ASD push to drill twin tunnels under the delta, that is, under the Bradley acres where Patrick's company had built another housing complex. Patrick saw the sale as a new source of water for his ranch estates. Which meant another fight, and he was getting tired of fighting the environmentalists, the biologists, and the Fish and Wildlife warden Elisa Martinez. He wondered how much cash it would take to make them go away.

Then again, no one who wanted to keep his job at Smith Farm would answer questions about their methods with fertilizer in the canals. When Patrick refused to open the books, the environmentalists would probably subpoena all the way to a federal grand jury, but Fish and Wildlife would react sluggishly, backing Smith Farm in the end. The director of the spill team would say the high level of ammonia that showed up in tests of the water were no more than a natural byproduct of the shad dying.

Of course, weeks after she found the shad, Elisa Martinez had found the damn grebes. Wouldn't you know they fed on the fish and were too sick to dive into the water, as Patrick was sure any living being would when Elisa Martinez came within a mile.

But Patrick knew Fish and Wildlife would be unable to pinpoint the party responsible for the ammonia found in his water because of the millions of pounds of chemicals he and his "neighbors" applied every year. More worrisome was that the old state pesticide regulator had recently gone to work for Clorox and the new one was none other than Patrick's daughter Samantha, who had settled in Sacramento, where she could loom over her father like a cormorant drying its wings on a telephone pole. Patrick hoped he was dead and gone before his own flesh and blood hit her stride.

A decade earlier there had been Elisa Martinez's predecessor, who came snooping around the duck eggs in Smith's evaporation ponds and found the same bird deformities that shut down the reservoir in the middle of a wildlife refuge in the Saltsink Water District. Samantha had asked about that too.

"It's selenium," he said in his own defense. "A natural compound in the soil."

"It's fertilizer," she countered, "that throws the natural level of selenium out of whack." Samantha was waving one hand while accepting another spoonful of her mother's potato gratin. "What caused the deformities at the refuge?" she asked. "Selenium, leached from farm soils."

"Love the gratin," Patrick said to Genevieve in an effort to drown out their daughter, but she rattled on, her talk about food-chain poisoning causing his own testicles to retreat into his groin.

Patrick had gone ahead and challenged the Fish and Wildlife biologist's findings on his evaporation ponds, and when the biologist defended his own numbers, Fish and Wildlife had banned him from Tulare County.

Now environmentalists were calling for an end to the use of evaporation ponds, but the state had given landowners four years just to complete their impact reports. And the eighty-five-year-old Patrick had just flown with his pilot and Genevieve to the state capitol to attend a dinner where the governor congratulated him and handed him a plaque from the Department of Water Resources.

"Remind me what the award is for?" Genevieve asked in the hotel room after dinner. She was sitting on the bed unstrapping her sandals.

"For recycling water," said Patrick, unable to contain his glee, and he saw a trace of a smile on his wife's face as she tossed her sandals in the direction of the closet.

Genevieve filled the bath with bubbles and sank into them. Loosening his bowtie and dipping a hand in the bubbles, Patrick contemplated how Smith Farm had done its "recycling." He'd used subsidized water to extract oil, treated the water, applied it to his fields, and sold the excess. But the evaporation ponds were becoming a problem. Unlined, they sat atop the colossal water bank Patrick and Lawrence had built underground, then purchased from the state. And it was taking more and more of what was a huge commodity on the open market to extract the oil that remained. Maybe it was time to cash in with the conservationists and expand the thirty-three hundred acres of Buena Vista wetlands on his property.

As Genevieve refreshed the bath with hot water, it occurred to Patrick that flooding the basin again would cost a hell of a lot less than building another dam somewhere. The swamp would filter the water so farmers didn't have to waste money cleaning it, and it would swell the water bank.

When the bath started to cool again, Genevieve stood, bubbles sliding off her skin, and leaned on her husband as she stepped from the tub. He handed her a towel, removed his pants, and folded them over a hanger. After drying off, Genevieve wrapped herself in a white robe and kicked her sandals all the way into the closet, because at their age it was about economy of motion and kicking was easier than bending to the floor.

That was what time did. As his marriage progressed Patrick was able to hold out longer during sex, once in a while long enough for Genevieve. It all slowed, including the frequency, but even now an evening out was almost a guarantee.

As Genevieve slipped out of the robe and under the sheets, Patrick mulled over his options. Maybe he should collude with

Elisa Martinez and the eco-terrorists, dynamite the dams he'd finagled, and leave this world in a series of grand explosions. He could see the water barreling down, filling the Tulare Basin and flooding the town of Hatfield: rakes, barbecues, and caulking guns floating out of Steve's hardware store, river water filling the old hunting cabin on the preserve, and Robert's beer cans bobbing out the door.

He could see his wife high and dry on the roof of the Hatfield Library, waving, gin and tonic in hand. Granting her father's last wish, Maxine would lay the three old men in the floor of the canoe, launching it on the same course they'd taken when they were young and virile, up through Tulare, Goose, and Vista lakes. The pintails and mallards, geese and herons would land in great numbers as they used to, while the canoe made its way at last to the sea and the birds took off all at once so you couldn't see the sky.

SAN JOAQUIN RIVER

32

On a warm afternoon in the foothills above Millerton Lake, a spider the size of a fist wandered across the rocky grassland, which, with spring rains long since past, had turned brittle and dry. The tarantula was black and hairy, and while his bite was not normally poisonous to humans, the venom was paralyzing to the insects, frogs, and mice that were his prey.

The tarantula was looking for a female. As she might eat him after they mated, she was one of his few potential enemies—except for the wasp whose sting rivaled his.

With a metallic blue-black body and orange wings, the wasp warned her predators that the meal was not worth the danger. She fed on the nectar of lupine, poppies, and baby blue eyes that covered these hills in spring, but she needed the spider as a resting place to lay her eggs. She spotted the tarantula and began circling, prodding him repeatedly with her antennae.

The spider fended her off with his legs and retreated, but she chased him, and it was only a matter of time before she got under him, turned him over, and shocked him with her stinger. The tarantula was paralyzed, and she dragged him off to her burrow.

Just below her burrow, the San Joaquin River ran through a granite canyon, and surrounding the canyon were the pine-oak woodland and chaparral of the foothills. Looming above the canyon were the flat rock tables formed by an ancient volcano whose lava had flowed down an old channel of the river. The proprietors, the Bureau of Land Management, allowed cattle grazing, hunting, and fishing, and the Yokut and the Mono still brought their children there to teach them the old ways.

The San Joaquin had always been the Yokuts' source of water. But after the Millerton dam was built, they were not allowed to take water from the lake. In the hot summer months, though, they still came down and camped on the river. The men left during the day to work on ranches and farms, while the women cleaned, salted, and dried the salmon that only native tribes were still allowed to spear. Along with their heart-shaped leaves, the redbuds growing near the river had thin, knotted branches that made good baskets. The women worked their fingers to the bone making the baskets, and it took months just to finish one.

Farmers tending smaller plots of land on the east side of the San Joaquin Valley were the designated recipients of water from the dam, until Lawrence Scheffield wrangled much of it for himself. But in the summer of 2008, increased pumping from both the river and the ground left even the valley's biggest landholders with no water to bank or buy. A smudge of sickly grey smog covered the valley floor, and the canal running south from Millerton shrank to a mossy dribble, while the one running north was dry.

Lawrence Scheffield's response to a massive overdrawing of the aquifers, in an area where land levels had dropped as much as twenty feet, was predictable. "Growers," he said, "have a right to farm just as much as anyone, regardless of the area."

Patrick Smith drilled five new wells that were the depth of two Empire State Buildings stacked underground. This was while residents in their districts had water coming into their houses at a trickle and were unable to flush their toilets.

Lawrence and Patrick's next recourse was to try to expand Millerton Lake, which would drown the canyon trails. And with allocations exceeding by nearly ten times the average runoff, water would never make it to the eastside farmers.

It was two years later when rain returned to the state that Buzz's lawyer son Henry prepared to fight the Saltsink and Kern water agencies over their plans for Millerton. The wasp using the belly of the tarantula to lay her eggs, Henry made sure the Environmental Impact Report—with its long list of endangered species like the monkey-flower and yellow-legged frog—cost the state more than a new dam would.

For the river defenders, the next step would be to get Patrick Smith to convert his oil-waste dumps to percolation ponds, with marshes providing natural filtration and wildlife habitat. Percolation ponds would recharge the aquifers, which, unlike dams, had unlimited capacity.

But the state loved dams, and as they forged ahead with the tunnels they planned to use to move the water stored in their new dams, Henry was preparing to face Patrick and Lawrence in court.

33

September 2010

Slipping into the gallery of the Stockton courtroom, Lawrence spotted Buzz two rows back, sitting next to his daughter Alice, and, behind them, the San Francisco reporter whose story about Buzz and Henry's surprise appearance at a closed meeting had been picked up by the *Sacramento Bee*. *Well, let them report.* Patrick, who was relying on Lawrence to brief him on the judge's ruling, said this case was "a slam dunk" for the Kern and Saltsink water agencies.

Henry stood at the front of the courtroom wearing a bright blue tie covered in ducks. Of course he was. Presiding over the court was the Honorable Sophia Emerald, whose eyes were the color of the stone itself and whose direct approach was a credit to her thirty years on the bench.

"Good morning, everybody," she began. "Before us is the matter of Defend Our Natural Resources versus the Saltsink and Kern County water agencies. When everyone is settled, please identify yourselves for the record."

Wearing a grey Sergio suit that fit his slim build, Pete Newell stood. "Yes, Your Honor, Pete Newell, representing the Saltsink and Kern County water agencies."

"Good morning, Your Honor, Henry Eberstark with Defend Our Natural Resources."

"Thank you, and you all may take a seat. Mr. Eberstark, would you like to begin?"

"Yes, your Honor. What is the basis for sustaining the objection to Exhibit 1?"

"I don't think it's relevant," the judge said.

"And we believe it is. The exhibit is an editorial written for a newspaper by the Saltsink Water District, in order to persuade the public as to why their delta island purchases are a good idea. It also shows there are impacts anticipated to the environment once the properties are purchased."

"Mr. Newell?"

"There is no commitment in the editorial," Pete said. "It simply uses the terms 'could,' 'would,' 'potential,' and 'possibilities.' All my clients have done is authorize purchase of the properties. They have not yet selected a project."

"Would," Lawrence thought, *was the operative word, and "potential," if the court decided in their favor, would become "done."*

"Do you maintain the objection to Exhibit 1, Mr. Newell?"

"Yes, Your Honor."

"Objection sustained." One point scored for the Saltsink Water District.

Henry continued, "Then I'd like to point out that the guidelines stating Environmental Quality—that is CEQA compliance—should be completed prior to land acquisition for a public project."

"Is there a case you found that says assurance of CEQA compliance is a prerequisite to purchasing the property?" the judge asked.

"No," Henry said. "But the Saltsink and Kern County water agencies filed a notice of exemption, which would prevent petitioners from challenging future projects, including habitat restoration and rehabilitation. These *sound* environmentally beneficial, but if you look at the list of items that the tunnel plans mention, all of them are water-driven. How is it that two of our state's largest water contractors have invested a hundred million dollars in a charity habitat project hundreds of miles from their districts? The answer is that three of the islands in the purchase are directly in the path of the planned tunnels. This is not a speculative matter."

He paused and stood straighter. "Once the sale is complete and escrow closes, it will drive the consideration of the tunnels before the public has an opportunity to weigh in."

"Mr. Newell?"

"Yes, Your Honor. All my clients have agreed to is the purchase. When we decide to make any physical changes to the property, we are bound by law to do the CEQA review."

"I'd like to note," Henry said, "that the water district for Los Angeles, which will bear a significant burden of the cost of the tunnels, wrote in a letter from its board of directors: 'The cost of the project that our district will inevitably incur is motivation enough to oppose the purchase of these islands being rushed for reasons that are not apparent.' And so, Your Honor, even decision-makers in Southern California are concerned about the consequences of imprudently rushing toward completion of this sale."

"Mr. Newell?"

"We don't know if we will ever use this property for the tunnels because they have not been approved. They'll likely be delayed by litigation and challenges."

That, Lawrence thought, shifting in his seat, *was certainly true.*

"We keep coming back to the same thing," the judge said. "How can the Saltsink and Kern County agencies research the environmental impact of their role in tunnels that haven't yet been approved? And how can we say that this is a project when nothing has been authorized other than the purchase of the islands?"

"I would respectfully disagree," Henry said. "This is a project that is substantially well defined. There have been two rounds of environmental review, the comment period has closed, and the Department of Water is within weeks of approving the project. Saltsink itself has repeatedly said the purchase will allow the tunnels to move forward. So to say that this purchase is proceeding in a vacuum is simply not true."

"Your Honor," said Pete, "my clients have not approved a restoration project. We're not bound by what we put in the notice of exemption, nor were we required to file one. We did so in an abundance of caution. We would request that you deny the preliminary injunction."

"If I may, Your Honor," Henry said, "I refer you to the map in Exhibit 11 that has a dotted line showing the path of the proposed tunnels going through Graham, Fogline, and Joseph Islands. The declaration cites water transfers, flood storage, an emergency fresh water pathway, and the tunnels. To say that this is not water-related is a lie."

"My clients," Pete said, "have never denied that they may have a water-related use for the property, but they have not determined which one of those uses might become a project."

"I don't think residents of the delta," Henry snapped, "would be heartened to know the purchasers are simply deciding which of their water-driven purposes will deplete the estuary."

"All right," the judge said. "If that's all, I'd like to take a brief recess."

Lawrence got up and headed for the restroom. He had just finished washing his hands when Buzz walked in.

"Lawrence," Buzz said.

"Buzz," Lawrence returned, crinkling up the paper towel, like paper on rock in Roshambo, and tossing it in the trash. As he exited, he saw the nonagenarian staring at him in the mirror from the urinal. Literally full of piss and vinegar.

When they reconvened, the judge said, "I have heard the arguments and considered all the prior evidence and exhibits presented. The court finds there is no approved public project for which CEQA review applies at this time. If and when the purchasers commit to any specific use of the property, environmental assessment will clearly be required. For now, the preliminary injunction request is denied."

Lawrence tried to hurry out of the courtroom, but despite his old age Buzz was right behind him. Lawrence found himself in the elevator with the man and his daughter. The confines of an elevator were worse than the restroom.

Alice pushed the button for the garage and, as they descended, Buzz said coldly, "Henry will take this to the court of appeals."

"The judge will deny the injunction," Lawrence said.

"Then he'll take it to the state supreme court."

The elevator dinged and they exited into the cool of the parking garage. As Lawrence walked toward his Buick, clicking the unlock button on his keys, he savored Pete Newell's words from the day before, that both justices would deny the injunction.

SACRAMENTO RIVER

34

October 2010

Dropping into the delta town of Stockwell at dawn, Nate turned onto Graham Island just as the sun was rising. Ahead of him on the crumbling levee road, a shepherd's truck disrupted a flock of sandhill cranes, transformed in their noisy takeoff to shadows against an orange backdrop of sky.

Below the road on one side was the Mokelumne River. On the other side were the fields, lower than the river by twenty-five feet. Water was constantly seeping into the islands and had to be drained, which caused the islands to sink below sea level. But as Nate drove on, the fields of dried cornhusks rose up to meet the road. That's when he pulled over and stopped, mesmerized by the sound of a thousand rustling skirts dancing in the wind.

Conservancy of Biological Resources was leasing Graham Island from a Swiss company, not so much for the corn as for the state's plan to build its tunnels beneath the island. Now unimpeded by an injunction, Lawrence Scheffield and Patrick Smith's purchase of Graham and the three other islands was moving forward.

Nate started the engine again and drove along the levee to a field where a combine was harvesting. He was awed by the power and ingenuity of the machinery. As the combine plowed through the cornhusks, all he saw of the machine-hands picking, husking, and separating were hundreds of pounds of fat grain pouring from the arm of the combine into a bin that rolled alongside in the shaven portion of the field.

He lifted a pair of binoculars and focused on two cranes further down the shaven edge, strutting on double-jointed legs and jabbing at kernels the combine had left behind.

The Conservancy of Biological Resources liked to brag that the corn they grew on the island wasn't genetically modified, but the real reason they grew non-GMO corn was that countries like Mexico rejected GMO product. A market for their corn was what kept many delta farmers from selling out to developers.

Nate had seen it on the pasture Patrick Smith's land company purchased in the south delta town of Bradley: grazing land plowed up and paved for streets named Sheep Creek Lane and Grassy Way, a housing complex people left every weekday morning before dawn to join the string of headlights crawling over Altamont Pass to get to their jobs in the Bay Area. In big storms rain raced across the hard-packed ground that was once permeable soil, poured into storm drains, and joined the roiling waters of a rising river. Employees at the massive new sporting goods store—the lucky ones from the housing complex who didn't have to commute—filled burlap sacks with sand and stacked them up against the doorways.

On his way off the island, Nate found himself behind the same shepherd's truck he'd been following at dawn. The CBR may have used grazing sheep for weed control and avoided genetically modified crops, but they used herbicides and insecticides on the corn seed. That was the kind of thing that made him seek out Elisa Martinez. "Why bother," he had said one sleep-deprived afternoon after their last final exam.

"Bother," she shot back, "because if you don't, they'll win. You know Defend Our Natural Resources?"

"Of course," he said, bolstered already by her energy.

"They win. All the time. They spend decades in court fighting their cases, and they never ask, 'Why bother.'" She quickly added, "I don't want to be an attorney, though. I need to be outside."

"Nobody would question you," he said, "even if you didn't wear a gun."

Nate wondered how he'd fallen in love with Ana when he liked nothing more than to spar with Elisa, or, for that matter, T Bone, who just that morning had worn a puzzled look on her face as he poured his coffee.

"Did you tell me your wife was living on the southern tip of Africa?" she asked.

"Yes. And she's not my wife for much longer."

She nodded, as if his comment confirmed something.

T Bone's scrutiny rattled him, and he spilled coffee on the counter. That's when she smiled out of one side of her mouth and said, "Careful there."

It felt good being teased, reminding him of the lightness he'd felt after getting rid of Ana's things. Sending her the divorce papers and moving in with T Bone had marked the resumption of his life. It didn't matter anymore what Ana wanted because Nate knew what *he* wanted. And as he headed east from Graham Island, crossed the slough on the first ferry, and drove down the levee road, he thought about how if rivers were what he cared about, then as Elisa said, he had to bother.

It was like the second ferry on which he was about to embark. Standing at the edge of the Sacramento Deepwater Ship Channel as the sun reached the apex of its burning trajectory, he saw the man in the watchtower come into focus as the boat rumbled over the water. When it landed and dropped its ramp, all he could do was get in his truck, roll onto the deck, and let it carry him to the other side. To the highway: past the wind farm on hills that were two hundred feet above sea level but seemed higher; past Grizzly Island where the vast acres of marsh were home to tens of thousands of species of shorebirds and waterfowl, where he knew there were steelhead because he'd helped tag them in the marsh, had followed their migration upstream, removed the tags, and released them alive. Like the hatchery salmon who were never as strong as the wild ones, it would always be a matter of starting from where they were, not from where they had been.

35

Kimura Farm, Joseph Island
October 2010

As they stood in the cool, dark barn on the final day of the harvest watching the last of the pears go into the storage bin, John turned to Lupe and said, "Nearly five hundred tons this season. A good year for fruit."

"*Gracias a Dios* for the rain," Lupe said.

She shed the apron pouch, hung it up, and walked back to the cabin, her shoulders still feeling the pouch full of pears, the weight like a baby outgrowing its carrier. Normally she walked or Manuel dropped her off before wrapping up his foreman duties. But that evening, looking straight into the sun, she saw the outline of a man walking toward her, and the stiff-back swagger told her it was her husband. A surprise meeting with Manuel still took her breath away.

Shirt covered in dirt and sweat, he reached his arms around her and kissed her, lips cold from the late October air.

"*¿Donde está el camion?*"

He turned and pointed at the cabin, where she saw the outline of his truck. "I finished the repairs early," he said.

Savoring the moment, they sat down on the narrow strip of porch with their boots in the dirt.

"The baby gets her twelve-month immunizations soon," Manuel said in Spanish. Social Services was helping him fill out the many papers required for adoption. "And Sherry says she's getting fat."

Lupe laughed, remembering the baby sucking down the bottle they'd given her that first night. They knew nothing of her history, and Lupe worried. But the doctor said she was healthy.

They had been careful not to name her. Anything could happen in the months it took to process the papers, and there would be plenty of time after the papers went through to give her a name.

"Where will we go," she asked, eyes following their long shadows across the ground, "if we have to leave Kimura Farm?"

Kimura Farm was where she had met Manuel, where they had found the baby. If the adoption didn't go through, or *ojalá que no*, if Kimura Farm were no more, she was unsure what they would do.

"Sunrise is hiring," he said. They both knew this because her sister Juana worked for Lawrence Scheffield.

Lupe sucked in her breath. She didn't want to go back to spraying chemical fertilizer. On Kimura Farm they let mustard grow wild between the trees, picked bruised apricots alive with flavor, and put up boxes so that owls moved into the orchard and hunted gophers eating the roots of the trees. But even on Kimura Farm, the labor, in the dirt and rain, in stifling heat, with biting flies and stinging fire ants, was what Lupe did for a paycheck. She loved the hours off the field best, when she drove to and from the supermarket, unloaded the groceries, and made dinner, when they prayed and fell exhausted into bed. She loved Sundays when they went to church, then gathered with the workers who lived in the row of cabins next to theirs for barbecues. Between the families in the other cabins and her sister Juana in Highland, there were always births and baptisms to celebrate.

Lupe wanted to watch her own child kick a soccer ball or write in the dirt with a stick, while Manuel used a fork to turn carne asada on the grill—wanted their child to go to school so she wouldn't have to work in the fields.

That night Lupe dreamt the pouch full of pears was a baby girl, and when she woke her arms ached. Manuel seemed to know. Pulling her to him, he whispered, "*Paciencia, va a pasar.*" It will happen.

"*Reza duro,*" he always said when they talked about the adoption. Pray hard. Now they needed to pray not just for the baby but for Joseph Island. If farm labor was what they did, she didn't know of a better place to work and raise a child than this little cabin in the middle of an orchard.

36

Ruby was eating a bowl of cereal when Nate entered the kitchen and pulled a banana from the bunch on the counter.

"Mom, can I have a banana?" Ruby asked.

"Those are Nate's," her mother said.

Nate tossed one to Ruby and grabbed a second one. He poured coffee into his car mug from the pot T Bone made every morning and stuck a protein bar in his pocket. Then he pulled a bag from the refrigerator and slid it into his pack.

"Ready when you two are," he said. Today he had rounds at the Cosumnes Refuge, one of his favorite places, and T Bone was taking the morning off work to join him.

They packed into the cab of Nate's truck, T Bone and Ruby's bikes in the back, dropped Ruby at school, and drove south to the delta. They crossed the bridge spanning the Sacramento River, then the Mokelumne and Little Potato Slough, before getting in line with the trucks rumbling north on the wide ribbon of interstate. They saw walnut orchards whose leaves had turned, a field harvested, plowed, and ready for planting, and the sun shining at a slant across acres of dying sunflowers.

Squinting happily into the light, T Bone said, "I feel like a kid skipping school."

Nate turned off the highway into the town of Randall, where they passed an old gas station, a sign that said Deli, and a warehouse that was once a fruit-packing shed. Within a block they were driving through the vineyards and orchards that surrounded the Cosumnes Refuge. Days like this, where he got to monitor the nest boxes, were what Nate loved most about his job.

They pulled into the parking area and Nate grabbed his pack. As they approached the walking bridge, there was a rustle in the leaves below an oak tree, and they caught sight of a cottontail as it scurried into the brush. Below the bridge, tule and cattails, willow and buttonbush pushed up from every available space in the marsh. The Cosumnes was the only river descending into the valley whose flow was unregulated by a dam, and the ancient valley oaks benefited from the rich soil whenever the river flooded its banks.

They turned onto a path shaded by the massive oaks. The path skirted the slough on one side and on the other the grasslands, where volunteers had planted hundreds of oaks to replace the many that had been lost when woodlands were cleared for farming and, more recently, when a mysterious disease had infected them. They heard the chirrup of a goldfinch, the ribbed vibration of a thousand cicadas, the faint drone of highway traffic, and, in the distance, a helicopter.

"Probably looking for weed," Nate said. Cannabis grew plentifully in the rich peat soil and helped a few struggling delta farmers make ends meet. But like grapes and cotton, outside the delta it sucked a lot of water, and north of them, pesticides from illegal forest growths were contaminating the streams.

Where the trail circumnavigated the grasslands, Nate and T Bone stood watching tree swallows, white breasts and blue wings soaring under an open sky. A dragonfly floated and dipped over the grape leaves turning orange at their feet. They saw three people—a man peering at birds through his binoculars, and a woman with a little boy—and in that whole time said little to each other.

"It's good to be with someone who's comfortable with silence," Nate said. Not Ana's kind of silence that shut him out, but a quiet they seemed to occupy together.

"I live with a twelve-year-old chatterbox," T Bone said. "Actually, *we* live with a twelve-year-old. Silence is nice."

They joined a looping trail at the fork of the Slough and the Cosumnes River and soon reached the first box tied to the trunk of an oak tree. Nate cleaned out the nest wood ducks had built in the box the previous spring.

At the next box on the bank of the river, they watched a great blue heron take off from the reeds, fly over the water, and disappear into the trees. The river was lower this time of year, and Nate pointed out an indentation in the mud above the water line.

"What is that?" T Bone asked.

"A slide made by the beavers and otters."

T Bone was incredulous and laughed.

Walking over to a bench under the woven canopy of an ancient oak, they sat down. Nate opened his pack and handed her a wedge of cheese wrapped in paper.

"Where'd this come from?" she asked.

Then he produced two pears and a box of crackers. The pears smelled sweet and grassy, and T Bone bit into one. Examining it, she said, "I can't figure out why your wife would move to the other side of the planet."

He looked at her.

"She's missing out." T Bone took another bite of the pear.

He bit into his own pear to hide the smile her comment had elicited. They listened to the song of a house wren under the dome of branches and the rapid-fire tapping of a woodpecker in the distance.

Later, after Nate parked in the campus lot, T Bone didn't ride away. Instead, she walked with her bike while Nate walked alongside her.

“Ruby rides home from dance at four thirty,” she said. “I’ll be home at five.”

They passed his favorite redbud, its heart-shaped leaves fluttering in the breeze.

“Thanks for letting me tag along. Best morning at work I've ever had.” She grinned.

“But no amount of refuge,” she went on, “can save the fish if they drain the river. Remember last year, when the pumps took so much water the San Joaquin flowed backward? My babies can’t avoid that kind of suction.”

“Speaking of which,” Nate said, “it’s my turn to cook tonight.”

“No jokes about barbecued smelt,” she said, locking the bike outside her office. “I already know them all.”

37

Nate pulled an envelope out of the mail, slipped it in his pocket, and dropped his keys and the rest of mail on the table by the door.

T Bone was standing in the dining room, holding a beer and gazing at the front door.

"Everything okay?" he asked.

"I think I'll shower before dinner," she said, and ducked into the bathroom.

Nate washed his hands at the kitchen sink and pulled lettuce and coho salmon out of the fridge. He'd finished poaching the salmon and the rice was just about done when T Bone appeared in holey sweatpants and a T-shirt that was brown like her eyes.

"You look nice," he said.

Ruby, who was right behind her mother, looked as if she couldn't disagree more.

Nate divided the salmon on three plates and added a scoop of rice. He tossed olive oil and balsamic in a bowl of greens and set it on the table. Ruby laid out the silverware and lit the candles.

"Sit here," T Bone said quickly, dropping into Ruby's usual seat so she had to sit between her mother and Nate.

"Mom, are you okay?"

She didn't answer, and Nate held up a bottle of Chardonnay.

"None for me," she said, covering the glass with one hand and taking a gulp of Ruby's water with the other. Ruby stared.

"Have you finished your math?" T Bone asked.

"Yes," she said, looking hurt.

"It's delicious," T Bone said, not meeting Nate's eyes. The barbecue dried out the coho, which was why he'd poached it.

"I don't really like salmon," Ruby commented. "Sorry, Nate."

T Bone said. "It's full of omega—"

"Omega-three fatty acids," Ruby said. "I know. May I be excused?"

Nate noticed she had eaten everything on her plate.

"I have something to show you," he said after Ruby went upstairs.

He pulled the envelope out of his pocket. It bore an airmail label and stamps from Namibia.

T Bone frowned. "You haven't opened it."

"I know what it is." He used his knife to open it and pulled out the divorce papers. Ana had signed them. He laid them on the table for T Bone to see.

Her face relaxed, and she punched him lightly on the arm. "What if you'd pulled them out and she hadn't signed them?"

He shrugged. "Then I'd be up a creek."

T Bone laughed. "Well, congratulations. Is that what you say to someone who's divorced?"

"In this case, yes."

"Did she send a note or anything?"

"No. She really didn't want to be married."

T Bone clinked her glass of water against his and met his eyes but only for a second. "This calls for me doing the dishes."

Nate decided that, once Ruby excused herself the next night, he would ask T Bone why she was acting weird. As it turned out, Ruby woke up with a low-grade fever and spent the day on the couch. Her mother managed to get her to drink a glass of cranberry juice before sending her to bed.

It was T Bone's turn to cook, and she put Nate to work chopping broccoli. It was as good a time as any to ask questions.

He waited until she was chopping and said, "Tell me about Ruby's father."

She was stirring onions in the wok with the same intent expression she always wore.

"It's not a secret," she said about the man she hadn't mentioned in the ten months Nate had lived there. "His name is Eduardo, and in high school we were in love. The one time we gave in, the condom broke and I got pregnant."

Nate handed her the cutting board and she dumped the broccoli into the wok.

"Wine or sparkling water?" he asked, opening the fridge.

"Sparkling water."

"Me too."

Nate lit the candles and set the table, which was normally Ruby's job.

T Bone handed him a plate of steaming rice and vegetables. "I tell Ruby all the time she was the best mistake I ever made."

"Here's to Ruby," Nate said, and they clinked glasses. "Where's Eduardo now?"

"He graduated from the university while washing dishes at night. Now he's apprenticing for a solar company. It's what I wanted for both of us, to graduate college."

"Does he see Ruby?"

"Since we moved here, only at Christmas. Ruby loves being with her other family." T Bone looked sad as she said this.

"Why didn't you get married?"

"We were sixteen. And because he got drunk at a party and bragged to his friends that I was going to have his baby."

T Bone was another father coyote, Nate thought, pitching her tent outside the circle.

"My mom Nora would say God gave me a choice, and I know it's true. Ruby was the choice."

"I wanted to have a baby with Ana right away," Nate said bitterly. "If she'd left, it would have been hard on a kid."

"Which is why I made a promise a long time ago that I'd be married to the next man I slept with."

Nate shook his head. "I disagree. If I hadn't been so focused on abstinence, Ana and I wouldn't have gotten married."

"She still would have broken your heart," T Bone said. "So what's the difference? You're here now." She was actually looking at him, and the candlelight danced in her eyes.

Then she was swooping in to pick up his plate. In the kitchen, he filled the sink with soapy water.

"Goodnight, Nate," she said, and he was not expecting what she did next. She kissed him on the cheek, then walked out of the kitchen and into her room, the door clicking shut behind her.

He was getting mixed signals and wondered what was going on. Anyway, what was he doing? She was twenty-seven and he was twenty-three. She was his landlord and he was her tenant. But Ana had returned the divorce papers, and that made him happy.

He decided to do what was in front of him and sank dishes into the soapy water. Later, as he passed her room, the light under her door pierced the dark hallway.

38

The next night, T Bone asked, "What are you doing for your birthday tomorrow?"

He shrugged. "Just a normal day. Work. I thought I'd go for a run."

"Are you planning to eat?"

"If you're offering to cook, I accept."

"I have a better idea. Adelaide's."

"I've never been."

"What do you say I treat you? We can even walk there."

Nate told himself she was just being nice because it was his birthday.

In the morning he stepped outside into the cool October air and ran toward campus and the grove in the arboretum. There were a hundred different species of oak in the grove, but his favorites were two that thrived in the valley: the live oak with its evergreen prickly leaves, and the valley oak with its deciduous fingered leaves. Both were immune to the disease that had taken out so many California oaks, their trunks spreading to impressive heights with canopies that made him feel protected when he stood beneath them.

After the arboretum, Nate stopped at the gym and lifted weights for half an hour. Then he ran home, showered, dressed, and was reaching for his usual protein bar when T Bone and Ruby stepped into the kitchen.

"Happy Birthday," Ruby said, handing him a bag. T Bone pulled the protein bar out of his pocket and tossed it across the counter.

"Blueberry?" he asked. That was Ruby's favorite.

She nodded and he took a bite.

That night T Bone made Ruby her favorite dinner, grilled cheese sandwich dipped in tomato soup. Nate wore jeans so it wouldn't look like he was overthinking dinner, but he couldn't resist tan oxfords or a bottle-green button-down shirt that matched his eyes.

"We'll be back!" T Bone said to Ruby. They stepped outside and she locked the door. She was grinning under the porch light.

They started walking as the first stars appeared in the deepening blue of the sky. The air smelled faintly of exhaust from the evening traffic. When they arrived downtown at the small building that housed Adelaide's, the Japanese maple in front was stripped bare save a few dangling red leaves. The hostess greeted them and led them to the last open table.

T Bone ordered risotto, Nate ordered lamb, and they chose a Zinfandel grown in the delta. As the waiter filled their glasses she asked Nate, "How far did you run this morning?"

"Just to campus. I went to the gym."

"I run around the block to get warmed up for kickboxing," she said, and in that moment it seemed obvious what hadn't registered before, that his housemate had the compact, slightly hungry build of a kickboxer.

"I would definitely not mess with you if I met you in a dark alley," he said.

"It's something I felt I needed to do. Moving here with Ruby was an adjustment. Growing up, I was so protected by my parents, and my dad's partner Jim is a big guy. They all watched over Ruby."

"Kickboxing should take care of it," Nate said.

"I took martial arts growing up. Did you run in high school?"

"My dad's shop sponsored my Little League team, and that was the only reason I played. I once missed a fly ball because I was rescuing a frog."

"Thus foretelling your future."

The waiter laid down a steaming bowl of risotto and a half rack of lamb with polenta and spinach. T Bone fed a forkful of risotto to Nate.

"*Mmm.* I did run in high school, cross-country. My favorite place to train was a trail on the Yuba River."

"I can see why. It's weird," she said, "growing up on the ocean I thought I'd never leave it, but I think I love rivers more."

"I'm happy to hear that. Besides, they're the same. Freshwater is just what evaporates from the ocean and falls as snow and rain."

"I never thought of it that way."

He cut off a piece of lamb raised in Bradley and put it on her plate. Bradley was the town in the southwest pocket of the delta where Patrick Smith had torn out a large chunk of pasture for his housing development. It also abutted the tract of water he and Lawrence Scheffield wanted to expand for storage, but Nate didn't want to dwell on that topic, with a perfect evening that seemed to be pointing them in a new direction.

For dessert they chose the warm bread pudding. Nate took a bite of crusty bread poking out from a scoop of vanilla ice cream and pushed the plate toward T Bone. In no time they'd polished it off and sat back to finish their wine.

"Are you sure you're only twenty-three?" she asked.

"Twenty-four today. Did you forget you were paying for dinner?"

"Of course not! Your birthday was just an excuse." She reached over and ruffled his hair. The curls had grown back on the head he'd shaved smooth eight months before.

"T Bone," he said, before he lost his nerve, "what's going on?"

"I don't know. What do *you* think's going on?"

"I think moving in with you and Ruby was the best thing I could have done, and I don't want to mess it up."

The waiter brought the check, and T Bone counted out some bills. They put on their jackets, and when they stepped outside Nate took her hand. Venus glowed in the sky just above the coastal range. During the walk home he had to remind himself to breathe.

Inside the house it was quiet, and she crept up the stairs. Nate was standing at the bottom, and when she came back down he kissed her. Warmth spread through his body, and she pulled him closer. When they untangled themselves, she said, "The promise I made is going to be harder than I thought."

"You don't have to keep it, you know. If I hadn't made that promise I'd never have been married."

"*Shh,*" T Bone said, pressing her finger to his lips. "If you hadn't married her, you wouldn't have been lost and come looking for me."

"That's true."

"Everything happens for a reason," she said, pulling him toward her room. Then she stopped and said, "This is where we say goodnight," kissing him again before closing the door behind her.

Nate fell back on the couch as the thoughts that had been jumbled in his head slid into place. From the moment he'd seen this house it had felt like a place of safety. For him, a weight lifted. But something had changed, and *he* was the father coyote the mother was keeping out of the den. T Bone was right, sleeping together was not part of the equation.

After his blueberry muffin that morning, he'd arrived early for a meeting on campus and ducked into the bookstore, where he'd seen prints that were an artist's rendition of delta fish. He'd found two black-and-white sketches of smelt and bought them, supposedly as a birthday present to himself.

But the smelt were T Bone's "babies." He went to his room, picked up the sketches, and turned one upside down so they were facing one another. Finding some tape in the kitchen, he attached them and drew heart bubbles rising. In each bubble he drew a letter, spelling "Hello" above each of their heads. To lighten the moment when the air felt charged.

He slipped the drawings under T Bone's door.

39

The Kimura house was dark in the hour before dawn. Shep, their five-year-old collie mix, lay under the desk, and John nestled his stockinged feet under her warm fur.

Thanksgiving was just another day of work for John, although the state capital shut down for the holiday. Yet December hadn't even begun when John and his neighbor Eric both received notice from the Department of Water that their farms, about a hundred acres each, were located where one of the pipes would be laid for the "state water pipeline." Now that escrow had closed on the four islands, project approval seemed to be a foregone conclusion, and the state was forging ahead.

After Eiji's friend stopped growing asparagus, Wes had leased the land to Eric's dad, who'd planted olive trees. And before they finished high school, Eric and John had made their pact, promising to do everything in their power to keep Sutton and Kimura Farms alive.

When Wes died, his children sold Joseph Island to the Swiss company that had just sold it to the Saltsink and Kern County water agencies. Now Eric and John were up against the state, and they needed to face off together. He clicked on the desk lamp and typed an email to Jamie Cannigan.

From: John Kimura
Sent: Dec. 7, 2010, at 5:04 a.m.
To: Jamie Cannigan
Cc: Eric Sutton
Subject: Preferred Location DCAP315

Jamie,
I am wondering if it would be possible to move DCAP-315 pipe to the east edge of the Kimura property as indicated on the attached map. Where it is currently located is in the middle of my family's graves.

May I stress that as longtime farmers on the property, my neighbor and I want no part of this project, and I am only exploring ways to mitigate the damage if this is forced upon us.

John Kimura

At nine forty, hours after John had left for the field, his computer chimed the arrival of Jamie's reply.

From: Jamie Cannigan
Sent: Dec. 7, 2010, at 9:40 a.m.
To: John Kimura
Subject: RE: Preferred Location DCAP 315

John,

I agree it is better for you to have input than for a court to dictate. Thank you for being proactive with your communication.

If the Tunnel goes forward your crops will be impacted. Kimura and Sutton Farms are located within a proposed shaft for Intake #2, as well as proposed storage for the project. But the Department of Water will negotiate a temporary easement and with the property owners move the drill site on DCAP-315 to your constituents' preferred location.

Please let me know if you have any additional concerns.

Jamie

When he came in for lunch John fired off a quick reply.

I will avoid any puns about DW giving us the shaft.

Neither I nor Mr. Sutton was able to attend the meeting the Department of Water held with delta property owners. Would you be willing to debrief me on the meeting?

Jamie replied:

The morning agenda exceeded the allotted time, and delta property owners' requests were pushed to the afternoon. Some of the property owners were unable to stay. Others sat all day waiting to address the DWR.

The bottom line will be whether the DWR and the owners, or tenants like yourselves, make a good faith effort to negotiate. We are asking all of you to engage the DWR, and have suggested those ignoring our notices contact us ASAP.

Good faith, John thought at nine thirty that night when he read the email. *There wasn't a single delta farmer who placed faith in the Department of Water.*

40

A week later, when Alexis was reading in bed, Benji was grading papers, and John was getting ready for his nightly visit with his mother, they heard pounding feet on the porch and a loud knock. Shep jumped up barking. John peered through the curtains at the front window and saw a man, six feet tall and muscly, with a shaved head and a ring in his eyebrow. Tattoos covered the Popeye arms under his nylon T-shirt. Shep growled and lunged at the door.

"Mr. Kimura," the man hollered, "Open the door! I have a notification from the State."

"Daddy?" came Alexis's voice.

Benji hurried toward Alexis's bedroom. "It's okay, Lex," she said through the door. "Stay there, and I'll come see you in a minute."

"Okay," Alexis said quietly.

Another bang on the door. When John opened the curtain, the man held up the papers. Benji grabbed Shep by the collar, and John opened the door just wide enough for the dog to shove his muzzle through the crack.

"Mr. Kimura?" The man's face was as smooth-shaven as his head, and he had acne.

Alexis had not made a peep since Benji'd told her to stay in her room.

"Could you hold off the dog? I have a notification to serve you."

"What for?" Benji asked, not letting go of Shep.

The man waved the papers as if to say his job was to deliver them, not read them. As he wedged his body into the opening in the doorway, John saw the tattoo of a dagger on the side of his neck pointing toward his ear. Shep, straining at the collar, snarled and bared his teeth.

Leaning his weight against the door, John was grateful for the years of labor that had given him enough muscle to hold off a six-foot process server on steroids.

"I'm sorry," he said sarcastically. "Were we expecting you? It's late."

"I need to leave these papers," the man said, reaching around the door, his softball-size fist holding the papers.

John was surprised to smell soap, when he'd assumed a man that menacing would smell bad. As the dog continued to growl, he snatched the papers, and the man was gone. The notification, John knew, informed him and Benji of their right to due process of law in case of the state taking over private property for public use. But the Kimuras and the Suttons were not the property owners, which meant their only recourse was to hope the state honored their wishes and moved the intakes, on the slim chance that they would be able to continue farming.

John slammed the door and locked it. Shep was panting and circling the hallway. John peeked out the window and saw a beat-up old two-door sedan. A gym rat with a night job.

He watched until the taillights faded at the end of the orchard, then he and Benji collapsed on the sofa. Shep stopped pacing and sat, leaning against them.

"Good boy," Benji said, taking a deep breath. She was trying to calm herself so she could go reassure Alexis.

She and John went to the door together. As light from the hallway flooded the darkened room, they saw Alexis huddled under the covers, eyes wide open.

"It's okay, honey," Benji said, sitting on the edge of the bed and smoothing her daughter's flyaway hair. Shep lay down at the foot of the bed.

"Who was that man?"

"He came looking for Dad. But he's gone now."

"What did he want?"

"It has to do with the farm," Benji said.

"You won't let them take our farm, will you Dad?"

John sighed.

"We just lease the land," Benji told her daughter. "But your dad's putting up a good fight."

Alexis was silent. Then she turned over and lifted her nightgown so her mom could graze her fingers lightly over her back. It was what calmed their daughter most. John wondered, with the adolescent years upon them, how much longer she would let her mother tickle her back.

Alexis's breathing slowed. "Want me to leave Shep?" Benji whispered. Shep slept at the foot of her bed whenever Alexis needed him.

"Uh huh," she said. The dog lay his head on his paws.

They closed the door, and John picked up the papers.

"I was hoping Shep would take a chunk out of his tree-trunk legs," Benji said.

John let out a nervous laugh.

"What happens now?"

"I don't know," he said. "But this is bullshit. There is no approval for the tunnels and the state's already at our doorstep."

"Literally." Benji shuddered. Then unable to keep the anger from seeping in, she said, "It's nine o'clock. Are you going to the nursing home?"

It wasn't Keiko Benji was mad at. It was all the demands on their time that pulled them in opposite directions like runaway vines. At night when Benji finished her work and stumbled off to bed, John still had to drive to the nursing home, and after that, answer his emails. Two hours' difference in bedtime was not conducive to intimacy, and Benji often woke up hostile at dawn.

"It's too late," John said. "I'll call and let them know I'm not coming." He felt the tension in the room melt away. "But I have to email the DWR."

Benji frowned. "I know. What they are doing isn't right."

After she went upstairs, John sat down at his computer.

Jamie,

I thought the DWR was going to negotiate in "good faith," and that we were having a conversation. Instead, tonight as I was getting ready for my nightly visit with my eighty-four-year-old mother, my wife and I and our ten-year-old daughter were invaded by a tattooed, scary-looking process server. He was banging on the door as if he had a warrant for the arrest of a dangerous criminal.

This is entirely inappropriate for your agency. When unknown people on steroids visit us in an isolated rural home after dark, it is fair to assume they are up to no good.

This will be the first night since I moved her to the nursing home that I do not see my mother, who is in the late stages of Alzheimer's and takes great comfort in my visits. All because of papers you could have served during the daylight hours. Frankly, you could have PDF'd them.

In your email you talked about "engaging the DWR" and keeping the conversation going. Why, when it was your

> intention to confront us and force us to do what you demand? I should not have expected honesty and professional behavior from your agency.
>
> It's late, I'm tired and angry. I will deal with the papers in the morning.

John shut off the desk lamp and sat in the dark. The Saltsink and Kern water agencies had said Joseph Island was perfect for stockpiling fill dirt. And a man whose father Lon had profited from Takashi's forced labor on Tulare soil would sink Takashi deeper in his delta grave.

Imagining dump trucks burying Kimura and Sutton Farms under hundreds of thousands of tons of dirt was unbearable, so John turned his thoughts to the southern islands where the state planned to expand Floyd's Tract for "wildlife habitat." But that was a joke, because the islands were twenty to thirty feet below sea level and would form a lake, not marshland. Conveniently, that lake would be located at the site of the new pumps.

John hoisted himself out of the chair and made his way upstairs. Letting his clothes drop to the floor, he climbed in bed and spooned against Benji.

"You're cold!" she complained, and he held on tighter, letting the warmth of her body seep into his.

Working in the soil was in John's DNA, and he would never stop. Even if fill dirt and crumbling levees sank the delta, the descendants of Eiji Kimura would find a way remain above water.

41

December 2010

Marie was in the cherry orchard bundled against the cold, the last of the leaves scattered on the ground around her. The seasons of the tree fruit started in a frenzy, with the cherries and apricots they hurried to pick before the birds ate them. Then as summer turned to fall, things slowed to a less frenzied clip with the gathering of pears and figs. But it was the pruning in the dormant season that set in motion the flurry of harvest.

Standing on the middle rung of the ladder, she used a hand pruner to cut the younger branches crossing over older ones. Both mature and new wood were needed to produce the deep red cherries, the Blenheim apricots that held all the flavor, and the firm pears with spotted skin.

The same could be said for the quiet hours Marie spent among those trees. There was new wood that allowed for complete otherness. But the old wood was what named the tree and held up the new. This would be the second Christmas without Lydia, holding both memories and tradition, while offering up the chance to do something different. She had been invited to have dinner with Manuel and Lupe.

A week before Christmas, Manuel and Lupe brought home the baby. Marie was waiting with the families from the other cabins when they pulled up in the truck and Mother Lupe climbed out holding Lupita. The women surrounded her, and their children hovered, pulling back the baby's blanket to get a peek at her face. The men hugged Manuel and clapped him on the back.

The women left gifts for the baby under the little tree Lupe had decorated with red tinsel. Marie's, wrapped in gold paper, was a set of three toddler T-shirts with a farm theme, one with a buzzing bee, the second with chicken eggs, and the third with a tractor.

The occupants of the other cabins left for Christmas in Mexico, and Lupe's sister Juana, who lived in Highland, moved with her family into one of the cabins, which the sisters used for overflow cooking. For the next three days they prepped and cooked the mole and tamales, beans, and rice. After Christmas Eve Mass they all gathered at Manuel and Lupe's for dinner.

When Marie walked in Lupe was dressing a salad with lemon, and Manuel was sitting on the couch feeding Lupita a bottle.

"I pulled her from a duffel bag," he said in Spanish, "the night we found her." It was a boast that was both bravado and tenderness. "Good thing Lupe and I were there," he said to Father Larry. "You didn't know what to do."

"I called the police," Larry said. "Otherwise you would have run off with the baby."

The other men laughed.

"We waited a whole year," Manuel said. The bottle was nearly empty and Lupita's eyes were growing heavy.

Lupe took the baby from Manuel and laid her on the bed between two pillows, where she cried half-heartedly for a minute, then fell asleep.

The adults sat down at the two tables they had pushed together, and the kids sat on the sofa with paper plates on their laps. Lupe said a prayer in Spanish, softly and rapidly. Larry followed with his own special prayer: "Lord, thank you for delivering Lupita to the doorstep of our church, and bless

Manuel and Lupe's first Christmas with her. Thank you for this bountiful dinner Lupe and Juana have prepared, as we gather in your name. Amen."

Everyone said amen, and as Larry tucked into his mole, he kept repeating the word "Delicious."

"It takes days to make," Manuel said. "Not two minutes like the box macaroni and cheese you have every night."

"That's why I'm going to have another helping," Larry said.

Lupe jumped to fill his plate, and the baby woke up crying.

Juana picked her up and carried her around the room while Lupe finished the dishes. Then Lupe changed the baby and sat at the table with a plate of rice along with a few beans. The baby pawed at the rice, and soon there was rice in her hair, on the floor, and pieces of smashed bean on the table. When she finished eating, Lupe cleaned her up and carried her to the sofa, where Manuel was drinking a beer with his friends. Lupita was enraptured by the older children, watching as they stood a set of dominoes in a long chain. When they pushed over the first domino, she laughed as they fell one by one.

"Thank you," Marie said to Lupe when it was time to go.

"De nada," Lupe said. For her it was nothing to invite Marie for Christmas Eve dinner.

Marie walked slowly to her cabin, a veil of clouds darkening the sky. She knew she couldn't get out from under the shadow of Lydia and didn't want to as long as she felt Lydia there. Not feeling Lydia's presence would have cast heavier clouds. But with her gone and the future of Kimura Farm unknown, the December miracle was more than the baby Lupita. For Marie the miracle was breaking bread with Lupe and Manuel.

She brushed her teeth, shed her clothes, and climbed into bed.

"Feliz Navidad," she said to nobody, and fell into a dreamless sleep.

42

Santa Cruz, California
June 2011

Reverend Isabelle McKenzie, tall and muscular and wearing a brightly colored shawl over her sleeveless dress, stood under the ancient live oak where the couple would exchange their vows. As the groom made his way toward her across Evan and Jim's patio, stepping onto the small patch of grass where forty people were beginning to squeeze together for the ceremony, he fiddled nervously with his tie.

"How are you doing?" Isabelle asked.

"There are more people here than the first time I did this," Nate said, taking a deep breath.

She put a hand on his shoulder. "Only a few dozen more people, and they all love you."

Jim's voice boomed above the bodies spilling onto the flowerbeds. "It's just ground cover, people. Walking on it won't kill it."

T Bone's dad steered the guests away from the path his daughter would use to make her way to Nate, while Jim took his place under the oak tree next to Isabelle.

The chattering group hushed as T Bone appeared, wearing a champagne silk dress, her brown hair tied back with a few small stems of freesia. Her mother, Nora, dark hair and eyes like T Bone's, walked on one side of her, and her father, Evan, not much taller than Nora but sinewy with red hair, walked on the other.

Behind them strode Ruby, freesias tucked into the waves of her auburn hair.

The tension dissolved from Nate when he saw T Bone coming down the path. He reached for her hand as they took their place in front of Isabelle. She gazed at them and said quietly, "Remember to breathe."

Then she began. "We are gathered on this June day to celebrate both the gifts and demands of love. Even on the wedding day love demands something of us. Nate and T Bone, we can see how happy you are, but marriage is about holiness as much as happiness.

"In ancient times the couple was called upon to be part of the village and the larger family, to create in their home godly traditions like hospitality. This is what it means to be made holy.

"Without the village, the marriage has to meet the needs of both people, a weight it can't bear on its own. Which is why you've asked your tribe here today, to enter with you into a covenant. And T Bone has asked Jim to read a poem."

Jim brushed his mustache with his fingers and reached into the pocket of his blue suit. He pulled out a folded piece of paper with some lines from the poem, *A Concordance of Leaves* by Philip Metres, which Nate and T Bone had chosen for the occasion. Nerves made his baritone voice rumble as he read:

> Because there is a word for love in this tongue
> that entwines two people as one
> and there is a word for love in this tongue
> that nests in the chambers of the heart
> and a word for love in this tongue that wanders
> the earth, for love in this tongue in which you lose
> yourself in this tongue and a word that carries
> sorrow within its vowels and a word for love
> that exudes from your pores and a word
> for love that shares its name with falling.

Jim smiled at T Bone and slipped the poem back in his pocket.

"Today," Isabelle said, "you exchange rings. They are round without beginning or end, like the commitment you have made to each other."

Ruby reached out a palm holding the rings. Nate and T Bone slipped them on each other's fingers and kissed.

"Nathaniel and Therese," Isabelle announced to the crowd, "husband and wife."

As Nate and T Bone turned toward the crowd, Evan, Jim, and Nora closed in for a hug, followed by Ruby and Isabelle, then Nate's mom and sister Deni.

After they broke apart Jim looked at Evan and nodded.

"When people in this country come to their senses," Evan said to Isabelle, "Jim and I would like you to marry us."

"I'd be honored," she said. And three years later, when the federal court ruled that the California law banning their marriage was unconstitutional, she would perform the ceremony under the very oak tree where Evan and Jim now stood.

Within moments the band started up on the second-story deck of the house. On the other side of the French doors the dining room had been cleared of furniture, and Evan began to dance with his daughter. Marie and Nora, carrying trays of food to the living room, where the sofas had been cleared and replaced with tables set up for dinner, stopped to watch.

Tables overflowed into the hallway, and caterers bustled around with champagne, appetizers, and more trays of food. Nate danced with T Bone, Nora with Evan, then Evan with Jim as the dance floor filled with people.

There were toasts and dinner, then apricot pie because Nate didn't like cake. There was more dancing, and then it was time for him and T Bone to go.

They'd decided to spend their honeymoon in the Sierra Buttes because T Bone said she wanted time on the river and trails where Nate had grown up. But they were spending their wedding night in a hotel with a view of the ocean.

"Be good," T Bone said when she hugged Ruby, who was having a slumber party with Nora. Nora held firmly to T Bone, then pulled away and grabbed onto Nate.

T Bone hugged her dad, then Jim, and when Nate held out his hand, the bride and groom walked toward Nate's truck. He had spent the week before cleaning it inside and out. Now he brushed aside the rose petals sprinkled on the seat, and holding up her dress, T Bone stepped in. As he started the engine, he looked out the back window and saw a flash of faces—Ruby's, Jim's, Evan's—and empty hands as the last rose petals fluttered behind the departing car.

When they came to the bottom of the driveway that wound away from the house, a new moon hung just above the web of an oak tree. Nate looked over at T Bone. A Central Valley boy, he was like the Chinook salmon: Born in fresh water, he would die in fresh water. T Bone, on the other hand, was more like her lab babies, the salmon's distant relatives that once spawned in the ocean under a moon just like this one, only to evolve into that elusive delta species with its own freshwater migration.

As they sped down the highway Nate reached across the seat for her hand.

43

September 2011

In July, three years after the drought sucked the Millerton canals dry, bulldozers came to Joseph Island. They came to build up the levee roads so they could hold trucks bearing heavy materials and dirt. The road was reduced to one lane, causing long waits on the way into town. The noise was constant, and the wood ducks, normally congregating by the dozens in the willows, scattered.

As promised, the state had moved the shaft drill site to John's "preferred" location.

"They moved it away from the Kimura graves," he told Benji, "and into the pear orchard. As far as I'm concerned, it's still over Dad's dead body and it's going to be over mine."

On a Saturday in September, the bulldozers showed up. Benji, who was finishing a lesson plan before breakfast, called John, and he came roaring back from the tomato field. Manuel, with Marie in his truck, was not far behind.

Lupe came outside carrying a squirming Lupita. Fearing the baby would run straight for the bulldozer, she threw a worried glance at Manuel.

Alexis, who had fled outside in her pajamas, shouted, "Don't let them, Dad! What are they doing?"

"Taking our trees to make room for the intakes," John told her.

"What intakes?"

Benji, who had appeared next to her daughter, said, "It's where they lower the machine to dig a tunnel."

"I can't just stand here and watch," John said.

"Neither can I." Benji pulled the barefoot Alexis toward the truck.

"I want to stay," Alexis said, but Benji walked faster, holding firmly to her daughter's hand.

"*Ya me voy*," Lupe told Manuel, and followed Benji to the truck. But before she even got the seatbelt over herself and Lupita, the bulldozer toppled the first tree. John heard Alexis scream, which scared the baby, who began to cry.

Benji started the engine and drove slowly down the road, pulling over just around the bend. The bulldozer backed up and, digging into the ground, yanked up a web of roots. Knobs of green fruit rolled like severed heads.

John trudged toward the bulldozer, Manuel and Marie on either side of him, and lay down between a standing tree and the line of fallen ones.

Marie felt the sun-warmed earth seep through her clothing. Her heart pounded. She was ready to die under the bulldozer, as she had been the day the mountain lion came out of nowhere. For John and Manuel, it was different. They would lie down and fight for the soil where Eiji had planted these trees, but they wouldn't abandon their families.

The bulldozer engine roared, then choked to a stop. "Holy shit!" yelled the man on the seat. "I almost ran you over!"

"Do it," John said.

A dusty white truck came tearing down the road and screeched to a stop. A man in a hard hat jumped out. "What in the hell do you think you're doing?" he asked, stumbling over a hole in the dirt as he made his way toward the three bodies in the orchard.

"Did you run over our wives and children when you came flying down the road?" John asked.

"*You* are about to be run over by a tractor, do you realize that?"

"We do," John said.

The man in the hard hat signaled at the bulldozer operator, and the engine started again.

The three bodies didn't move. The bulldozer didn't move. The man in the hard hat pointed to the next row of trees. The bulldozer backed up, moved two rows over, and knocked down the first pear tree.

John stood up and clapped the dust from his clothes. Manuel and Marie stood, and the three of them walked two rows over and lay down between the standing tree and the fallen one.

The man in the hard hat signaled to the next row and the bulldozer moved over. The three bodies moved over. This happened again before the bulldozer operator killed the engine, and his supervisor approached the three bodies.

"What are you trying to do."

"These trees," John said, "were planted by my grandfather when my father was four years old."

The man in the hard hat shook his head. "It's not right, I know. But this is my job, and we'll be back tomorrow. With the sheriff. And yes, I did see your wives and children. Do you want to leave them widows and orphans?"

But leaving her a widow was not part of the plan John had made with Benji. Nor was it part of the plan his neighbor Eric had made with his wife, who, along with their adult-age children, had lain in the path of the bulldozer in their olive orchard. The next day when the man in the hard hat returned with the sheriff, John texted his neighbor, and Eric drove over.

"Do I need to take you into custody?" the sheriff asked them both.

John and Eric shook their heads and walked away from the fallen trees.

That was before the dump trucks came with what the state generously called RTM, or Reusable Tunnel Material, as if they had a better plan for the fill dirt from twelve tunnel shafts than drowning John's orchards, along with Eric's.

"Even if the state keeps its promise to leave the Kimura graves intact," John told Eric one evening when he drove over to his neighbor's farm, "this kind of obliteration unearths them."

Eric shook his head. "They did it for *me*," he said of his children lying in the path of the bulldozer. "They did it because they love the farm. But the boy just graduated from art school, and his sister wants to be an engineer. I'm taking this opportunity to get out of the olive business."

"What will you do?" John asked.

"I don't know." Eric looked at his neighbor the same way he looked down the scope of a rifle when he took out a deer eating the leaves off his trees. "But I've got to do something. We have tuitions to pay off."

Walking back to his truck with the sun in his eyes, John knew he had to find a way to keep the promise Takashi had made to his own father.

Two months later John Kimura drove away from the farm for the last time. In a caravan loaded down with their possessions, pulling the tractor on a trailer, he drove with Benji and Alexis beside him. The bee boxes were packed snug in the truck bed, their lids secured tight.

Manuel and Lupe drove behind them, and Marie completed the caravan. That was as many workers as John could take with him to the thirty acres he'd leased in Woodland, open farmland with an aging, overgrown orchard, where he and his family would live in a drafty house. Marie had agreed to live in what was essentially a shed with an outhouse.

"We'll install plumbing in the slow season," John said, his voice growing heavy on the word *slow*.

"Lydia and I turned a shed into a darkroom," she told John. "I know how to make a sink out of a plastic tub and a garden hose."

The trailer where Manuel and Lupe would live already had plumbing, and if there were leaks, John would fix them.

The property belonged to a friend of Buzz's who was too old to keep farming and didn't want to see the land sold to developers.

The day John signed the lease, Alice drove Buzz out to see it. Buzz teared up as he stood looking east toward the river. "All that time on the North Canal District and I couldn't save your farm."

"No," John said, looking down. "But it's thanks to you that I get to start over here with my family and my three best workers."

And between the delta and Woodland there were other farmers still carrying on. The caravan of trucks driving from Kimura Farm passed a stack of hay bales at the far end of a harvested field, and an orchard of almond trees losing their leaves.

Lupita pointed at the leaves from her car seat. "*Amarillo*," she said. Yellow.

"*Sí*," Manuel told his daughter.

"*Peras*," Lupita said. Of course she would think they were pear trees.

In the truck in front of them, Alexis asked, "Is there a pear orchard on our new farm?"

John shook his head, blinking away tears.

"Cherries?"

"No. There's a prune orchard."

Alexis wrinkled her nose.

"And tomatoes." He looked sideways at his daughter, and Benji squeezed her hand.

"Yellow tomatoes?" Alexis asked.

Her dad nodded. "What else would you like to grow?"

Because she had always loved the surprise of them being unearthed by the hoe, Alexis said, "Potatoes." Then she said, "Squash! And chard!"

Inside the hives, the bees hummed.

Sources

In researching my novel, I read many books, online articles, and articles in the *San Francisco Chronicle* written by Glen Martin, Jeremy Miller, Kelly Zito, Peter Flimrite, and Carolyn Lochhead. I also learned from the Record Searchlight about the Winnemem Wintu's fight for sacred land in and around Lake Shasta.

The kind people at Lundberg Family Farms served as a model for the rice farm in my novel.

The books listed below were my favorites and were the most influential.

Mark Arax, *Dreamtland*
Mark Arax, *The King of California*
Editors Joell and Coke Hallowell, *Take Me to the River*
Gerald Haslam, *The Other California*
Robert Kelley, *Battling the Inland Sea*
Mike Madison, *Walking the Flatlands*
David Mas Masumoto, *Wisdom of the Last Farmer*
Marc Reisner, *Cadillac Desert*
Ted Simon, *The River Stops Here*
Charlie Soderquist, *Sturgeon Tales*
Gary Soto, *Jessie De La Cruz*

Acknowledgments

Thanks to BEST and FDT for instilling in me a love of reading, and for supporting me in my pursuit of writing, even after you were both gone from this earth. Gratitude to my mentor, Joe Di Prisco, for your kindness, encouragement, and maybe most of all, your sense of humor. To Elizabeth Trupin-Pulli, for hanging in there with me through the subpar drafts, and for your deep knowledge of the publishing industry.

Thank you to Jenny Pritchett for helping me weed out extraneous nonfiction, and for clarifying the role focus plays in the structure of a novel. To Monica Wesolowska for your careful reads and thoughtful feedback. And to Joe Ortiz for your work with me way back when on the Old Overholdt chapter, as well as to Sara Crampton for inspiration on the story of Margaret getting lost.

Much gratitude to Bill Darsie for your Delta tours and the trove of information you shared. I could not have written this book without the kindness you showed a childhood friend.

To Brett Baker for your willingness to share all you know and love about the Delta.

And to Mark Arax, whose writing on the Central Valley laid the foundation for my story.

A nod to Matt and Sara Bishop for your love story that inspired mine for Nate and T Bone.

Thank you to Brooke Warner, Addison Gallegos, and She Writes Press for the community of women writers and your commitment to excellence.

Finally, thank you to Blue for your love and support. I could not ask for anything more than to be able to travel this life journey with you.

About the Author

Victoria Tatum received her Master's in Creative Writing from SF State, and her Master's in Secondary Education from UC Santa Cruz. Her first novel, *The Virgin's Children,* was released in Canada by Rain Books in 2006. *More Than Any River* is her second novel.

Looking for your next great read?

We can help!

Visit www.shewritespress.com/next-read
or scan the QR code below for a list
of our recommended titles.